GEMINI

STAR TREK®

GEMINI

Mike W. Barr

**Based upon STAR TREK
created by Gene Roddenberry**

POCKET BOOKS
New York London Toronto Sydney Singapore

This book is a work of fiction. Names, characters, places and incidents are products of the author's imagination or are used fictitiously. Any resemblance to actual events or locales or persons, living or dead, is entirely coincidental.

An *Original* Publication of POCKET BOOKS

POCKET BOOKS, a division of Simon & Schuster, Inc.
1230 Avenue of the Americas, New York, NY 10020

Copyright © 2003 by Paramount Pictures. All Rights Reserved.

STAR TREK is a Registered Trademark of Paramount Pictures.

This book is published by Pocket Books, a division of Simon & Schuster, Inc., under exclusive license from Paramount Pictures.

ISBN: 0-7434-0074-7

First Pocket Books printing February 2003

10 9 8 7 6 5 4 3 2 1

POCKET and colophon are registered trademarks of Simon & Schuster, Inc.

For information regarding special discounts for bulk purchases, please contact Simon & Schuster Special Sales at 1-800-456-6798 or business@simonandschuster.com

Printed in the U.S.A.

To Laurie S. Sutton,
who can have any posting she wants
on my starship

Acknowledgments

Thanks to Gene Roddenberry, for boldly going, and taking us along.

"He's not really dead, as long as we remember him."
—*Dr. Leonard McCoy,* Star Trek II: The Wrath of Khan

Chapter One

Captain's log, Stardate 3375.3

   While en route to the planet Nador, as per our orders, I have decided to try something of an experiment, with, I am confident, the full support of my senior staff.

"I'M TELLING YOU, JIM," said Dr. Leonard H. McCoy, "this is *not* a good idea!"

"Diagnosis noted, Doctor," replied Captain James T. Kirk, in that tone that indicated Kirk hadn't heard him at all.

Kirk exited the turbolift and strode onto deck six, stopping after a few steps to turn and look behind him. "Coming, Bones?"

"I might as well," said McCoy, with a sigh of resignation. "I have a feeling someone's going to need medical attention."

Kirk turned right at the door labeled MESS HALL and entered as the door hissed open before him. Despite his apparent bravado, McCoy suspected Kirk had deliberately chosen this time of day—rather late for lunch—hoping the hall would be almost deserted. Of all the tables in the room, only one was occupied, and that by only four crew members. Kirk entered, seemingly paying them no more attention then he had McCoy's advice.

"Chicken sandwich and coffee," he said to the food slot. Lights flashed, sounds warbled, and a moment later the dispenser panel opened. Kirk took his meal, cocking an eyebrow to McCoy, a look the doctor knew was part curiosity, part challenge.

"Cobb salad, extra dressing, with iced tea," said McCoy, finally. He considered ordering a mint julep, extra strong, but thought better of it; he might need his wits about him.

Across the room the four crew members tried not to look at though they were eyeing Kirk and McCoy, and had been from the moment the two officers entered. But now, with Kirk approaching them, to avoid contact would have been rude, not to mention insubordinate. The four pushed back their chairs and began to rise as Kirk neared. McCoy remembered them from their physicals upon being assigned to the *Enterprise,* new crew members picked up at Starbase 7.

"Please," said Kirk, with his most charming smile, "at ease. May we join you?"

The four crew members exchanged furtive, nervous glances. It seemed to McCoy they were asking each other, *What have we done?*

"Of course, sir," said Lieutenant Sherwood, a trim strawberry blonde, keeping her voice as even as circumstances permitted.

The four sank back into their chairs uneasily as, to their dread, Kirk took the head chair at the table. A moment later Dr. McCoy sat down at the other end, cutting off that avenue of escape, as well.

McCoy nodded and smiled sympathetically, an attempt to put the young crew at ease that did anything but.

"Should be an interesting mission, don't you think?" asked Kirk, picking up his cup of coffee.

"Sir!" said Trask, an ensign assigned to engineering, springing to his feet with such energy that Kirk nearly wound up wearing his coffee. "The *U.S.S. Enterprise* is headed for planet Nador to review the Nadorians' vote to decide whether or not to become a member of the Federation, *sir!*"

"Sit down, Mr. Trask ," said Kirk, gently. "I was just asking—"

"Sir," said Ensign Fox. His soup spoon sounded a discordant note as it struck his tray when he dropped it. He remained seated, but stared straight ahead, hands at his side. McCoy noted this with interest; he had never seen a crewman *sitting* at attention before. "We are also ordered to provide transit to Federation Commissioner Roget and his wife, sir."

"Yes, of course," said Kirk, trying to keep the desperation from his voice. "But I was just asking how you thought the mission might—"

"Sir," said Sinclair, a young lieutenant with a manner of currying favor that McCoy didn't cotton to, "if the captain wishes, I can prepare a dossier with the salient points of planet Nador, sir. For example, Nador has been judged a B-minus on the Richter cultural scale—"

"That won't be necessary, Sinclair," replied Kirk, patiently. "I was just asking if—"

McCoy saw the bafflement in Kirk's eyes as he surveyed the four crew members, all sitting stiffly, teeth clenched, brows furrowing, then unfurrowing when they realized they were showing too much stress. He wouldn't have taken any bets as to which of the five had the highest blood pressure at that moment. This had been fun, in a certain mildly sadistic kind of way, but he began wishing for a diversion that would break the tension he could cut with an exoscalpel.

Across the room the hailing whistle came from the intercom, and a cool, measured voice said, *"Bridge to captain."* McCoy had rarely seen Kirk move as quickly.

"Kirk here. Have we entered Nadorian space yet?"

"Still some minutes out, Captain," replied Mr. Spock, *"but we have encountered a ship broadcasting no identification beam and which refuses to answer our hail. She bears no known markings and is of unknown design."*

McCoy was at Kirk's side now, thumbing a drop of dressing from the corner of his mouth. "Hostile actions?" asked Kirk.

"Not as yet. She is attempting to elude us, however. Our shields were raised automatically."

"Intercept course," said Kirk. It could be nothing, but with the relations between Nador and the Federation at such a crucial state, nothing could be left to chance. "Yellow alert. I'll be right up."

To McCoy, the sighs of relief from the four seated at the table sounded like those of a plow horse at the end of a long, hard day.

"Bridge," said Kirk moments later to the turbolift grid, and the car hummed smoothly upward, the alert panels strobing yellow. He cleared his throat twice, then turned to McCoy. "Not exactly the response I'd hoped for."

"What *did* you hope for, Jim?" asked McCoy. "You've got a crew that would walk through fire for you—and has, on occasion. What were you trying to prove, hobnobbing with green recruits like those? They're not as familiar with you as the rest of the crew. You nearly gave them all strokes."

"I'm not sure," said Kirk, avoiding McCoy's gaze. "I was just trying to be a little more . . . outgoing with the crew. If Captain Garrovick had wanted to dine with us when we served on the *Farragut*—"

"You'd have been as tense as those kids were," interrupted McCoy. "They're your crew, Jim, they can't be your friends, too." He looked at Kirk and grinned. "That's why you have me."

"Prescription noted," said Kirk, dryly, as the lift slowed. "You coming?"

McCoy shook his head. "I'd better make sure sickbay's ready, just in case."

Kirk nodded as the lift slid to a stop and the doors parted. Before they closed, McCoy saw Spock rising from the captain's chair before Kirk's presence could even be announced, and he wondered, not for the first time, or for the hundredth, how Spock knew Kirk was there. He wondered if the Vulcan's olfactory sense was as keen as his damn hearing. The noise of the crew preparing for yellow alert would have drowned out the hiss of the lift door, and the carpeting on the bridge would have silenced any footsteps.

McCoy shook his head as the door closed. Damned if he knew, and he sure as hell wasn't going to give Spock the satisfaction of asking. "Sickbay," he said, hoping, not for the first time, or for the hundredth, that his services wouldn't be needed.

"Status," said Kirk, lowering himself into the center seat.

"No change since the last report, Captain," replied

Mr. Spock. "We encountered the unidentified ship as we neared Nadorian space. They attempted evasive action and we gave pursuit. The ship is out there—we can catch occasional glimpses of it on sensors—but it eludes full detection."

Kirk nodded, leaning forward slightly, and scanned the viewscreen, as though his own eyes could detect something the ship's sensor spread could not. Around him the crew performed their duties, with a precision that would have done credit to a ballet company. Spock moved to his science station, Chekov in turn moved to his chair at the helm, while the relief navigator moved to an unoccupied perimeter station and began processing data. In any other circumstances, it would have been rather absurd, like an adult game of tag.

"Normal lighting," he said at last, and the alert panels dimmed. "Do we know who they are?" he asked.

"Not with any certainty," replied Spock. "Possibly smugglers, or other traffickers in contraband."

"Open a channel to the ship," said Kirk. "All standard frequencies."

"Go ahead, Captain," Uhura said from behind him.

"This is Captain James T. Kirk of the Federation Starship *Enterprise*," he said, crisply. "No unidentified vessels are permitted in this space. You are ordered to stand down and identify yourself." Kirk jerked his right hand sharply, thumb out, and Uhura cut the transmission. On the viewscreen sprawled only endless blackness, dusted with silver. "Spock, why can't we see them?"

"I can offer speculation only, Captain," began Spock. "It may be that their shields or hull are configured so as to refract our sensors. It may be that the ship is somehow able to phase in and out of space, eluding sensors."

"Maybe they have some kind of a cloaking device,"

said Sulu, from his post next to Chekov's, "like the Romulans."

"Possible, Mr. Sulu," said Kirk, gnawing on a knuckle while he thought. "The Romulans are the only fleet we know of to have a cloaking device. But they're on the other side of the galaxy, and not known for sharing their technology."

"I have a brief glimpse of them on sensors, Captain," said Spock, peering into the viewer at his station. "Off the port bow."

"Tractor beam, those coordinates," said Kirk, urgently.

"Ineffective," said Spock, a moment later.

"Why haven't they attacked?" asked Chekov, tensely.

"If you were a vessel that size, would you want to take on a starship?" replied Sulu. "They're probably trying to put as much space between us as possible."

"Don't make that assumption, Mr. Sulu," said Kirk. "Appearances can be deceiving, after all."

"Aye, sir," said Sulu, suitably abashed.

Kirk hoped they wouldn't have to learn that lesson the hard way. Even as he sat he felt his blood rise, and his pulse quicken. As there had always been when these physiological signs made themselves known in humans since they first crawled out of the sea, there was a choice to be made, panic or fight. Kirk had learned the hard way, many years ago, that only fight would do them any good. More, he had to be an example to his bridge crew. The threat seemed minor, yes, but the one foe you turned your back on would be the one to stab you there.

"Spock," Kirk said, "link tractor beam to sensors, so they function together."

"Understood," said Spock coolly. He continued to peer into his viewer as his long fingers worked the buttons at his console, not unlike a pianist at his keyboard. "Accomplished, Captain," he said, a moment later.

Kirk nodded. "Now if sensors get a taste of them, we'll—"

Almost instantly Spock's console beeped. "We have them," said Spock.

"Expand tractor field, divert all available power to it," snapped Kirk.

"They're firing," said Sulu.

A moment later the bridge rocked like a sailing ship on choppy seas. The crew reeled a little, but maintained their positions.

"I read their weaponry as missiles," said Spock, turning from his console. "Conventional, but quite powerful."

"We can take a little punishment, just keep our grip on him," said Kirk. "Go to red alert."

"They are attempting to break free," said Spock, working his console quickly.

Kirk punched a button on his chair arm. "Engineering," he rasped, "increase power to tractor beam."

"We're tryin', Captain." Montgomery Scott's voice crackled over the intercom. *"But she's fightin' like a fish on a line. Hard t'believe a ship that small can have that much power."* On the viewscreen, tractor beams struggled to contain something between them, like hands groping in the dark. Kirk peered anxiously as, within the tractor field, the configurations of a vessel began to firm. . . .

"Establish phaser lock," said Kirk, urgently, "raise shields and fire!"

The *Enterprise* lurched again as, on the viewscreen, the tractor beams dissolved.

"Damage report," said Kirk.

"Minor damage to the port hull," replied Spock, after a moment. "Unless they are able to mount a concerted attack, their assaults are more annoying than efficacious, unless our shields collapse or we are incapacitated."

"Neither is a state of affairs I anticipate," said Kirk, stiffly. But he left his chair and strode the bridge, bearing a frown of concentration, trying to quiet the pounding of his blood. To let them escape would weaken the name of the Federation in this section of space (and if it occurred to James Kirk that the same risk existed to his personal reputation, he did not acknowledge it).

"Too bad we can't just cast a net for them," said Sulu, under his breath.

Then he turned, to see Kirk smiling. "Perhaps we can, Mr. Sulu," said Kirk. "Spock, all available power to sensors, widest possible dispersal."

"Captain, such dispersal will be virtually useless with our shields up—"

Kirk nodded, tautly. "I did say 'all available power,' Mr. Spock. Drop shields."

Spock's fingers played over his console effortlessly.

"And link *phasers* to sensors," said Kirk, softly.

Spock's left brow notched up a bit, as he nodded.

"Uhura, tie your console in with Spock's," said Kirk. "Monitor those sensors. If so much as a stray meteorite touches them, I want to—"

"Contact, Captain," said Spock. "Sensors have been breached."

The ship shimmied slightly as the phasers fired, seemingly toward open space. For a long moment, it seemed they would simply disperse into random background radiation . . .

. . . then a flash of energy as they struck something.

"Fire," said Kirk, clenching a fist.

Another fusillade and something became visible out there. "Maximum magnification," said Kirk, urgently.

There it was, a ship, small but capable-looking, listing to one side like a man staggering from a blow.

"Tractor beam," said Kirk. "Before they can—"

"I'm reading transporters," said Spock.

In an instant, Kirk was back at his chair. "Kirk to transporter room! Intercept that transporter beam! Don't let them—"

"Sorry, sir," crackled back the voice of Mr. Kyle. *"They were too quick for us. They're gone."*

"Raise shields!" said Kirk. "They'll—"

Abruptly, the ship erupted like a giant piñata struck by an unseen bat. For a long moment black space was painted purest white, as if by a minor star that coalesced, ignited and went nova all in the span of an eyeblink.

Even though the viewscreen automatically dimmed, the flash was still painful. Then nothing was left but floating debris.

"No organic remains," said Spock, peering into his viewer. "Mr. Kyle was correct, its crew is gone. Quite probably to planet Nador, which is barely within transporter range."

"Beam in as much of that debris as you can get," said Kirk, pointing at the screen. "I want all available knowledge about these people."

"Acknowledged, Captain."

"Damage report?"

"Minimal," replied Spock, after checking the reports coming in from the ship. "The missles were unable to penetrate our shields, or our hull when we were unshielded. No appreciable damage."

"Except to our pride," muttered Kirk, seating himself. Then he took a deep breath. Their assailants had escaped, but the ship and crew were safe. Maybe McCoy was right, maybe he was too hard on himself. Maybe. "Secure from red alert. Viewer ahead, continue plotted course."

The planet Nador occupied the center of the screen now, growing larger with each second, a piebald sphere of blues and greens, not unlike a place across the galaxy which most of the *Enterprise* crew called home.

"Standard orbit, Mr. Sulu. Lieutenant Uhura, open a channel to the Nadorian palace. Standard greetings."

"Transmitted, sir, I have a response," replied Uhura several seconds later.

"On screen."

The lovely view of the planet they now orbited dissolved, to be replaced by the interior of what was obviously some sort of official building. In the background Kirk caught a glimpse of what he thought was a human figure, but was instead an elegantly carved statue, then turned his attention to the face of the magistrate, which occupied most of the screen. A middle-aged man bordering on elderly, he had the uncertain air of a man who had been used to commanding authority, but had found, rather recently, that his power base had eroded out from under him. The man on the viewscreen began the conversation with an odd mixture of sympathy, respect, and very mild contempt for his subject.

"Captain Kirk, welcome to Nador. I am Lonal, acting regent for Their Serene Highnesses, Princes Abon and Delor." He said this firmly and courteously, then, at the end, added a rather incongruous and—Kirk

thought—rather servile smile, almost as an afterthought.

"Greetings, Regent Lonal," said Kirk, putting on his diplomat's face. "Captain James T. Kirk of the *U.S.S. Enterprise,* representing the United Federation of Planets. I bring you best wishes from the Federation Council."

"Most welcome, I am sure. May I convey the wish of Their Serene Highnesses to your and your senior staff to dine at the Royal Palace this evening? Their Highnesses are quite anxious to meet you."

"Thank you for the invitation, Regent Lonal. We look forward to meeting Their Serene Highnesses. Kirk out."

The screen want blank and Kirk turned to Spock. "*'Their* Serene Highnesses'? They rule this planet jointly?"

"They have, and will again," replied Spock, "if the populace decides to reject Federation membership. Little is known of the princes aside from the facts that they are identical twins and are, if I am correct, thirty years of age."

"I am sure your figures are quite correct," said Kirk dryly.

"Thank you, Captain," said Spock, with no trace of irony.

"Captain," said Sulu, turning in his chair, "why not ask the regent about that ship?"

"I'd rather broach a subject like that face-to-face," said Kirk. "I assure you, that matter has not been forgotten. In fact . . . Uhura, open a channel to Commissioner Roget's quarters."

"I have him, sir."

"On screen." The screen flashed on again, this time

to show a definitely elderly man whose white hair was retreating rapidly, leaving behind large blue eyes and a wide, smiling mouth, as if the features of his face were expanding to take up the space left by the retreat of his hairline. Kirk noted another statue in the background of the expansive room, placed between a bookcase and a huge desk that looked from its sheen to be of a fine Saurian hardwood. It was something of an effort, Kirk realized, with minor irritation, to keep his concentration on Commissioner Sylvan Roget; the workmanship of this statue, like the one in Regent Lonal's office, was such that he kept watching it out of his eyes, almost expecting it to move at any second.

"Commissioner Roget, I'm Captain—"

"Captain James T. Kirk." The old man smiled warmly. *"Good to see you, Captain. The palace just transmitted details of the banquet tonight. My wife and I look forward to making your acquaintance here, and on the journey back to Earth."*

"Thank you, Commissioner, the *Enterprise* and my crew are at your service. I wonder, before the banquet tonight, if I might consult with you on a somewhat delicate matter?"

If Roget was taken aback by this request, his years of ambassadorial training would not permit him to show it. *"Certainly, Captain. Why don't you beam down to the embassy and we'll discuss it?"*

"Captain," came the voice of Spock, "according to strict protocol, your first footfall on the planet should be to greet representatives of the planet's government."

"Thank you, Mr. Spock, I'm aware of that," replied Kirk, patiently. Spock was a good friend and the best first officer in the fleet, but he had an occasional tendency to state the obvious. "Commissioner, why don't you be my guest aboard the *Enterprise?* We can have a quite proper talk, with—" He did not look at Spock. "—all the i's dotted and the t's crossed."

"I'd like that very much, Captain. Would it be too much of an imposition if we began beaming aboard a few crates of our personal effects?"

"Not at all, Commissioner. See you in a few minutes, Kirk out." He stood thinking for a moment, then punched a button on his chair's arm. "Kirk to sickbay. Bones, any customers after that little dustup?"

"Not a one, Jim. Who were they, anyway?"

"We're still trying to puzzle that out. Have time for a little unofficial reception for Commissioner Roget?"

"Absolutely."

"Good. Meet us in the transporter room in ten minutes. Kirk out."

Chapter Two

"THIS IS REALLY excellent ale, Captain," said Commissioner Roget. He held his glass up to the light in the officers' lounge, and it seemed as though the blue aura of his glass was conferred not from the room's lighting filtering through the liquid, but from his eyes, the eyes of a young man. "Romulan, I presume?"

"If I were to answer that, " said Kirk, blandly, "I would make the commissioner complicit in a crime. The possession of Romulan alc is, of course, illegal."

"Then, since I have no wish for my last act as a Federation official to be the arrest of a starship captain, we had better do all we can do dispose of the evidence," replied Roget, reaching for the bottle.

"Allow me," said McCoy, pouring the commissioner a generous measure of the liquid, and a dash more for himself.

"Then you do plan to retire, Commissioner?" asked Spock.

"I've had a wonderful career," said Roget. "I've been witness to history and upheld my post as best I could.

Yes, the admission of Nador to the Federation is an admirable last act for my career."

"You're sure Nador wants to be admitted?" asked Kirk.

"It'd be damned ungrateful of them if they didn't," said Scotty, emptying his glass. He professed no fondness for Romulan ale but, Kirk noticed, he didn't often turn it down. "After all, the Federation spent years helpin' them improve their planet by education, industrialization, cultivation—"

"True, Mr. Scott," said Commissioner Roget, patiently, "but the Nadorians do have the right to turn down membership. And to force them would be against everything the Federation stands for."

"Aye," grumbled Scotty, "but it would still be damned ungrateful of 'em."

"Scotty's an engineer, not a diplomat," said McCoy, dryly.

"And thank God for it," said Scotty, fervently, reaching for the bottle. "Give me a warp-drive engine, cranky and temperamental as she may be, instead of a room o' bureaucrats any day o' the week—" He stopped, remembering his audience, and looked up, sheepishly. "Beggin' your pardon, Commissioner, I meant no offense . . ."

"None taken, Mr. Scott," said Commissioner Roget, with a smile. "I have to admit, there have been many days in the last thirty years when I've thought the exact same thing. The Nadorians can be a very stubborn people. And," he said, cautiously, after a brief pause, "there are some rather obstreperous political factions you should know about."

Kirk and Spock exchanged a brief glance. "Go ahead, Commissioner," urged Kirk. "We know the population of the planet's main continent was composed primarily of two major tribes who've spent the majority of the past few centuries trying to wipe each other out."

"Must put you in mind of the good old days on Vulcan, Mr. Spock," said McCoy, blandly.

"Indeed," nodded Spock, evenly. Kirk smiled to himself; Spock's refusal to rise to the bait would irritate McCoy more than McCoy's barb had irritated him. "That similarity between the two planets as warring cultures does exist, as does another, more pleasant similarity. As I recall from my reading of your summary of Nadorian history, Commissioner, the tribal leaders finally realized that their culture's progress was coming to a virtual standstill. It was then that the tribal leaders finally realized, when they were first contacted by the Federation, that their efforts would be better spent in working together rather than against each other. Quite commendable; it speaks highly of them as a people."

"Exactly right, Mr. Spock," said Roget, with the enthusiasm of an expert in an obscure subject who has found a kindred spirit. "To that end, the prince of one tribe and the princess of the second married. It is their sons who are next in line for the throne, though to all intents and purposes they rule the planet now."

"Yes, 'Their Serene Highnesses' Abon and Delor," said Kirk. "I recall that they were named for the tribes they were descended from, the Abonians and the Delorites. But from your lead-in, I'm afraid things aren't running as smoothly as all that."

"Unfortunately, that seems to be the case. Though most natives have accepted the idea of a united planet to keep themselves competitive in this shrinking galaxy, there are a few diehards who still like things the way they were."

"There always are," said McCoy, glumly.

"There are some unpleasant constants in diplomacy, Doctor," said Roget with a resigned sigh. "The two representatives of the tribes are Counselors Docos and Hanor—Docos representing the Abonians and Hanor the Delorites. Those posts as 'representatives' are entirely self-granted, but they do serve on the Planetary Council, and they do carry great influence among the people as a whole."

"Well, what about this Regent Lonal?" asked Scotty, in a tone of mild irritation. Kirk smiled slightly. A practical man, in his own way Scotty hated inefficiency as much as Spock. "Isn't his job to make 'em sit down and play nice?"

"I often think Regent Lonal would like nothing more than that, Mr. Scott," said Roget, "but he, too, is a politician and is doing his best to hold the fabric of Nadorian society together."

"Their Serene Highnesses aren't much good at that?" asked Kirk.

"They are still young men, Captain, with little actual experience at ruling a people, much less a people so divided, though the Nadorians do put a great deal of store in them as figureheads. And, of course," he said, shaking his head, "there's the physical situation—"

Kirk couldn't help interrupting. "But there are several thousand Federation citizens on the planet, how are they taking all this political intrigue?"

Commissioner Roget sighed. "As well as can be expected. Their safety has been often my major concern, of late. Nador's most radical separatists have even attacked some of the Federation citizens. In response, some of the more indignant Federation citizens who have put down roots here have formed an activist group of their own, feeling themselves at risk. But don't worry, Captain," he said, quickly, "such instances are rare. Your nephew is quite safe."

"Thank you, Commissioner," replied Kirk, avoiding McCoy's suddenly intent gaze. "One last question—are any of these groups ardent enough in their beliefs to take armed action?"

The laugh lines of Roget's face disappeared, and he seemed to pale. "What do you mean?"

"We encountered an unidentified ship. Small, but fast and heavily armed. Spock, have you been able to learn anything from the debris?"

"All attempts at analysis have proven inconclusive," replied his first officer. "The hull samples retrieved are composed of various alloys common to starship construction across several inhabited systems. Nor have any of the unidentified ship's energy frequencies produced any usable information as to its place of origin."

"Please keep me posted on this," said Roget. The softness of his voice was belied by the urgency of his speech. "The situation is critical enough without bringing armed vessels into it."

"You'll be the first to know," said Kirk. Throughout this exchange, Kirk could feel McCoy's eyes on him. Peripherally, Kirk saw McCoy's mouth about to open when the table intercom sounded.

"Kirk here."

"Uhura, Captain. Cargo bay reports that Commissioner Roget's effects have been secured. And I have a message for the commissioner from his wife."

Roget chuckled. "She probably thinks she needs to remind me of the banquet tonight."

"I'm glad someone reminded me," said Kirk, rising. "We'll give you some privacy, Commissioner, and look forward to seeing you later tonight."

"Thank you, Captain," said Roget, warmly shaking hands with all of them, save Spock; Kirk wondered if he had ever served on Vulcan.

"Why didn't you tell me your nephew was on Nador?" asked McCoy, in an accusatory tone, once they were outside.

"I thought I had mentioned it," replied Kirk, innocently. "At any rate, you know now. What of it, Bones?"

"Nothing," said McCoy, a little too easily. Then he chuckled. "If he's a real Kirk, he's probably got a girl he wants you to meet. How'd he wind up on Nador?"

"I pulled a few strings," said Kirk. Spock joined them as they headed toward the turbolift. "Sam and Aurelan knew Commissioner Roget, and it didn't take much coaxing to get them to agree to let Peter join the Federation party here as a kind of junior adjutant." He felt McCoy's concerned gaze on him as he spoke of his late brother and his wife and all he had lost on the planet Deneva, but he was all right. "They say he's getting along fine."

"I would not find that surprising," said Spock. "The boy seemed resilient."

Kirk smiled, tapping the side of his head. "He's a Kirk, complete with a very thick skull."

"Let's hope he doesn't need it," said McCoy. "I don't like this talk of Federation citizens being attacked."

Spock nodded. "Such news is most alarming."

"Let's not go looking for trouble, gentlemen," said Kirk, grimly. Experience had taught him that trouble, more often than not, found them on its own.

Chapter Three

CONSTITUTION-CLASS STARSHIPS were wonderful creations, with their myriad devices for enabling humankind to travel with relative safety in space. Their marvels extended past the basic mechanism of travel to the environmental programming, with, among other wonders, the subliminal tapes of the sounds of animals and bodies of water that they still couldn't live without (and hopefully, would never learn to).

But there was nothing to compare with the native air of a Class-M planet. They could mix anything they wanted into the air on the *Enterprise,* but it would never smell quite like the surface of Nador did when Kirk and his landing party beamed down. It was an olfactory dream, a combination of pleasant odors, some familiar, some unique.

Kirk looked around to find himself in a partially enclosed plaza on the periphery of the grounds of the royal palace of Nador. Beneath and before them stretched a length of what Kirk took to be some variety of native rock; it was partially translucent, with veins of color and—he looked again—yes, that was some sort of wood growing through it. He made a mental note to ask Spock about it. Beyond the plaza was a well-maintained swath of forestry, tended just enough to give it that untended look, studded with a few sizable boulders. And beyond that was a high wall, enclosing the palace grounds. It seemed to Kirk that beyond that he could hear an urgent murmur of voices, but he could distinguish nothing particular, and he could see only samples—doubtless carefully chosen—of native architecture, a kind of long, curved, design sense that seemed to sweep down, then up, drawing the observer's eye, giving the impression of a rising that continued past the scope of the structure itself.

Approaching them was Regent Lonal, wearing the bland smile familiar to every career diplomat Kirk had ever met, followed by a number of functionaries, including a lovely young woman, with blond hair and a shy smile that seemed to flicker on and off like a ray of sun trying to peer from behind a cloud.

"Captain Kirk," said Lonal, making a precise bow, "the planet and people of Nador wish you and your fellow travelers all the peace and plenty our globe contains."

"Thank you, Regent Lonal," Kirk said, with a warmth that was genuinely felt. "I bring greetings from my ship and the entire United Federation of Planets, in the hope that Nador will soon be joining us."

"Ah, but that is a matter for wiser heads than ours to decide," replied Lonal, heartily. "Please, may I present some of my loyal and most capable staff—" He reeled off several names of stiff-looking courtiers, who bowed with equal rigidity. Kirk greeted them as though each was the most important person he had ever met, though he couldn't have recalled any of their names five minutes later. "—and the Lady Pataal."

The young woman Kirk had noted stepped forward and curtsied charmingly. She was wearing something flowing and diaphanous that seemed to gather around her body like a cloud. Her eyes were the color of warm almonds, her forehead high and broad, her features proud and aristocratic. Nonetheless, she barely lifted her head to meet their gazes, though her on-again-off-again smile reappeared briefly.

"We are delighted to meet you," said Kirk, with feeling. "May I present my first officer, Mr. Spock, our ship's surgeon, Dr. Leonard McCoy, and Yeoman Tonia Barrows." Kirk had wanted one of the rank and file present to enhance Starfleet's democratic image, and, secretly a matchmaker at heart, saw no reason why such a lovely planet shouldn't be visited by both Dr. McCoy and the yeoman, who seemed to be circling each other in a perpetual, unconsummated, mating dance since their experience on that amusement park planet, earlier this year. *What kind of captain,* he thought, *would let such a valuable member of his crew continue to endure that? What kind of friend?*

Scotty, who loathed state functions to the depths of his simple soul, had practically begged to stay aboard the *Enterprise.* And, considering their encounter with that mystery ship earlier in the day, Kirk was glad to have an experienced hand on the bridge, just in case. Scotty had said he planned to spend the time trying to program the food slots for haggis. Kirk dearly hoped he was kidding, but with Scotty's often dour countenance, it was difficult to tell. Kirk still got a grin out of the time Scotty had sent a new hand all over the ship looking for a left-handed dilithium crystal articulation frame.

"If you will permit us," said Regent Lonal, moving to one side as he bowed and extended an arm toward the interior of the palace. Kirk returned the gesture, permitting Lonal and his party to precede them. As planned, both parties started for the palace archway, mingling as they proceeded.

Kirk contrived to find himself next to the blond young woman, to, he was sure, the surprise of neither Spock nor McCoy. "Your planet is quite lovely, Lady Pataal."

"Thank you, Captain." She smiled, but when she finally looked up, the smile vanished like a wary animal who wasn't certain if it was wanted or not. "I hope you will find our planet hospitable."

"I'm already finding its people so," said Kirk, gallantly.

"She's quite lovely," Yeoman Barrows commented to McCoy, his arm through hers, "don't you think?"

"She's nowhere near the most attractive woman in this gathering," Kirk heard McCoy say, his Southern accent suddenly more prominent.

"That's sweet, but I mean it," said Barrows. "Pataal, her name is? I wonder what she does here?"

"I don't know, but five to one says Jim winds up sitting next to her at the banquet," whispered McCoy, tugging unconsciously at the collar of his dress uniform. "Any takers?" he added, to Spock, not far behind.

"It would be unfair of me to accept that wager, Doctor," replied Spock. "I am in possession of facts you are not."

"What 'facts'?"

"Your name is Pataal?" Kirk was asking. "That's a lovely name, it's almost musical."

"I am glad you like it," said the young girl, dimpling. "Their Serene Highnesses also like it."

"What do you do here at the palace?" asked Kirk, as they were led through a high archway into the structure itself.

"I am Their Serene Highnesses' consort."

"Oh, those facts," said McCoy, expression deadpan.

"Really?" said Kirk, after a moment. "Then Their Serene Highnesses are extremely lucky men."

"You are kind," smiled Pataal, touching his arm.

"Merely truthful," responded Kirk, wondering if this planet's customs attached any special significance to such a simple touch. It hadn't been so long since he had been tricked into dueling nearly to the death with Spock over a minute point of planetary protocol, and he had no desire to engage in another joust over the finer points of ambassadorial rules. Surely Spock would have warned him if—

Kirk's attention was abruptly seized by the chamber they had entered. It was wide and spacious. A small band of musicians at one end of the room played what he took to be the Nadorian equivalent of chamber music, compositions he found to be unusual, but melodic. As he entered, he had thought the chamber already occupied by several persons, but now, as he neared what he had taken to be the room's occupants, he found them to be statues, apparently—the fine arts weren't his strong point—of the same style as those he had seen earlier in Commissioner Roget's quarters and Regent Lonal's office.

"Excuse me," whispered Pataal. "I must help prepare Their Serene Highnesses for their entrance. I hope we shall have a chance to talk later. Your starship must have taken you to many exciting places."

"I'd like that," replied Kirk, satisfied that no breaches of interplanetary protocol had been committed—yet. She curtsied and was gone.

"Charming girl," said McCoy, absently, as he, Spock and Barrows caught up to him.

"Delightful," said Kirk, evenly. "Spock, these statues—"

"Excellent examples of ancient Nadorian sculpture, Captain," said Spock. He stood before one now, and Kirk noted that the statue stood simply on the antechamber floor, unprotected and unseparated from the crowd in any way.

"It is beautiful, but they're asking for something to happen to it, leaving it out this way," said McCoy.

"It is the Nadorian custom to display their statuary in this manner, Doctor," replied Spock, examining the sculpture closely. "Far more civilized than attempting to view such an objet d'art from afar."

"I agree, I just hope they don't have much problem with vandalism."

Spock shook his head slightly. "The Nadorians are taught from an early age to value and appreciate art."

A liveried servant bearing a tray of drinks approached them. They took slender glasses with hinged lids, inside which was a bubbling liquid that seemed to be on the verge of evaporating before their eyes.

"Vapor dew," said Yeoman Barrows, excitedly. "They're really treating us like royalty."

"And I'm sure they expect the same," said McCoy. He thumbed the small handle, lifting the lid of his glass, and inhaled the vapor produced by the volatile liquid. "And I'll be happy to," he added, smiling. "This is excellent."

"Spock, do you know how these statues are sculpted?" Kirk asked, lowering the lid on his own drink.

"Through the use of psionics, Captain," replied

Spock. "Though the past tense would be more appropriate."

"Hang on a minute, Spock," McCoy said indignantly. "The medical reports on the Nadorians indicate that their telekinetic potential is little different from that of humans."

Spock nodded. "In the present, that is quite correct, Doctor," said Spock. He continued to stare at the statue, gesturing with an index finger whose motion followed its lines. "But should you examine the history of the Nadorians, you will find that, as recently as ten centuries ago, their ancestors were indeed possessed of formidable telekinetic powers. Many of them turned their hand—"

"Or their minds," said Kirk with a smile.

"—to the fine arts. Many hundreds of such statues have been unearthed, and experts feel many remain to be yet discovered. Such statues command high prices across the galaxy in those rare instances when they become available."

"But I read every one of the Starfleet planetary surveys of Nador, and there wasn't a word about psionic powers," said McCoy.

"Such data is to be found only in the historical reports of the planet, Doctor," replied Spock, evenly. "As the various tribes mingled and intermarried, such psionic powers were gradually bred out of the race. Experts theorize that such abilities were needed in ancient times, but no longer when Nadorian society reached a certain level of civilization."

"It's happened before," said McCoy, thinking it over. "The theory is that humans once had a third eye, certain species of the dryworm of Antos IV have been found with the remnants of gills, and, of course, there's the Vulcan inner eyelid."

"Which, happily, has not been bred out of the race," said Spock. McCoy smiled at that, no doubt remembering the events of Deneva. Those events of some months back called to Kirk's mind first and foremost his late brother, Sam, and his nephew, Peter, and he scanned the crowd for any sign of the boy, but found none.

"So they can't carve any more statues like these?" asked Yeoman Barrows, sadly. "What a shame. The grace, the form . . . it's remarkable. Almost like a living being, caught in stasis."

"And so the Nadorian aesthetic makes another conquest," said a voice behind them, in the tones of one who had long ago succumbed to the same desire. They turned, to see Commissioner Roget approaching, escorting a woman near to his own age. "Captain James T. Kirk, my wife, Janine."

"An honor, Mrs. Roget," said Kirk. "May I present my staff?"

Janine Roget was an elderly woman who had obviously come to terms years ago with the fact of her aging, and had made no pretensions about holding on to her vanished youth. As a consequence, with her nearly elfin features, surmounted by a pair of green eyes and a mane of gray hair, making no attempt to seem young, she seemed younger than most beautiful women Kirk had known who fruitlessly clung to their departing years. The Rogets were holding hands, a gesture Kirk found sweetly endearing.

"It will be a pleasure to return home to Earth," said Janine Roget after Kirk finished the introductions, "though I must confess I shall regret having to leave such beautiful things behind."

"Janine's working on a history of Nadorian sculpture," said Roget, proudly. "As for leaving beautiful things behind, dear, from my perspective, I'm taking this planet's most comely treasure with me." He squeezed her hand, and she actually blushed as the rest of Kirk's crew exchanged an appreciative smile (with the exception, of course, of Spock).

A servant circulated among them again, collecting the containers of vapor dew and distributing glasses containing a green liquid. "What's this?" asked McCoy, sniffing it carefully. "It looks like a glass of algae."

"I shouldn't drink that just yet, Doctor," said Commissioner Roget, taking glasses for himself and his wife. "It's for the ceremonial introduction of Their Serene Highnesses."

"Tell me, Commissioner," asked Kirk, before the ceremonies started in earnest, "have you seen my nephew, Peter? I was hoping he'd be here."

"He told me he would be, Captain," replied Roget, looking toward something else. "He was quite looking forward to seeing you. I wouldn't worry, I'm sure he's just—"

Roget was interrupted by a flare of louder music from the band of musicians as they began playing a piece of music Kirk actually recognized—the planetary anthem of Nador. Regent Lonal emerged from the crowd and stood next to a huge pair of double doors. The music stopped as Lonal gestured to them, and Kirk realized that even in here he could still hear the murmuring of voices he had noted earlier. He was wondering idly who they were, when Lonal cleared his throat.

"My friends and allies of Nador," he said, "I thank you all for your gracious presence here tonight as we greet our honored guests, Captain James Kirk and his crew of the Federation starship *Enterprise*." There was a smattering of applause, which Kirk nodded to, gratefully.

"And now," said Regent Lonal, warming to his subject, "I have the honor to present the cherished rulers of the planet Nador, they whose wisdom and grace illumines our every day, Their Serene Highnesses, Prince Abon and Prince Delor." Lonal stepped to one side of the double doors as they swung open and a single figure walked forward. Kirk was a little surprised on seeing the figure's bulk, which belied the youthful age of the princes—and didn't Lonal introduce them both . . . ?

Then the figure emerged fully into the light. The glasses of those assembled were raised in tribute, save those of Kirk's entourage, most of whom were as startled as Kirk was.

A single figure stood in the doorway, a tall young man whose features contrived to be at once noble and attractively rough-hewn. Yet there seemed to be another person standing right behind him . . .

. . . Then the single figure turned, and Kirk realized the figure he had taken as one individual was actually two. Two men, who pivoted gracefully, letting the room take them in. Two men, as alike as two halves of an apple.

Two men, identical twins, joined at the spinal column.

Chapter Four

"FASCINATING," SAID SPOCK, with a slight catch to his voice which told Kirk he had actually been taken by surprise, though he knew the Vulcan would never admit it.

"You're becoming predictable, Mr. Spock," said McCoy, under his breath. But his voice held the same startled quality as had Spock's; he clung to his perpetual baiting of Spock as a sane man would cling to a single known fact in a universe that had gone otherwise mad.

"Science is a matter of determining predictables, Doctor," replied Spock, his equanimity restored.

"Gentlemen," Kirk said with a hiss, "shut up." He remembered the glass he was holding, raised it, then drank; later he would try to recall what he had imbibed, and fail. He recalled Roget's beginning a statement about "the physical situation" concerning the princes, and wished he had let him finish.

The Princes Abon and Delor had now turned sideways to the reception, giving the crowd an equal opportunity to see them both. They nodded and smiled, waving at the crowd, and gracing certain citizens with eye contact and a knowing smile. Of the two, it seemed to Kirk that Abon—if Kirk had properly distinguished them—bore the public greeting with better grace. Delor, though smiling politely enough, betrayed a certain impatience, a longing to have the thing done. Kirk recognized this expression because he had worn it many times himself during functions just like this one.

A palace functionary, dressed in clothes of the same royal blue and burnt orange color as the princes', though of course of a different style, approached Kirk. He bowed politely and asked, with the spread of a hand, for Kirk to follow him. Kirk moved off and nodded to Spock, McCoy, and Barrows, who followed.

"This I have got to see," said McCoy to Spock.

"I, too, confess much curiosity, Doctor," replied Spock.

Commissioner Roget, who had preceded them to the princes, half-bowed, with his eyes raised to meet the gaze of the monarchs. Kirk waited at a respectful distance, patiently.

"Your Highnesses," said Roget, formally, "I have the singular privilege of presenting the representative of the United Federation of Planets, Captain James T. Kirk of the *U.S.S. Enterprise.*"

Kirk approached and imitated Roget's bow. The twins had turned, so only Delor (Kirk thought) now faced him. Should he wait for them to speak, or—

"The honor is ours, Captain," said Delor, and it occurred to Kirk that of all the royalty he had met in his duties, Abon and Delor were the first who were justified in referring to themselves in the first-person plural. "How do you find Nador?"

"I've not had the pleasure of seeing much of it, Your

Highness," said Kirk, "but I've seen enough that I look forward to seeing more."

"We hope you shall," replied Delor, almost absently. Then—probably by some prearranged signal Kirk knew nothing of—the princes took two steps to their right, with the precision of marching troops, placing Kirk face-to-face with Abon. It was oddly like seeing the carved wooden figures in his grandmother's cuckoo clock back in Iowa spin around to announce the striking of the hour.

"Captain," said Abon with a smile, extending a hand in a reasonable, if somewhat stiff, version of an Earth handshake. Kirk took Abon's hand and pumped it twice. "Your presence honors us. We spend many hours scanning the night skies—you must tell us all about your travels."

"It is *you* who spend hours in the study of astronomy, Abon," said Delor, wearily. This was, Kirk realized, his first confirmation that he had the twins straight. "I think our time would be spent in far better uses."

"This is my first officer, Mr. Spock," said Kirk quickly, "my chief medical officer, Dr. Leonard McCoy, and Yeoman Tonia Barrows." All approached Abon and bowed similarly; then Abon turned and the process was repeated with Delor, who seemed particularly taken with Spock.

"If time permits, I should be grateful for the opportunity to discuss the science of logic as expounded upon by Nador's most prominent philosophers," said Delor.

"I would find such a discussion most interesting," replied Spock, "particularly in the position your philosophers have assigned to the superaltern as it affects the subalternate—"

"Not until Mr. Spock and I discuss the movements of

planetary bodies," came Abon's voice, from behind Delor.

Kirk glanced at Pataal, seeing dread growing in her eyes.

"I'm certain our visit will be long enough to accommodate all your desires, Your Highnesses," said Kirk.

"Their Serene Highnesses shall proceed us into the Great Hall," said Regent Lonal, somehow bowing submissively and urging the princes forward at the same time. Kirk wondered how they would proceed—with a kind of sideways crablike shuffle, or one possibly carrying the other? Instead, Delor took the lead with Abon backing behind him, in perfect synchronized footsteps, Abon stepping back with his right foot when Delor stepped forward with his left, with Abon's arms folded over his torso, eyes open, but staring into space, making no contact. *And they've lived their entire lives that way,* he thought. Rather than pity, which he suspected the princes would hate, Kirk's feelings were those of profound respect. Kirk and Commissioner and Mrs. Roget followed, with Spock, McCoy, and Barrows behind him.

"Most remarkable," Kirk heard Spock say, in a low voice.

"I'll say," came McCoy's awed reply, his tones equally hushed. "Did you see how gracefully they move? Like one person. I wonder if that's just practice or if their cerebral systems are connected, too. My God, I'd love to have a look at their medical chart."

"An interesting speculation," said Spock. "Perhaps observing which twin primarily utilizes which hand will prove informative. One could argue, in their condition, that their favored hands would be mirror images of each other, but there is a case to be made for—"

Kirk decided they were more fun when they were arguing.

Given the nature of the princes' handicap, Kirk wondered if the seating arrangements of the banquet would be awkward. He realized, once ushered into the high-ceilinged, spacious dining hall, that any and all possible socially embarrassing situations would have been foreseen and eliminated, given that Their Serene Highnesses had been living this way from the day of their births. The dining table was a massive four-sided structure fashioned from a faintly aromatic wood with a delicate bluish tinge which Kirk assumed was native to the planet. At the middle of the table's head was a kind of circular booth, able to swivel independently without disturbing the rest of the table, presumably so the princes could then converse with parties on either side of them. He was seated to the right of the princes' chair, with McCoy next to him and Spock seated to the princes' left. Kirk was grateful to see the two separated; not only was their newfound shared curiosity not fun, but the constant conversational undertones were beginning to drive him mad:

"On Earth they were called 'Siamese twins' for decades, after the nationality of the first pair to attain any kind of fame. Chang and Eng, I think they were named."

"When we return to the ship, we must scan all medical banks for any data as to the cause of the disability. There may be some genetic trait shared by humans and Nadorians that will shed light on Their Serene Highnesses' unique condition."

Kirk didn't recall who it was who said another person's shop talk is always fascinating, but he wished he were here now.

Too, he was beginning to wonder about the appropriateness of the term "disability." The princes seemed totally at home with their condition, able to navigate and engage in social situations with the best of them. It wasn't that you forgot their condition after seeing them for a while, Kirk realized, it was just that it ceased to make them seem that much different. As a child, Kirk had had a dog, Ranger, that had lost a leg in an accident. Young Jimmy had watched over the animal for days, bringing it food and carrying it around with him. It was Sam who finally convinced him that the dog had to learn to get around on its own. It soon did, causing them to call it "Tripod" from then on.

Sam. Blast it, where was Peter, anyway?

Kirk had not been surprised to find himself asked to make a toast—persons all over the galaxy attached a certain gravitas to the gold braid on Kirk's sleeve. As he rose, he realized part of his mind had been working on it for several minutes. Not that it would go down with the Fundamental Declaration of the Martian Colonies . . .

"In the name of the United Federation of Planets and Starfleet Command, I thank you all for your friendship and hospitality. I pray this is the first of many such occasions where we will meet as trusted allies and as friends."

But it wasn't bad. As he raised his glass, after tilting it toward the princes, Kirk noticed a genuine smile on the face of Abon, but a rather forced, dutiful version of that same expression worn by Delor. Kirk felt he had his work cut out for him.

The meal was excellent; some sort of native fish that seemed naturally boneless, served in a piquant sauce. They had even provided a vegetarian dish for Spock.

Glancing around the table when he had a moment's respite from fielding questions from Their Serene Highnesses, who seemed nearly to fight over Kirk's attention, he noticed Yeoman Barrows sharing some small joke with the Lady Pataal. Seeing a quizzical expression on the face of Dr. McCoy, Kirk had a hunch who they were discussing.

After the banquet came a formal dance. Kirk shared Scotty's reluctance for these functions. Though there were generally many attractive women present he wouldn't have minded dancing with, the gold braid also attracted many women of—he thought delicately—a more mature vintage, whom he dutifully accepted being dragged around the floor by. He noticed Spock in a graceful, if somewhat overly precise, pirouette with the Lady Pataal, but it was, as seemed to be the case tonight, the Princes Abon and Delor who drew the most attention. Not only did they dance, they danced with a skilled lightness that Kirk found remarkable. When only one had a partner, the other clasped his hands across his chest and closed his eyes, letting the other "lead" in a faultless exhibition of rhythm. This would have been remarkable enough, but then Abon extended a hand to Mrs. Roget, and Delor to the Lady Pataal. The four of them then joined in a simple yet skilled variation of what Roget told Kirk was a native dance in which Abon and Delor often exchanged the role of lead dancer with a frequency that sent Kirk's head spinning almost faster than theirs. He stole a glance at Spock, who was watching the proceedings in the mirrored ceiling, no doubt admiring their geometrical precision. At the end of the dance, the audience broke into spontaneous applause, which Kirk appreciatively joined.

Things were going well. Diplomatic matters had not

yet been broached, but Kirk knew these things take their own time and had developed the patience, and the necessary carapace, to let such things move at their own pace. Kirk had just finished a dance with Yeoman Barrows—under the watchful eye of Dr. McCoy, who was trying and failing to affect an aura of utter nonchalance—when he was approached by Commissioner Roget and Regent Lonal. With them were two persons who appeared to be in late middle age. One, a burly man with incongruously delicate features, to whom the matters of diplomacy did not seem to come easy, was introduced to Kirk as Counselor Docos, a member of the Nadorian Planetary Council. The other, a woman who was not beautiful, but acted as though she were, was Counselor Hanor. Each had been introduced to Kirk as the head of one of the tribes from which the princes had descended, Hanor the Delorites and Docos the Abonians. Kirk had thought their roles largely ceremonial, though they played their allegiances to the hilt. Hanor's robe was the color of burnt oranges, while Docos wore royal blue, both colors that had been incorporated into the garb of Their Serene Highnesses for reasons, Kirk now knew, that held greater relevance than fashion. Kirk had thought himself expected to dance with Counselor Hanor, dutifully offered her his arm, but was rebuffed—not an experience he was used to.

"Perhaps later, Captain Kirk," said Counselor Hanor, in a tone that said she'd be doing Kirk a favor. "Right now, there is a matter of much importance to be discussed." She was not only not beautiful, noted Kirk, with an almost technical interest, but quite frankly ugly, her hatchet face giving the impression of having been hewn by that same instrument.

"Counselor Hanor is correct," said Docos, his tone

seeming to grudgingly admit this fact. Seeing them, Kirk noticed that each possessed certain features that seemed hereditary, and were blended pleasantly in the features of the royal twins. "Concerning certain citizens of your Federation residing on Nador." *From his tone, you would think he was discussing internal parasites,* thought Kirk.

"It's the matter we touched on earlier, Captain," said Roget. "I know we were scheduled to meet with the local Federation citizens tomorrow, concerning their fears that their rights are endangered, but a sizable contingent of them seemed to have gathered on the palace grounds—"

"'A sizable contingent'?" said Counselor Hanor with a contemptuous snort. "They are a mob! They threaten the princes and the entire royal court."

"I'm sure threatening anyone is the farthest thing from their minds," said Kirk, gently. "Why were they permitted to gather on the palace grounds?"

"It is the custom of Their Royal Highnesses to tolerate dissent," said Docos, in a tone that said he doubted Their Royal Highnesses' wisdom. "Such groups are often permitted on the outer perimeter of the grounds, though no farther, of course, should such a contingent get out of hand—"

"You seem preoccupied with the threat of violence, Counselor," said Kirk, blandly.

"I'm sure it won't come to violence," interjected Roget, his eyes darting from one counselor to the other, "but there is that possibility, Captain. I've often spoken to them, so often that any influence I might have had seems to no longer carry—"

"You'd like me to speak to them," said Kirk with a nod.

"Something must be done," said Docos, "if not by you, then by the palace guard. They will not take an incursion into the palace grounds lightly. On the other hand," and he shrugged mildly, "it has been some time since they had any practice, so perhaps this would be a good time to—"

"I assure the counselor, such an incident would be looked upon with extreme distaste by the Federation Council," said Roget quickly, his tone conveying the proper combination of thoroughgoing distaste and warning, yet somehow without seeming threatening. "Captain, would you—?"

"Of course," said Kirk.

"I understand your starship carries many security troops," said Docos, blandly. "Perhaps it would be wise to utilize a few."

"We're trained as diplomats, too, Counselor Docos," replied Kirk, as they strolled through the crowd, toward the palace gates. "I'll try the option of the carrot before we bring out the stick."

The night air had grown cooler, yet it was not so cold as to be uncomfortable. The city lights had been ignited, bathing the graceful architecture in a lambent glow. From this distance, Kirk thought, as Counselor Docos and Commissioner Roget accompanied him, the gathered crowd seemed like normal citizens out for a fine night's walk. It was only when he drew closer that the sounds of angry muttering came to him, a low murmur that became louder as the mob recognized Roget.

"There are Nadorian separatists here, too," Roget whispered to Kirk, urgently.

Kirk nodded, knowing from experience that the Nadorians were probably waiting—or hoping—for the Federation citizens to try something.

"Citizens of Nador and of the Federation," said Commissioner Roget, from behind the gates, "I empathize with your cause and, as a man who in many ways is a citizen of both bodies, I assure you all that your cries will be heard."

This noble speech resulted in only an increase in the mob's rowdiness. Kirk saw some elements in the crowd shove others, who, in keeping with mob psychology, shoved back.

"Very well," said Roget, spreading an arm toward Kirk, "if you will no longer listen to me, perhaps you will heed the words of Captain James T. Kirk, of the Starship *Enterprise*."

This introduction brought at least a temporary respite in the roiling crowd. Kirk saw hundreds of pairs of eyes turned toward him, faces filled with pain, bewilderment, and need. He had seen such faces turned to him many times during his command, whether on the bridge during combat when it looked as though all was lost, or while under siege by Klingon warriors, outnumbered ten to one. Though his Starfleet psychological profile showed him to be emotionally quite stable—he could not otherwise have been promoted to the captaincy of a *Constitution*-class starship—he wondered, in situations like this, if he was stable enough to guide his people through one more crisis. And then he realized that that doubt was itself another indicator of his emotional stability; only a fool thinks himself incapable of failure.

"People of the Federation and of Nador," Kirk said, as an overture. He used the old orator's trick, learned from Professor Gill at the Academy, of slightly lowering his voice to make the crowd strain to hear his words. "I am here to assure you that the Federation will ensure full protection for its citizens, while respecting the rights of the native Nadorians." During the crowd's hush, he heard footsteps next to him; Spock and McCoy. He should have expected them to notice his departure.

"You say that now," cried a husky voice from the crowd, "but you and the commissioner will soon leave, and *then* where will we be?"

"I promise you, we will not leave Federation citizens in danger," said Kirk, emphatically. He paused; many of the crowd whom he judged to be Federation citizens had stopped and spoke intently to each other, occasionally gesturing at Kirk.

"Of course you can make that promise with assurance," called another voice, in which Kirk detected a Nadorian timbre, "for you intend to make Nador another of the growing line of puppet monarchies that dangle from the Federation's strings!"

Kirk scanned the crowd to try to determine who had spoken. Instead, he noted, on the edge of the crowd, a woman whose movements were so graceful as to belie their furtiveness. She was swathed from head to toe in some kind of dark, flowing garment whose purpose, Kirk assumed, was to conceal her identity. In one sense, it failed, and miserably: once he'd seen it, he would have noticed that supple figure anywhere. He told himself it was the purposefulness of her movements, so rare in an assemblage whose opinions could sway like a reed in a windstorm, rather than the allure of her person that drew his attention, and he believed it, owing to what happened next.

For as Kirk's gaze followed the woman, it was caught by another figure that she passed in front of. A figure with an achingly familiar hairline, and a set to the jaw that Kirk had, over the course of his life, wanted to disjoint several times, or at least as often as any younger brother had wanted to thrash his elder.

Sam's features, but younger, softened a little. So like Sam, yet . . .

. . . *Peter.*

"Your planet is free to choose its own destiny," replied Kirk, shouting now over the renewed roar of the crowd. He tried to keep track of Peter, but he was soon as lost as a stone thrown into a stormy sea. "Our presence here as guests, not as conquerors, should be proof of—"

"Captain, look out!" called Spock, suddenly. The Vulcan was at Kirk's side in a moment, pushing him roughly. Kirk heard something fly by his head, nearly missing him, something heavy enough to have done considerable damage, had it struck.

"Counselor Docos, Commissioner Roget," said Kirk, urgently, "please withdraw to the palace immediately."

"People of Nador," said Docos, instead moving forward, "I ask you to end this chaos! Do not act like those outlanders who—" An instant later, Docos stopped speaking. A projectile of some sort had struck him in the head; he dropped to the ground, flailing awkwardly, blood spurting like a fountain from the side of his head.

"Bones!" called Kirk. But McCoy had already started forward and was at Docos's side almost in time to catch him. The whirring of McCoy's medical tricorder went unheard over the renewed cries of the mob, hundreds of different voices keening heavenward in one cry of chaos.

"Captain, I suggest withdrawal," said Spock.

Kirk silently agreed. The mob was by now slamming itself against the palace gates, some of its members willingly assaulting the threshold, others pushed forward by others behind them. Those forced against their will, of course, turned and returned the gesture.

Not far ahead McCoy was half-carrying Docos back to the palace. Kirk joined them while Spock saw to Roget. "Counselor Docos," said Kirk, into the ear of the Nadorian that wasn't bleeding, "you had better close the palace immediately, before—"

Too late. With a screech like a banshee's, the palace gates caved inward.

The mob boiled onto the palace grounds.

Chapter Five

KIRK HAD BY NO MEANS forgotten his nephew, but he had a job to do. He glanced around to see Spock and McCoy spreading the word to palace officials and the partygoers. Just behind them, Commissioner Roget was bearing the bulk of Counselor Docos to safety. That was good of him; few would have blamed him had he simply run to his quarters and locked the door.

Kirk turned and saw that the mob was not far behind him. In fact, it seemed to be gaining, as if its collective rage gave it extra speed. Kirk whipped out his communicator with one hand, his phaser with the other. "Kirk to *Enterprise*. Emergency."

"Scott here, Captain. Shall I beam you up?"

"Negative," said Kirk. He turned a corner and stopped. "Beam down a contingent from security immediately, these coordinates—but tell them phasers on stun, only."

"Aye, sir!"

"And Scotty—experienced hands only. No rookies. Understood?"

"Aye, Captain," he replied, his tone betraying his uncertainty.

"Jim, what are you doing?" asked McCoy, now at his side. "We need all the help we can get!"

"We'll be fine, Doctor," said Kirk, in a tone McCoy appeared to find anything but convincing. "Where's Spock?"

"Here, Captain," said the science officer, approaching them. Heard over everything was the low mutter of the mob, growing in intensity as it neared them.

"Commissioner Roget?"

"Inside the palace, with Counselor Docos." Spock drew his phaser. "Phasers on stun, I presume?"

"Correct," said Kirk, grimly. The roar of the mob grew louder. It was like hearing the approach of a tidal wave.

"Isn't there any palace security?" asked McCoy, as he drew his own weapon.

"My very question to the commissioner," said Spock, adjusting his phaser as if McCoy has asked about the weather. "The palace indeed possesses a system to repel intruders, but such defenses are primarily concentrated on the perimeter. Once the protesters were let into the palace grounds, they would be unaffected by such measures."

"Shows the downside of a tolerant monarchy," said Kirk. He had to nearly shout to make himself heard as he whipped out his communicator. "Scotty, where are those—?"

Even over the keening drone of the mob the hum of the transporter made itself heard. Right then, it was the sweetest sound Kirk had ever heard. Security Chief Giotto materialized with phaser drawn, and five men. He looked around, immediately understanding the situation.

"We'll take our stand here, Chief," said Kirk. "Stun only. Many of them are Federation citizens."

Giotto replied, "Yes, sir." Giotto's handsome looks belied his skills as a security officer, but Kirk had seen him handle two men half again his own size without breaking a sweat. Kirk wouldn't have blamed him if he sweated this time, though. His men took their places around him, phasers drawn.

"Peter's with them," said Kirk urgently to Spock and McCoy. "If you see him, let me—"

"Here they come!" shouted Giotto.

"Fire!" said Kirk.

Around the corner of the palace hall they flooded, a human tide. As individuals they were loving husbands, sons, mothers, daughters, unique in their own right, each with something to contribute to society, given the chance. But they had forsaken their individuality when they joined the mob, and though Kirk hoped none of them would be severely hurt, he could make no promises.

Over the thunder of footfalls and shouts, phasers shrilled. A number of the mob went down, but not enough. Some of them in the forefront were nearly trampled by those behind them.

Kirk and his people continued to fire. They slowed the pack down somewhat, but didn't stop them. Rather than assaulting them directly, the crowd flowed around the *Enterprise* personnel, like a flood circumnavigating a crumbling breakwater.

But it did slow, and though many of the mob made it past them, many of them crumpled to the floor like empty suits of armor.

Kirk scanned the crowd as best he could, but he saw no sign of Peter. He did, however, catch a glimpse of the mysterious woman he had spied before, at the edge of the crowd. At this range he could tell that her eyes were nearly as dark as her garb. They flitted across him once, as if taking his measure, seeing there was nothing there to concern her, then moving on.

"Take over, Spock," shouted Kirk as he charged off, ignoring McCoy's shout of "Jim!?" behind him. Though unable to explain it—Spock and McCoy could hash it out later, and more power to them—he felt he had to head this woman off before something disastrous happened.

Kirk virtually dove sideways into the mob. One or two of them charged him, and were phasered. After that the others seemed to think better of interfering with him. Kirk headed for the far wall, which had a tapestry depicting some ancient event in Nadorian history. It seemed to be the coronation of one of Their Serene Highnesses' ancestors. He thought he had seen it move as the mob rushed by, pulling it to one side. He quickly realized why: there was an archway behind it.

A couple of the crowd tried to follow Kirk. He caught a glimpse of their eyes: there was nothing there, no curiosity, not even hatred, just sheer animal instinct and the will to smash. Kirk gave one of them a martial-arts chop and shoved his fist wrist-deep into the other's ample stomach. *Not as elegant as Spock's Vulcan nerve pinch,* he though wryly, *but it gets the job done.* Taking a few steps past the archway, he turned and played his phaser, now set far higher than stun, on the archway. The resulting shower of wreckage would make sure no one followed him; he could make a formal apology to the Nadorian government later. He made his way up the stairs, two at a time, through a cloud of rock dust.

As he thought, the stairway emptied onto a balcony he had noted earlier, overlooking the main banquet hall. The main floor's passage to the banquet hall had been very leisurely designed, with the intent of showing off the various palace treasures and artifacts placed there. But the stairway Kirk had just taken was, as he had hoped, a good deal more direct. Below he could see the diners vacating the hall at the bidding of palace security guards, in a none too orderly fashion. He noticed Yeoman Barrows standing over the princes, who had lost their balance in the furor; Their Serene Highnesses lay on the floor, limbs flailing like a scuttled crab.

Earlier in the evening, Kirk had admired their grace and poise and the resolve with which they had coped with their situation. Now, watching them jerk spasmodically as they tried to right themselves, he felt only pity, the last emotion the princes would wish bestowed upon them.

Through the archway leading to the banquet hall Kirk heard the rumble of footsteps closing the gap. He ran to the thick draperies on one side of the balcony, leaped, and began to climb down.

While clambering down, Kirk noted a figure entering the hall: the unknown woman he had noticed earlier. She dashed so swiftly that she seemed to be gliding over the floor, her feet unseen beneath her gown. Barrows, still grappling with the princes, gave no sign of seeing her.

"Barrows!" shouted Kirk, still a few feet from the floor. "Behind you!"

Barrows pivoted with admirable speed, phaser at the ready. Her quarry, however, had spun, drawing a hand weapon of a design Kirk didn't recognize, pointed directly at Kirk.

She fired, a second after making a minute adjustment in her aim. A controlled force beam, violet in hue, severed the drape Kirk was climbing down, bringing him to the floor much more quickly than he had expected. However, the remainder of the drapery he had yet to climb bunched under him, breaking his fall.

Caught briefly in the drapes, Kirk could do nothing to prevent the woman pushing Barrows away, roughly, and running for the princes herself. Kirk drew his own phaser, took aim—

—and halted. The mysterious woman had deftly, yet somehow respectfully, yanked Their Serene Highnesses into a standing position and began guiding them toward the far exit. Once on their feet again, their normal sense of balance reasserted itself. Delor took the lead, while Abon faced the rear, their short strides keeping their feet from becoming entangled, yet making good time.

"Who are you?" asked Kirk, as he neared the woman and Barrows.

"No time," she said, in a low, throaty tone. She brought out her weapon again, this time swinging it past Kirk and aiming it at the apex of the archway leading to the banquet hall. She fired, releasing another burst of violet energy. "Help me!" she commanded.

Kirk caught on soon enough. He nodded at Barrows's inquisitive gaze, and she and Kirk brought their phasers up, blending their force with that of their new ally.

The stone of the archway first quivered a bit, releasing trailing wisps of stone dust, then collapsed, just as the approaching mob surged around the corner. They halted as tons of stone crashed before them then, after a moment of panic, like that of a trapped animal, began to retrace their steps.

Too late. Over the top of the mound of rock, Kirk saw that the security contingent from the *Enterprise* had caught up with them, firing phasers at will, spraying them with stunning force. With nowhere to go, the crowd tried to turn upon its attackers, but it had no real chance of success.

Spock climbed over the pile of wreckage and bodies, dispelling trails of stone dust with his free hand. "Are the princes well, Captain?"

"Safe and sound."

"And you?"

"Somewhat the worse for wear," said Kirk, gingerly touching the spot where he had made contact with the floor of the banquet hall, "but under the circumstances, fine." Spock nodded and turned to help the security officers drag the unconscious rioters away, lest they smother one another.

"Give them a hand, Barrows," said Kirk.

Barrows's eyes jerked briefly toward the strange woman, then back to Kirk's. "Aye, sir," she said, holstering her phaser.

"McCoy," called Kirk, "check the princes, make sure they're all right." McCoy detached himself from the rest of the *Enterprise* personnel, climbed over the barrier of rubble, and made his way past Kirk.

Kirk turned to the woman, who had not yet put away her weapon. He still held his, not wishing to give her the upper hand. "Who are you? What was the idea of shooting me down like that?"

"Had I not," she replied, dryly, "you would not yet have attained the floor. I needed you down here. You climb like a girl." If that remark referred to this girl, Kirk realized, it would have been a compliment; from the agility he had seen her display, he was certain she could climb like a monkey.

"And my first question?" Kirk demanded.

She finally stowed her force-beam weapon in the depths of her garb and lifted her hands to her head, pulling back her hood and unwrapping the cloth that covered the bottom two-thirds of her face. "I am Llora," she said, "Chief Securitrix for Their Royal Highnesses."

"You have an odd way of attending to their security," said Kirk, tucking his phaser away.

"We have a saying on Nador," replied Llora. Freed of the scarf that had swathed her face, her voice was low and musical, with an accent Kirk had heard, in differing strengths and modulations, in other voices that evening. "'Better to crush approaching parasites with your feet than to pick them off your person with your hands.' I was infiltrating the mob, to try to learn their intent."

"Oh? Did you get any idea who's behind this unrest?"

Llora shrugged, her muscles rippling beautifully under her gown. "I'm not yet convinced there is any one person or will behind it. Nadorians are historically a dissatisfied people, and it takes little to exploit this."

"That must make your job rough," said Kirk, smiling slightly.

"It is of little consequence how difficult my task is," replied Llora, stiffly. "It is my job." She turned and stalked away.

"Just a moment," called Kirk. "I'm not—"

"Captain," came Spock's voice from behind him. "I believe you will be interested in seeing this particular protester."

Kirk pivoted to see a familiar face looking at him, smiling through a layer of dirt and rock dust with a sheepish, scapegrace grin he had seen many times in his life, both on the face of his brother Sam, and, if he were honest with himself, in a mirror.

"Peter!"

"Hi, Uncle Jim," said Peter, his voice slightly subdued. He obviously knew the predicament he was in, and the fact that a great deal of explaining was required.

There was a moment of uncertainty between them. It had been months since they had seen each other, and he seemed to have grown a foot. What was the proper greeting for a self-conscious young man caught with the wrong crowd from his properly official uncle?

The hell with it, Kirk decided. He reached out, wrapped Peter in the biggest, strongest hug he could muster, and was delighted to feel it returned.

"What the devil were you doing with these people?" asked Kirk, pushing Peter to arm's length. Now that he was sure the boy was safe, he could lay into him. "I'm going to assume you don't believe in the violent overthrow of an established monarchy, but did it ever occur to you that you could have been killed?"

Peter opened his mouth to reply, but was interrupted by the sound of Spock clearing his throat. "Captain, with your permission I will report our status to the ship."

Kirk nodded. "And check with McCoy, find out how the princes are."

"Understood," Spock said, and moved away. Beyond him, Kirk saw the *Enterprise* security officers picking the captured protesters out of the rubble, working side by side with the palace guard. Llora was having a discussion with Chief Giotto that seemed perhaps more animated than it needed to be. She was pointing in Kirk's direction. Kirk could guess why, and produced his communicator.

"Kirk to *Enterprise*. Two to beam up, immediately."

"Aye, sir," replied Scotty. Kirk heard only the opening syllables of Securitrix Llora's enraged shout before the entire scene dissolved around him.

Chapter Six

"Now," said Kirk, seating himself in a chair in the cabin that had been assigned to Peter aboard the *Enterprise,* "we'll continue the interrogation we began planetside."

"'Interrogation'?" asked Peter. He looked much better now, showered, with a change of clothes, his injuries—all of them minor, thank heaven—attended to by Nurse Chapel, whose disapproving looks at Peter's condition almost overshadowed her happiness at seeing him again.

Kirk had told Uhura and Scotty that he was incommunicado, to anyone south of the Federation president, "and particularly to a high-handed Nadorian security officer calling herself Llora. Refer her to Commissioner Roget. Blame sunspots, blame emissions from the central coil, blame the Great Bird of the Galaxy, just make it stick."

Nodding at his nephew, Kirk repeated, "Interrogation. You're my prisoner, mister, and if I don't like the answers to your questions, you'll find yourself in the brig—"

"That's not such a threat," said Peter, with a smile.

"—or back on Nador in the capable hands of Securitrix Llora. And I assure you, her methods of questioning will be a great deal more uncomfortable than mine. Is that understood?"

Peter gulped. "Yes, sir."

Kirk suppressed a smile of his own. With the fear of God properly installed, they could proceed.

"To continue," said Kirk, "what were you doing there?"

"I was spying," said Peter. This frankness had the desired effect; Kirk was silent for a moment. "On the dissidents," continued Peter, a moment before Kirk would have asked him to continue. He'd give his nephew that, he was good at brinkmanship.

"Why did you feel there was reason to spy on them?"

Peter shrugged uneasily. "I felt something was wrong. Too many of the Federation citizens with resident alien status on Nador were stirred up too easily, encouraged to violence too quickly. Uncle Jim, I think there's someone working them up behind the scenes."

"An agitator?"

Peter nodded. "Not that the Federationists don't have valid complaints. Lots of the Nadorians resent our presence, treat us as second-class citizens. The rumor is that when the planetary government is handed back to Nador, we'll be subject to a whole bunch of unfair 'alien' taxes and discriminatory laws, even if Nador becomes a member of the Federation. Not that rumors make violence acceptable," he added, after a pause.

"Of course not. But didn't any of the Federation citizens suspect you?"

"No." Peter shook his head, baffled. "Why should they?"

"Your name," said Kirk, impatiently. "You're my nephew."

"There are lots of Kirks in the Federation, Uncle Jim," said Peter. "You understand that, right?"

"Of course," said Kirk, quickly.

"And I hadn't told anyone we're related," continued Peter. "I wanted to fit in on my own. Good thing, too. I hoped to have a lot more information on whoever's stirring up the protesters to give you by this time. But everybody's playing it pretty close to their vests." He shook his head ruefully. "This undercover stuff is hard."

That time, Kirk did grin, but smothered it before Peter could see. "At least you found some way to make use of your free time," he said, dryly.

"Don't get me wrong," Peter said quickly, "Commissioner Roget had no idea what I was doing. Anything I did, I'm totally responsible for, no one else."

"Oh, I assumed that," said Kirk, rising. Still, the boy's sentiments did him credit.

The entry tone at the door sounded. "Come," said Kirk and Peter at the same time. They exchanged a glance, and smiled.

Spock and McCoy entered, Peter shaking hands with the physician happily, after McCoy gravely inspected Chapel's work.

"Status?" asked Kirk.

"Damage, some of it irreparable, to the ancient statuary of the palace," began Spock. Kirk watched McCoy out of the corner of his eye, waiting for him to take the bait.

"'The statuary'? Spock, what about—?"

"And only minor injuries sustained by the palace guests and staff. None of the rioters were severely injured," said Spock, as if McCoy had not spoken. "The rioters have been detained for questioning. Securitrix Llora is quite displeased with what she called your 'high-handedness' at removing one of the rioters before her eyes."

"Let the commissioner smooth things over," said Kirk with a shrug. "Spock, Peter seems to think there's a party deliberately agitating these riots. Did you get any impression that any of the rioters knew who was behind it?"

Spock shook his head. "No, Captain, once their rampage had been halted, they seemed bereft of direction and purpose. This would tally with the supposition that they were being used."

"If they had been able to injure the princes or any of the dignitaries present, it would have played hell with the negotiations," said McCoy.

"Thank you, Doctor," said Kirk. He rose and headed for the doorway, pivoting there to wag an index finger at Peter. "You're to consider yourself under house arrest, young man. You're not to leave the ship without my permission, is that understood?"

"Yes, sir," said Peter, contritely.

"Can you beat that?" said Kirk, to Spock and McCoy, as they headed for the turbolift. "He was spying on the rioters."

"Quite a chip off the old block," said McCoy.

"He is that," agreed Kirk. "His father would have been proud of him."

"Gentlemen," said Spock, in a tone of mild astonishment, "am I to understand that you tolerate this type of conduct? Had the boy been caught or injured, or worse, the negotiations with the Nadorians could have been severely set back."

"Of course, Spock," said Kirk. "But he showed initiative and creativity."

"And gumption," added McCoy, chin lifted in Spock's direction. "File it under 'illogical comma very,' Mr. Spock."

"That file is quite sizable, Doctor, but I believe I have room for yet another entry."

"Spock," asked Kirk, "why were we caught unaware by the princes' conjoined state? I gave our file a quick scan and there's no mention of it."

"I was almost taken by surprise myself," said Spock, ignoring, if he even saw, McCoy's dry glance at Kirk, "and discussed this matter with Regent Lonal. It seems that the princes, and the Nadorian people, are quite concerned with being perceived by the rest of the Federation as a 'normal' people, and did not wish us to prejudge them on the basis of the princes' conjoined status." Spock looked at McCoy, who had snorted loudly. "I quite agree, Doctor, that the term 'normal' means little, given the physical variegations of sentient beings present in the galaxy's inhabited planets, but such logic often holds little sway where emotion is concerned—as you should well be aware from personal experience. Even among their own people, the princes restrict their public appearances; most of the Federation citizens were unaware of the princes' unique nature."

"And tonight's banquet was deemed to be their 'coming-out party'?" asked Kirk. "The place where we got a good look at them? I hoped they'd hold a better opinion of us than that."

"Well, the first date's over," said McCoy. "If they're going to join the Federation, it's going to have to be 'warts and all.'"

"Bucolically stated, but at its essence, correct," said Spock.

"Jim, a word?" asked McCoy as the turbolift doors opened.

Kirk glanced at Spock. "I'll be right up." Spock nodded as he gripped the lift handle, and was gone.

"What's the trouble, Bones? I've got a lot of diplomacy to practice."

"What was that business about using only experienced security hands for riot control—'no rookies'?"

"Do I have to explain my command decisions to you?" asked Kirk.

"Don't answer a question with a question!" said McCoy, biting off the words angrily. "If more security troops had beamed down, the riot might have been contained with no injuries whatsoever."

"Except on the part of the security staff, had that ever occurred to you?"

"Of course it did, Jim. But it's part of their job."

"Perhaps they should have a chance to live a little first," replied Kirk. There was an odd tone to his voice, one McCoy couldn't identify. "Anything else, Doctor?" asked Kirk, as the turbolift returned for him, clearly not caring if there was anything else or not.

And before McCoy could reply, Kirk was gone.

McCoy returned to sickbay, feeling every bit as baffled by Kirk's actions as Spock could have been.

"I trust you weren't injured by any of the rioters' activities, Mrs. Roget?" asked Kirk solicitously. "I'm sorry I had to leave so abruptly, but—"

"Captain, please, I'm married to a diplomat," Janine Roget said with a laugh. "There's no need to apologize for doing your duty! Remind me to tell you about the time we escaped Rigel VI with nothing on our backs but our bedclothes."

Kirk smiled. "I look forward to hearing it."

"In the meantime, Captain," said Sylvan Roget, smiling fondly at his wife as he took her place on the viewscreen, "the decision of the Nadorians on whether or not to join the Federation is only four days away, and the handover ceremony only six. We have some rather major repairs to make in Federation-Nadorian relations."

"I know. Are Their Royal Highnesses quite perturbed?"

"To my surprise, they are not," said Roget. "While they realize the gravity of the situation, they also seem to have enjoyed it, in an anarchic kind of way."

"I don't suppose they've had much in the way of action in their lives," said Kirk.

"Nonetheless, the rest of their court is still quite angry over the participation of Federation citizens in the disturbance. Some sort of conciliatory gesture is in order, Captain. No one holds the Federation responsible for the riots, but—"

"I should hope not," said Kirk. "There were plenty of Nadorians citizens involved, too."

"Yes, but it does behoove us to take some action to show them that we do regret the damage it has done to the cause of diplomacy."

"Can't an apology be issued through normal diplomatic channels?"

"I've instituted just such an apology," said Roget, "but whether it will even reach the princes by the time the handover is to be determined is anyone's guess. They're quite insulated from day-to-day life, Captain."

"I'm sure." Kirk thought for a moment. Then, as he became aware of the faint but pervasive sounds always present on the bridge—the hum and beep of consoles, the click of switches, the drone of commands given and acknowledged, the multitude of sounds that he had learned to screen out, yet that had become so familiar—it suddenly became clear to him.

"Commissioner," he said, calmly, "at the banquet, Princes Abon and Delor seemed quite interested in the day-to-day operations of the *Enterprise*."

"I'm sure they are, Captain. After all, their lives have been quite cloistered, not only due to their social status but to their physical condition. They've been denied many of the normal emotional outlets most young men have. In many ways they're still boys."

"Just as I thought," nodded Kirk. "I have an idea . . ."

"You're going to invite the entire royal entourage aboard the *Enterprise,* Jim?"

"Why not, Bones?" Kirk poured himself a second finger of brandy, inclined the bottle toward McCoy and Spock, both of whom declined the refill, then set it down on the desk next to his bed. "Their Royal Highnesses seem very interested in the workings of the ship, isn't that right, Spock?"

"The majority of their conversation was confined to inquiries about life aboard a starship," said Spock.

"I hope I'm not alone here," said McCoy, in that martyr's voice whose tone belied his words, "but hasn't it occurred to you that it was only by a near-miracle that the princes weren't at least injured in the palace riot? If that mob had gotten to them—" He shook his head, drained his glass, and poured himself another couple of fingers after all.

"I believe the captain is well aware of that, Doctor," said Spock, looking at Kirk with the same expression he used when facing him across a chessboard. "In fact, I might go so far as to say that the captain is counting on such an occurrence."

"That's going a little far, Spock," said Kirk, sipping brandy and feeling its fire prowl through him. He rose, pacing back and forth. "While I agree it's my personal desire to see whoever is agitating the rioters—not to mention who was behind the attack on my ship—"

"Which is almost certainly the same party," said Spock.

"—which is almost certainly the same party, yes. While I would very much like to see them identified and brought to trial, I would be only slightly less satisfied if they faded into space and were never heard from again. The threat to the princes' lives and to the stability of Nador must be our primary concern."

"Not much chance of them fading away," said McCoy. "We've seen too many of their type, over too many planets."

"I unfortunately agree," said Kirk. "And it follows that, given the . . . efficiency of their kind, that the easiest way to destabilize Nador and blacken the eye of the Federation would be to kill the princes. Regicide."

"Actually, that term refers precisely to the murder of a king, from its root, *regis,* from your Latin," said Spock. "Barbaric, but often effective."

"Brutally so, Spock. Faced with that probability, then, doesn't it make sense to bring the princes to an environment where we can virtually assure their continued good health?"

"Logical," said McCoy, not looking at Spock.

"Indeed," said Spock, emptying his glass and placing

it on Kirk's desk. "And if some sort of attempt is made on the lives of the princes while they are aboard the *Enterprise*—"

"Then we'll have greatly narrowed the field of suspects, won't we?" smiled Kirk, refilling his officers' glasses and hoisting his own. "Gentlemen, to success."

Both Spock and McCoy drank to the sentiment, but it seemed to Kirk that neither looked particularly confident.

It took some persuading to get everyone on board— literally as well as figuratively. Kirk knew that Princes Abon and Delor would virtually leap at the chance to accept Kirk's invitation to come aboard the *Enterprise,* but, as always seemed to be the case in these matters, the most direct course was the one most ensnarled by red tape. Kirk first issued the invitation through Commissioner Roget's office, who would in turn extend it to Regent Lonal, for eventual transmission to Their Royal Highnesses.

So in the end, Kirk was not surprised to have his invitation turned down. He would not have been surprised to find that it had never made it past Regent Lonal to Their Royal Highnesses.

"You played your best cards," said McCoy. "Now what do we do?"

"We're not out of aces yet," replied Kirk, with a sly smile that made McCoy feel sorry for whoever it was directed at. "Bones, don't take this the wrong way, but I'm going to pay a social call on Yeoman Barrows."

"And what way should I take it?" said McCoy, irritably.

* * *

"Pataal?"

"This is she." The voice of the young consort sounded through the speaker. *"Who is this?"*

"It's Tonia. Tonia Barrows. I'd hoped you wouldn't mind if I called you on your private—"

"Tonia! Oh, of course not!" The girl practically gushed with relief. *"It's so good to talk to you! I was so sorry about that silly diplomatic incident."*

"Oh, me, too," said Barrows. "You know, we're probably violating their silly 'protocol' right now. I just called to say I'm sorry you won't be able to attend."

"Attend? Attend what?"

"Captain Kirk had the idea of inviting Their Royal Highnesses aboard the *Enterprise* for a banquet tomorrow night, to apologize for the role the Federation citizens played in the riot. But, of course that won't happen—"

"Won't it?" said Pataal. *"May I speak to you later?"*

Yeoman Barrows closed the connection, and the viewscreen in her quarters went dark. "I feel just awful," she said, turning. "Pataal's my friend."

"Sometimes friends have to do things that may not seem very friendly, at first," said Kirk, who had been standing out of range. "Just ask Spock and McCoy. But not in each other's hearing."

"Captain Kirk?"

"Yes, Commissioner Roget. How are you, sir?"

"Very well, thank you. I'm calling to say that Princes Abon and Delor have accepted your offer of a state dinner and tour of the Enterprise."

"I'm delighted to hear it."

"How did you ever get through to them?"

"The shortest distance between two points," said Kirk, innocently.

"But what about the security issues involved, Captain?" Scotty asked, plaintively. "These people have barely discovered warp drive. Isn't showin' 'em engineerin' a violation of the Prime Directive—or somethin'?"

"I'm quite familiar with the finer points of Starfleet General Order One, Scotty," said Kirk, with no trace of irony, "but trust me, it doesn't apply here. I know you don't like having strangers in engineering, but it won't be for long."

"Well, if I must," said Scotty, with a manful shake of his head.

"That's the spirit," said Kirk, clapping him on the shoulder. "I knew I could count on you."

"Aye, sir," said Scotty with a sigh. "You can that," though it could be inferred from his manner that he would rather give the visitors a peek up his kilt.

The night of the state dinner found Kirk in virtually every corner of the *Enterprise* at once. The crew often thought of him as omnipresent, but this was the first time anyone could recall him actually attempting to achieve it.

Even Peter, who seemed to see his uncle every time he turned around. To this point, Peter Kirk had enjoyed his house arrest aboard the *Enterprise,* reacquainting himself with old friends and making some new ones, roaming the ship as he pleased. That all came to a stop one night when he returned to his cabin after a stint in the gym to find Kirk waiting for him.

"Peter." His uncle smiled, too quickly. "I suppose you've heard what's going on tonight?"

"Yes, sir," replied Peter, after a moment's thought. He wasn't sure if this was a trap; if so, was it better to feign ignorance or admit to the truth? Well, he had always been a bad liar.

"Did you have any plans?"

"Uh . . . nothing major, sir."

"Good." His uncle smiled the smile he used when he got his own way. "Because tonight, you're confined to quarters."

"But, Uncle Jim—sir," he corrected, seeing Kirk's smile morph instantly to a steely frown, "I had plans tonight. Lieutenant Sulu was going to show me some fencing moves, and—"

"Sulu's got bridge duty—he volunteered," added Kirk, at his nephew's expression, which seemed more than a little suspicious. "I told him I'd tell you."

"But why?" asked Peter.

"We've got lots of guests coming—Nadorian guests. You're still something of a sore point with them, and I want to make sure nothing happens to aggravate that wound until I can smooth things over with the Nadorians. You bouncing all around the ship, enjoying yourself, would be the last thing I need them to see, right now. Do you understand?"

"I guess." He nearly sighed, until he realized that would have been the action of a little boy; the next words out of a child's mouth would have been: "But it isn't fair!" But Peter Kirk was no longer a child.

"Good," said Kirk. "Thank you. I'll make it up to you. Oh," he added, as a seeming afterthought, "the Nadorians may want a statement taken of your activities planetside—"

"I won't—"

"No one's asking you to turn in your friends," said Kirk, in a soothing voice, "just a statement concerning your activities. Why don't you get started on that tonight?"

"Yes, sir."

Kirk nodded reassuringly and headed for the door. "And Peter—thank you."

"You already thanked me."

"Not for that." He smiled, and Peter saw something of his father in the sparkle in Kirk's eyes. "For not saying 'It isn't fair.'"

Peter stood for a moment after the door closed, thinking, then roused himself and sat before the cabin's computer.

The quantity of transporter rooms aboard the *Enterprise* was probably sufficient to beam up the entire entourage of Princes Abon and Delor at once; such a display of Starfleet efficiency would almost certainly have impressed them. Nonetheless, Kirk chose to bring them up six at a time, in order to personally greet them.

"Gonna lay on the old charm, eh?" asked McCoy, skeptically.

"I wouldn't have put it in exactly those words," said Kirk, as they headed for the transporter room, "but that's pretty much the idea, yes. I intend to be the first thing they see when they step off the pad."

"Oh, given what happened the last time they saw you, that should be very reassuring."

They arrived at the transporter room just in time to see Commissioner and Mrs. Roget materializing. The commissioner looked resplendent in his black uniform

with silver trim, a color scheme that nicely comple-
mented the gown worn by Mrs. Roget, which seemed to
float around her like an argent mist. If Kirk was going
to "lay on the old charm," he thought, he might as well
start with such a charming subject.

"Good evening, Captain," said Roget, shaking hands
with Kirk. "The others are waiting below. Oh, by the
way—I took this opportunity to beam up a few more
crates to your cargo hold, was that all right?"

"I hope storing your gear is the worst problem we
have tonight," replied Kirk. "Mr. Scott?"

"Counselors Docos and Hanor and Regent Lonal are
signalin' ready for transport, sir," said Scotty, who
probably thought he owed himself a look at the
strangers who would be intruding in his domain. Spock
stood next to him, nodding and half-bowing to
Commissioner and Mrs. Roget. Scotty gazed at Kirk for
a moment, then said, "If you like, sir, I may be able to
lose them in a transporter loop for a few hours."

Kirk glared at Scotty; he had thought he was in better control of his features than that. "That won't be necessary, Mr. Scott," he said, pasting on a smile. "Beam
them aboard, nice and easy."

The air over the transporter platform shimmered,
then coalesced to form three figures. Counselors Docos
and Hanor immediately shot a sharp glance at each
other, as if each had suspected the other of planning
some sort of midtransport mischief. It was Regent
Lonal who was first to march off the transporter pad,
toward Kirk.

"Regent Lonal, Counselors Docos and Hanor, on
behalf of the United Federation of Planets and Starfleet
Command, may I welcome you aboard the *U.S.S.
Enterprise.*"

"You may," said the Regent. He met Kirk's gaze, but did not offer his hand. He looked around the room, slowly, then back at Kirk. "Is this your entire ship? It seems rather cramped."

Kirk spoke quickly, to drown out a strangled eruption of indignation from somewhere behind the transporter controls. "This is but one of hundreds of chambers, Regent. By the end of the evening, you'll know her as well as I do."

Counselor Hanor frankly shouldered Counselor Docos aside—*and with those shoulders, she could alter the course of an old Earth buffalo,* thought Kirk—and approached Kirk, offering her hand. Somewhat surprised by this coyness, Kirk gallantly took it and lightly kissed it, then shook hands with Docos, who offered his hand, in an obvious imitation of an Earth-style handshake, wearing a slightly embarrassed expression as he glanced at Hanor, as if to say, "What can you do?"

"Counselors, welcome to the *Enterprise,*" said Kirk. "I hope this is the first of many times our people travel together through the heavens."

"Thank you, Captain," said Docos, and he seemed to mean it.

Hanor smiled, said something indistinguishable, and headed to the edge of the crowd, to obtain a better view of the proceedings than Docos.

"The palace is signaling the princes are ready to come aboard, Captain," came Uhura's voice, from the transporter console.

"Then let's not delay this historic occasion any longer," said Kirk. "Mr. Scott, beam them aboard."

Once again the harnessed energies of the transporter hummed, and three figures materialized on the platform. No, four, Kirk corrected himself. The princes would naturally stand on the same pad. Flanking them on either side were the Lady Pataal, and—Kirk knew this to be unavoidable—Chief Securitrix Llora.

Kirk started forward to greet them, but was headed off by Llora, who seemed only to step from the platform but landed several feet from it. She scanned the room, dark eyes going from side to side, as if she expected phasers to pop out from behind every panel. Her energy weapon seemed to appear in her hand as if transported there. "Are you well, Your Highnesses?" she asked.

It was Delor who responded; Kirk knew this only because he was dressed primarily in blue. Otherwise, the twin princes seemed as alike to him as the conjoined figures on a playing card. "We are well, Securitrix," said Delor.

If there was irritation in the prince's tone, she decided not to hear it. Kirk smiled to himself; he had suffered that kind of selective deafness now and then. The princes rotated on the transporter platform, moving like two figures glued to a pivoting stick, taking in everything with a barely contained very unprincelike awe (which Kirk found rather charming), while Securitrix Llora faced Kirk, her superb brows arching. "Captain." In that single word was a challenge: *This isn't over yet.*

"Securitrix," replied Kirk, neutrally. "Welcome aboard the *Enterprise.* You, too, my lady."

"Oh, Captain, thank you." The Lady Pataal was also looking about, her glance more appreciative than that of her transporting companion. "What a wonderful ship! May I see more of it?"

"Of course," nodded Kirk, smiling appreciatively. Here was a woman who knew how to talk about a starship. Pataal joined the rest of the entourage, saying hello to McCoy, who welcomed the girl warmly, as Kirk approached the platform.

"Your Serene Highnesses," Kirk said, "welcome to the *U.S.S. Enterprise*. May the warmth of the welcome we give you in our domain match that of the welcome you gave us in yours."

"Thank you, Captain," said Abon. He took the lead as they stepped from the platform, nodding gratefully at Kirk's welcome, then offering his hand. Abon straightened his neck then, his head barely touching the back of Delor's, and the two rotated.

"We are most appreciative of this opportunity, Captain," said Delor. He did not offer his hand. The princes might have been identical physically, but, as with most twins, there were many differences beneath the surface—or, rather, surfaces. "We found the process you call 'transporting' quite unique—"

"—and delightful," said Abon. Had Kirk not been watching them, if would have been impossible to tell that two people were speaking.

"I'm glad you enjoyed it," replied Kirk. "You might wish to discuss it with Dr. McCoy, who has his own, equally strong views."

"We should enjoy that," said Abon. The princes had now taken one step sideways to the right, putting them equidistant from Kirk.

"Please, let me conduct you to the dining hall," said Kirk, sweeping a hand toward the door.

The princes followed, their entourage followed them, and the entire parade glided through the halls of the *Enterprise,* the heads of Their Serene Highnesses, and those of most of the Nadorians as well, turning so rapidly as they tried to take in every sight that Kirk feared Bones might have to repair some strained necks.

To their credit, Kirk's crew handled themselves well. Not just those chosen to attend the banquet, but those who, going about their normal duties in the ship's halls, had no idea the princes were aboard. Kirk had, during his years in space, noted the odd fact that human beings are likely to regard as more bizarre some deviation from the standard humanoid form than the weirdest abstract alien physique. Knowing this, he gave high marks to his crew, who barely cast a second glance at the princes, though it was obvious many of them wanted to, partly owing to their unique physical conjoining, but mainly to the unique grace with which the twins moved.

As Kirk escorted them down the halls of the *Enterprise,* some detail of the ship's design would occasionally strike the monarchs, requiring Kirk to deliver an explanation. Either the twins examined the object of interest while standing sideways before it, or one would bend to deliver a full scrutiny. Then, after a few seconds, the other would tap his twin on his left elbow, at which point they would rotate one hundred and eighty degrees, and repeat the process. Kirk regarded with admiration their achievement of learning how to exist with what could have been such a major handicap. Though he tried not to stare, he felt that Abon and Delor could not have been ignorant of the hundreds of eyes upon them. Abon, who seemed justly proud of the ease with which he and his twin navigated life, bore this with a greater grace than Delor, who, from a slight reticence in his manner, seemed to take great pains to make sure he was not performing for the crowd.

The seating arrangements for the banquet—to be held in the re-dressed officers' lounge on the aft side of deck four—could have proven tricky. No one in the princes' entourage had broached to Kirk the concept of seating the twins. Kirk felt certain that this had been a deliberate oversight on the part of certain elements in the government that wished him embarrassed. But when the princes entered the banquet hall, they were delighted to find in the place of honor a chair, specially constructed just for them, as fully functional as their own furniture on Nador, but designed along the cool, flowing lines of the *Enterprise*. Kirk had kept several of Scotty's most talented engineers busy with its design, based on specifications supplied by Spock, who remembered everything about the chair they had sat in during the reception planetside.

Kirk told the princes that the chair was a gift, then found himself startled, but gratified, to be on the receiving end of a Nadorian medal. It was engraved with the faces of Princes Abon and Delor, heads back-to-back, looking very much like the Roman god Janus, for meritorious service for his handling of the rioters, and the protection he had afforded Their Serene Highnesses. He made a short speech upon receiving it, having the good grace not to dwell too long on the gazes of the Counselors Docos and Hanor, Regent Lonal, or Securitrix Llora.

The entertainment for the evening had gone swimmingly, if Kirk said so himself. Feeling the Nadorian contingent would be curious about Earth culture, he had prevailed upon Scotty to render some Nadorian songs upon his beloved bagpipes which, Kirk admitted, he could take in small enough doses. The reception to this performance had been so enthusiastic that Scotty was about to begin another set, before he caught Kirk making a slashing motion across his throat, a gesture Scotty was all too sure could become more than symbolic if not obeyed.

After dinner the tour of the ship began. The princes seemed interested in literally every aspect of starship life, from the bridge to the hangar bay. The Lady Pataal and Yeoman Barrows seemed thicker than thieves, continually making that incomprehensible transition between capable grown women to giggling girls, then back again. He approached them at one point, purely to ask Pataal how she liked the tour, only to find her in earnest conversation with Barrows, apparently concerning some of the more intimate details of her physical relationship with Their Serene Highnesses. Kirk inquired courteously and briefly after her, then hastily reversed course.

Though Prince Abon, from his former statements, seemed to be the twin who had an interest in astronomy, both princes seemed most intrigued by the stellar cartography section of the ship. Spock took the lead here, calling up charts of many different systems across the galaxy, including those of Earth and Vulcan.

"Your Serene Highnesses may find this of personal interest," said Spock, fingers tapping keys without looking at them. On the screen before them appeared a pair of stars Kirk knew well. "Castor and Pollux in the constellation Gemini," said Spock, "a set of twin stars, named after twins from Earth mythology."

"I had heard of the stars," replied Abon, eyes fixed on the screen, "but I was unaware the names were from Terran culture."

"They shared the same mother, but different fathers," said Spock, "yet were identical twins, in the disregard for logic that myths often have. They were called the Dioscuri, 'Dio' from Dios, meaning 'god,' and 'kouroi,' or 'boys,' in the Earth Latin. 'Divine boys' is often the translation of the term."

"'Divine boys,'" said Abon with a laugh. "How our tutors would have disputed that designation, eh, Delor?" Delor made no response for several seconds (Kirk snuck a glance at the Lady Pataal, who seemed to be holding her breath), then:

"Quite the opposite, they would have claimed," said Delor, and the dour twin even managed a smile. The Nadorian contingent laughed expectedly, but even the *Enterprise* crew chuckled, and Kirk wondered what they must have been like as boys, realizing they were unique, yes, but therefore totally, utterly alone in their eternal togetherness.

They returned to the officers' lounge for dessert—something frigid with flames of lit Saurian brandy leaping from it, Kirk recalled—and the talk developed into a question-and-answer session about the *Enterprise.* Spock was quite capable of handling this, and Kirk excused himself as he saw a member of the palace entourage leave the room.

"Did you find the dessert a little too rich?" asked Kirk, catching up to her in the hall outside.

"No," replied Securitrix Llora, in a tone nearly as chilly as the dessert. "I simply wished to get some air, so to speak. I have little taste for sweets."

"I'm almost surprised you didn't sample the princes' food before they ate it," said Kirk, falling in beside her, quite unbidden.

"Now you mock me." Her dark eyes flashed dangerously.

"Not at all," said Kirk, seriously. "You take your job with palace security quite seriously; I admire that."

"You do?" The dark eyes shifted uncertainly; her full mouth twitched a little.

"I do," replied Kirk. "I take my job seriously, too. In

a way, our tasks are much alike—we both bear the responsibility for a great number of people."

"That is so," Llora said, precisely. She continued walking, the muscles of her long legs playing rhythmically under her leggings.

"I'm very much afraid we got off on the wrong foot, and I'd like to apologize. Here," he said, directing her down a hallway. He placed a hand on one of her elbows; she did not pull it away. He guided her to a wider portion of the hall, stopped before what appeared to be a bulkhead, and tapped a button set into it. The bulkhead slid silently to one side, revealing a large port. "We call this the observation deck."

Kirk knew what the view would be, so he watched Llora's face. Her eyes widened as she saw her home planet from space, for the first time as one of a thousand thousand celestial bodies, an azure globe swathed in its atmosphere, backdropped by the reaches of the endless universe.

She gasped; the cool blue light washed over her, softening her features delicately, and it occurred to Kirk that he had no idea what color her hair was. The wariness fell from her face, and she seemed as awestruck as a child seeing the sky for the first time.

"You wanted some air," Kirk said, softly. "I thought I'd give you a little space."

"It's so beautiful," she said, simply. Her voice was low, she seemed to have trouble breathing.

"Yes," said Kirk, bending toward her.

Just then, the wall intercom whistled. *"Bridge to captain,"* sounded Sulu's voice.

Sighing, Kirk turned from Llora.

"Kirk here, Mr. Sulu. This better be important." He glanced back at her. She hadn't moved, but one corner of her mouth lifted in a small, quizzical smile.

"Captain, shields have snapped on."

"Status," said Kirk, everything else in the universe forgotten.

"Sensors read some kind of missile attack, heading straight for us. Source and type of weaponry unknown."

"Sound red alert, all hands to battle stations."

"Aye, sir." A small panel in the wall console began flashing red.

In far less time than he could have described it, Kirk knew something was wrong. Sulu's response was absolutely right by the book, and yet the years he had spent in that center seat told him—

"Sulu!" he rasped. "Maximum power to *aft* shields! Prepare for—"

Suddenly, it was as if a giant hand slammed the *Enterprise* from one side, sending it reeling through space.

Chapter Seven

THAT ATTACK didn't come from forward, realized Kirk, as he picked himself up from the deck, *it came from aft.* He had been right, though as with many such decisions in his career, he would have given much to have been wrong.

The bulkhead had slid back over the transparent aluminum of the observation port as soon as battle stations had sounded, and the deck lighting had flickered momentarily at the moment of attack. So it was in brief darkness that Kirk sprang to his feet. "Llora!" he called.

"I am here," came a low voice from not far away. Lighting was restored, and Kirk saw she had been thrown against the bulkhead directly behind her.

"Can you—"

"I am well," she said, struggling to her feet, taking Kirk's outstretched hand. "What of the princes?"

"Come on." The observation port was on the other side of the deck from the officers' lounge. Kirk sprinted down the hallway, hearing Llora's light footfalls just behind him.

Just outside the lounge they met a group rushing

there from the other direction: Spock, Counselors Docos and Hanor, Commissioner Roget and his wife, Regent Lonal. "Some of the guests wished to see more of the ship," said the Vulcan, tersely.

"The princes?"

"Still inside, to my knowledge. With the doctor and Yeoman Barrows."

The rest of the princes' entourage had urgently flocked around them. "Their Highnesses—!" began Regent Lonal.

"Open this door!" said Counselor Hanor, banging uselessly against the hatch.

"Not so fast," said Kirk. He took Counselor Hanor's hands gently but firmly, and led her away. "Please, stay back." She stared at Kirk, but made no protest. Commissioner Roget later told Kirk it was the first time he had ever seen her speechless.

He returned to Spock, who was leaning against the door, placing an ear against it.

"Hull breach?" asked Kirk, urgently.

"If so, the breach seems to have been sealed," said Spock, after an eternal second. "I detect sound within the lounge." He put his back to the door, with Kirk joining him. For seconds the hatch refused to move. Then Kirk sensed another presence beside him. He glanced over to see Securitrix Llora also applying her strength to the door; they soon wrenched it open.

The lounge looked as though a tornado had coursed through it, which, Kirk realized as he surveyed the room, was very close to the truth. The far wall of the officers' lounge bore a huge crack from floor to ceiling, mute evidence of a breached hull. It was only a few inches across at its widest spot, but that was more than enough for escaping atmosphere to wreak havoc and, potentially, death. Like most seasoned spacehands, Kirk regarded a hull breach as very nearly the worst damage a spaceship could suffer.

But behind the huge sundering of the lounge wall was an expanse of dull gray metal. The emergency hull had slid into place as soon as escaping atmosphere was detected, hopefully keeping destruction to a minimum.

But what damage had been done was bad enough. The components of the sedate, civilized banquet to honor the princes had been transformed, by the chaos of escaping air, into something very much resembling a battlefield. Tables had been overturned as if by whim, silverware and broken dishes had been scattered randomly. The remnants of dessert were spread over every surface of the room. This last would have been comical, were it not for the circumstances.

Other debris, some of it still smoldering, some of it still retaining its rounded contours, littered the floor. This looked alien to the environments of the *Enterprise*. Kirk pointed to it as they passed, and Spock nodded.

Of the princes' entourage, only Pataal had remained behind. She bore a few scratches but seemed otherwise uninjured, though her skin was nearly as pale as her disheveled gown. A civilian, she was of course unused to combat, let alone space combat. The major damage to her was probably mental, Kirk realized, not so much physical. Barrows, her own arm bleeding from a large gash, was trying to comfort Pataal, whose mouth worked soundlessly, as she pointed toward the overturned banquet table.

The princes lay crumpled on the floor, like twin dolls flung there by a petulant child. But dolls didn't bleed. The twins lay with their spines at almost right angles to each other; Kirk knew that couldn't be good.

McCoy was barking orders into the wall intercom, ignoring the output from what looked like an ugly wound to his forehead. Near his feet lay a broken plate bearing the *Enterprise* insignia, one sharp edge spattered with blood. "Send up medics with an antigrav stretcher, Chapel! Prep for emergency surgery!" Before he returned to his patients, he and Kirk exchanged a brief glance, and McCoy shrugged: *I don't know.*

Seconds later a team of medics charged into the lounge, bearing the twin cylinders of an antigrav support stretcher, whose use would prevent further aggravation of the princes' spinal damage, if any. These cylinders were laid on either side of the still princes. Then, as they were activated, the princes' figures, twitching slightly, rose from the floor, and were guided out by the medical team. Kirk wasn't surprised to see Llora following.

Through all this, distant, harsh thuds were heard through the ship, as though they lived in the bottom of a kettledrum. The princes were in McCoy's hands now.

"Spock, you're with me," said Kirk.

"Acknowledged." The two of them headed for the turbolift.

Kirk's last view of the room was of the princes' entourage clustered around Commissioner Roget, besieging him with questions and demands—all except a lonely young girl who stood in the center of the room, head in her hands, ignored by everyone except for one concerned yeoman.

"Bridge, emergency override," rasped Kirk, as he and Spock entered the lift. The car shot upward smoothly, save for a slight shaking as a peal of thunder rolled through the ship.

"The old bait and switch," said Kirk, grimly, more

just to have something to say. "They sent a fusillade to distract our attention from another attack, from aft." He shook his head. "What a fool, to have fallen for that."

"Lieutenant Sulu is a fine officer," said Spock. "I do not believe the term 'fool' a fair assessment of—"

The lift opened onto the bridge. "I wasn't talking about him."

"Normal lighting," said Kirk, as he strode toward his chair. Sulu's skin was tightly drawn, and he seemed pale. Kirk met Sulu's gaze briefly and he shook his head. *It wasn't your fault.* "Status."

"We have not determined the location of our assailant, Captain," said Uhura. "We have returned fire."

"Shooting in the dark," said Kirk. "Shields?"

"Down to seventy-five percent, sir," said Chekov.

"Another missile approaching, Captain," said Sulu.

"Trace launch coordinates and return fire."

The ship shook again, but this time the bridge crew was braced for it.

"No sign of damage to the enemy craft, Captain," said Sulu.

"Shields at seventy-one percent, sir."

"Thank you, Mr. Chekov," said Kirk, patiently. "Report at five-percent increments." Their foe seemed to be using the same powerful missiles as before. Not fancy, but they certainly got the job done, as the aft wall of the officers' lounge could attest. "Any sign of them, Mr. Spock?"

"None, Captain. They remain as elusive as before."

"Yet they knew where to strike to attack the princes. . . . Uhura! Scan for a low-yield frequency signal coming from the *Enterprise,* something so faint you'd normally pass over it as static."

"Scanning, sir," said Uhura, her voice betraying only a slight thrill of anticipation as she tried to foresee Kirk's course of action.

"Another missile approaching, sir," Sulu said.

"Evasive action."

"Closing too rapidly, sir."

"All power to forward shields, then. Yes, forward shields. They won't try the same trick—" The rest of his sentence was cut off by the explosion of the enemy projectile. "Uhura?"

"I've got something, sir . . . but it's very faint. I'm not sure it isn't some kind of static or feedback."

"I'm sure," said Kirk. "Uhura, transfer data to the weapons console. Sulu, lock photon torpedoes on that frequency and fire."

"Torpedoes away, sir," said Sulu, a moment later. Kirk imagined rather than felt the slight backwash as the torpedoes were ejected; a moment later, he saw them surge onto the field of the viewscreen, and vanish into space, like a coin dropped into a bottomless pond.

For endless seconds he held his breath. Then, at the lower periphery of the screen, came a burst of energy, followed by a stream of debris. "There! Lock phasers and fire!"

"The ship appears to be gone, Captain," said Spock, peering into his scanner.

"Did we hit her again?"

"Our attack appears to have injured them, but not mortally. Pursuit would be fruitless."

"Isn't there any kind of trail we can—?"

"None, sir. A study of the debris may yield facts."

Kirk edged back in his chair and drew a breath for what seemed like the first time in hours. "Get a tractor beam on that debris, bring it in here for analysis. Secure from red alert. Damage report."

"How did you know, Captain?" asked Chekov.

"I assumed this was an attack on the princes," said Kirk. "But whoever was behind it—"

Uhura interrupted. "All sections reported, Captain. Some damage, nothing major."

"Any report from sickbay?"

"None, sir."

"Doctor," said Nurse Christine Chapel, "it's a woman, asking about the princes."

"Pataal?" Dr. McCoy shook his head irritably, but did not look up from the wreckage of two human beings that lay before him.

"No, it's—" Chapel looked up, then back at McCoy. "I think you should see for yourself, Doctor."

"Chapel, I don't have time for—" Whatever McCoy was about to say was lost, forgotten as he stared into the barrel of a Nadorian energy weapon.

"Doctor," said Securitrix Llora, her voice very low and very clear, "you will cease whatever manipulations you have begun upon Their Serene Highnesses and return them to the Royal Palace immediately."

"Doctor . . . ?"

"I'll handle this, Chapel. Keep prepping the patient—patients."

"Are you deaf?" asked Llora. "You will release them, now." The finger on the weapon's activator switch tightened perceptibly.

"You're aiming at the wrong person," said McCoy.

Her dark eyes widened. Of all the answers she had foreseen . . . "What?"

"You might as well eliminate the middleman and

shoot them. If you delay me any longer, both of them will die."

"Your transportation system is instantaneous—"

"Perhaps, but they'll never survive it. They're dying even now. Look." He pointed to the medical scanner over the bed. Llora's eyes followed it, but the barrel of the energy weapon remained steady on McCoy.

"What of it?"

"Do you see those indicator lights sinking? Hear the pulse slowing? Do your duties to your princes include watching them die, when you could have prevented it?"

"No, of course—"

"Then pull that trigger," said McCoy, his blue eyes now very cold, "or get the hell out of my sickbay."

Slowly the energy weapon sank, like a rock through a pool of quicksand. Llora withdrew, almost as slowly. "Save them, Doctor." The words were a command, but they were voiced as a plea.

"Get out of here! If you want to help, contact your palace and get me their medical records! *Now!*"

The operating room door hummed shut behind her. "Well, Nurse," said McCoy, "prepare for surgery."

"Notify me at once if McCoy calls," said Kirk, pulling himself back from thoughts of crumpled dolls. "At any rate, it seemed reasonable that someone targeting the princes that accurately was doing it by means of a signal—a low-frequency signal, almost too faint to register. And what can be transmitted can be traced." He shrugged, irritably. "I should have thought of it far sooner than I did. Uhura, any word from sickbay?"

"No, sir, should I—?"

"No, don't bother them."

"Yes, sir. And Captain, most of the Nadorian group are asking to return to their planet."

"And one in particular, I'll bet. Tell Giotto to herd them into the lounge and wait for me." He rose from his chair and turned to his right. "Spock, let's find some answers."

"Yes, sir."

"Mr. Sulu, you have the conn."

"Captain," said Uhura, as the lift doors opened, "sickbay."

"Bones?" said Kirk, into the chair intercom. "How are—?"

"Critical. They're being prepped now, I'm about to go into surgery."

"Can you save them?"

"If I don't try, we'll lose them both."

"Then try."

"I wasn't asking your permission." There was silence for a long moment, punctuated only by the familiar noises of the bridge. Then: *"Jim, I—"*

Such indecision was unusual in the physician's voice. "Yes, Bones?"

"Jim, I'm going to have to separate them."

Chapter Eight

"SEPARATE THEM?" Kirk whispered, but it seemed that his words echoed throughout the bridge. "Bones, are you sure you can?"

The response was prefaced by a harsh laugh. *"I guess we'll find out."* Then, more softly: *"Jim, I know what's riding on this. I'll do my best."*

"I'm sure," replied Kirk. "Good luck."

"Thanks, I—" Kirk heard Chapel's voice in the background, and the channel suddenly went dead.

Kirk stood there for a moment, brooding over matters he never discussed with anyone, not even his two best friends. Then he looked up, and headed for the lift doors. "Let's see if we can make ourselves useful, Spock. Bring your tricorder."

"Yes, sir," said Spock, at his heels. "According to damage reports, that area of the ship is secure. Mr. Scott says that repairs will begin immediately."

"After the damage has been done," mused Kirk. "You were with most of the party?"

"Yes, sir. I have formed no conjecture as to which of

them might have been responsible for signaling an attack on the princes—if any of them."

"Oh, it was one of them," said Kirk. "I feel it." For once, Spock let the obvious go unsaid. "When I met you in the hallway after the attack, you were returning with most of the princes' party."

"Yes, sir."

"Whoever signaled the attack would obviously have wanted to put some distance between themselves and the princes. Did anyone suggest you leave the lounge?"

"Yeoman Barrows," replied Spock.

"Sometimes they get lucky," said Kirk. "The guilty party was looking for a way to leave the room unobtrusively, and Barrows did his work for him. Well, here's where his luck ends."

The lift door opened, and they proceeded toward the lounge. Chief Giotto's men had already sealed it off, preventing anyone from entry or exit. The two guards nodded at Kirk and Spock, who passed into the room. The doorway had been restored to functionality, though its appearance still left something to be desired.

Gathered there was the entire party that had come aboard with Princes Abon and Delor—no, not quite all. Kirk noted Commissioner and Mrs. Roget, Regent Lonal, Counselors Docos and Hanor—seated as far away from each other as possible. The Lady Pataal was sobbing, her gown crumpled and creased like a wilted flower. Next to her, Barrows did her best to comfort her.

But one of them was missing.

Kirk nodded to Spock; the Vulcan activated his tricorder and began methodically crossing the room, watching its screen unblinkingly.

The lounge doors opened and Chief Giotto entered, with Securitrix Llora in tow. Actually, the woman walked slightly in front of Giotto, with the security head following warily, with the respect one expert in a field gives to another, even an adversary. Kirk didn't know if she was armed or not—wherever she had kept that energy weapon of hers, it was certainly well hidden.

"We found her wandering the halls, sir," said Giotto, not taking his eyes from her.

"I was not 'wandering,' I was attempting to return here. Thank you for escorting me," she said, sarcastically.

Regent Lonal suddenly sprang to his feet. "Where are our monarchs? Why have we not been allowed to see them, nor return them to Nador? Captain, I shall complain to the highest office in the Federation!"

"Regent Lonal, please," said Commissioner Roget with a sigh. He was holding his wife's pale hands in both of his, and it seemed that even the seemingly bottomless well of his diplomat's patience had almost been emptied. "I assure you, the princes are in the best of hands—isn't that true, Captain?"

"Their Serene Highnesses are being operated on even as we speak," said Kirk, gently, "for injuries sustained in the attack."

"No!" shrieked Pataal. She seemed exhausted, yet she rose from her seat as if lifted by an outside force. "I must go to them!" She started to head for the door.

"No one can leave just yet," said Kirk, intercepting her, gripping her shoulders. "There's nothing you can do."

"Their Highnesses are not being allowed visitors," said Llora, in an unidentifiable tone. "The doctor is trying to save their lives."

Pataal sobbed anew; Kirk felt her slump in his arms and had to help her back to her chair.

Spock was scanning the crowd now. He lowered his

tricorder and looked at Pataal. "Dr. McCoy is an excellent physician," he said. "Your monarchs could scarcely be in better hands." He looked at Kirk, and raised one eyebrow, the equivalent of a shrug. Despite the situation, or perhaps because of it, Kirk almost laughed.

"But what purpose is served by our detainment?" asked Regent Lonal. He seemed to have realized that with the princes down, he called the shots for the palace. His manner was more confident, less subservient, than Kirk had ever seen it.

"It was no coincidence that the attack upon the *Enterprise* came during your princes' visit," said Kirk, "nor that the only part of my ship to sustain significant damage was the section your princes occupied." He looked to his science officer. "Spock?"

"Results, Captain, but not as conclusive as we would like."

"What is he doing?" asked Counselor Hanor, her voice sounding much like the wail of a phaser going through steel.

"Coming to conclusions, Counselor," Kirk said. "Please remain where you are. Well, Spock?"

Spock stood next to Kirk, turned to address both his captain and the audience. "The missile which felled Princes Abon and Delor followed a specific coded frequency, sent by a minute transmitter," said Spock, lifting his tricorder to midchest height. "I have been attempting to ascertain the source of that transmission."

"And?" asked Kirk, impatiently. The Nadorians were all watching Spock. Was one of them unduly concerned, shifting his stance to make a break? Kirk wondered. But to turn to watch them, to have given any sign that they were being monitored, would have betrayed his intent. "Have you found the source, Spock?"

"I have, Captain," said the Vulcan. He turned, raised his right arm, and pointed at the specially constructed chair the princes had occupied.

Kirk said nothing. He didn't trust himself to speak. That guests aboard his ship, no matter their rank or social status, had been assaulted during his watch was bad enough. But for the medium of the attack to have been an item of comfort which he had personally ordered prepared for his guests . . .

"Proceed," he said, his lips barely moving.

"Yes, sir," said Spock, moving to the chair. He held the tricorder equidistant between himself and the chair for a few seconds. Then he produced a small probe from the pouch of his tricorder, knelt before the chair, and examined it, his long fingers probing the cushions and surface of the chair in a manner much like that of McCoy examining a patient.

"Blood pressure?" asked McCoy.

"Down five points, Doctor," said Nurse Chapel.

"I thought so," he said, shaking his head. For seeming hours he had stared into the abyss of spinal cords and connective tissue that formed the juncture of the twin princes. Under any other circumstances, he would have been happy to examine them, to learn how their systems had learned to accommodate the double load of messages from the brain, to coordinate shared physical impulses but to keep discrete impulses separate—but not like this.

What was it he had said? "I'd love to have a look at their medical chart." And what was it Uhura sometimes said? *Be careful what you wish for. . . .* He snorted, derisively.

"What was that, Doctor?"

"Nothing," said McCoy, shortly. "Physiostimulator."

"Captain," said Spock. It was the first sound that had been heard in the room in several minutes, save for the muffled sobbing of the Lady Pataal.

Kirk approached, and Spock held out a pair of tweezers that seemed to contain within their prongs a piece of solidified light. No, Kirk realized, as he took the tweezers, it was a small length of metal, thinner than a needle, slightly and irregularly bent from the explosion. Yet Kirk could make out on its surface small ridges and indentations, almost like—

"Circuitry?" he asked.

Spock nodded, straightening up. "A fine example of microcircuitry. A low-yield transmitter, emitting a signal every few seconds on a frequency so low that it nearly eludes detection, unless specifically sought."

Kirk looked up, as a sudden thought struck him. "It can't explode, can it?"

"I read no potential for destruction, Captain. Whoever brought it aboard surmised, almost certainly correctly, that an explosive device, even a diminutive one, would have been detected. This is merely a transmitter."

"Like the rats in the Black Plague," said Kirk.

"Sir?"

"Just a carrier." Kirk handed it back to him with an expression of disgust, as though it had been a roach. "Full analysis," he said, despite the fact that he knew the command was unnecessary.

Spock nodded, folding a length of sterile cloth around the microtransmitter, stowing it in the pouch of his tricorder, and leaving the chamber.

"Captain," said Regent Lonal, in the wake of Spock's departure, "there is no proof that one of our party planted that—that device. Anyone on board your ship could have done so."

"Anyone who possessed the technical wherewithal to create such a device," said Counselor Hanor, "which I emphatically do not."

"Whoever planted that device wouldn't have had to know how to make it," said Mrs. Roget, cutting off the reply Kirk was about to make, "only to know how to plant it."

"Janine," said her husband, his tone softly chiding.

"Well, it's true, Sylvan," she replied. In some part of his mind Kirk marveled at the endless patience and tolerance a diplomat's spouse had to present to the world. She probably used small comments like this to let off steam, and not often in the presence of official parties like this one.

"That is true," said Kirk. "I'm afraid you're all going to have to submit to searches before returning to Nador." There was a low murmur of protest, but it had no teeth to it.

"Please, Captain," said Pataal, "is there no word as to Abon and Delor?" If anyone else in the room realized she had broken palace protocol by referring to Their Serene Highnesses by their first names, no one called her on it. Given the circumstances, it seemed a small enough offense.

"Dr. McCoy will let us know," said Kirk. "I don't dare disturb him."

The first thing he learned in medical school, Leonard McCoy often said, was to hate the smell of blood. Not that he couldn't tolerate it, but he realized that if he had a whiff of that scent, if he had to perform physical surgery, he might already be too late.

Then he got to know the smell of cold blood, and learned how much he welcomed the smell of it warm.

"Damn nature anyway," said McCoy, fervently.

"Doctor?" asked Nurse Chapel.

"Yes, I know nature is the reason these two boys are still alive—the fact that their systems were able to adapt to their conjoined state—but it's also the reason they were born like this in the first place." His fingers continued to nimbly work over the exposed flesh as he spoke; he assumed Chapel was used to his seemingly aimless monologues during surgery. They seemed purposeless at their onset, but they always went somewhere. "No matter how well they've learned to adapt, despite the fact that they're the princes, and no one could comment on their condition, there's still the fact that they were born so different that to most people they're either the recipients of amazement or pity. If it weren't for their bloodline, they could have wound up in some Nadorian sideshow." He sighed, his fury momentarily spent. Despite his rage, his hands had never so much as quivered. "Signs?" he asked, his voice rasping.

"Stable but low," said Chapel. "The one on the left—"

"Abon. They have names, Nurse."

"Yes, sir. Prince Abon's signs are lower than Prince Delor's. I've removed the shrapnel and sealed his wounds, that should help."

"He was probably closest to the bulkhead when it blew," commented McCoy. He straightened up, took a deep breath and a sip of water from the antigrav thermos, then looked intently at Chapel. "Ready?"

Her reply was no less solemn. "Yes, Doctor."

"Make sure you have plenty of sterilite prepared," said McCoy. "Here we go." He bent over the tangled mass of nerves and ganglia that connected the twins, blue eyes examining them with an intensity no medical scanner could match. "Exoscalpel." He took the device from Chapel and began to probe, gently but thoroughly. "Make sure this is being recorded," he said, "I want to be able to prove to the Nadorian government that we had no other choice."

"Well?" asked Kirk, for the third time in five minutes.

"As I surmised, Captain," said Spock, looking up from the microscanner, "an uncommon, though not unique, job of microcircuitry, composed of high-quality alloys and wiring. An excellent job of craftsmanship." He paused for a moment. "Pardon me, I should have said, 'I presume it to have been an excellent job of craftsmanship.'"

"It's not now?"

"No, sir. Most of its circuits have been fused beyond any functional state, doubtless due to a self-destruct signal sent after the transmitter had accomplished the task it was designed for."

"There's no way of tracing it?" asked Kirk.

"Not to the possession of any one person, no, sir. The transmitter itself is composed of an alloy whose molecules bond extremely tightly, leaving virtually no surface room for exterior elements to cling to."

"In other words, it's very, very smooth."

"Your words, Captain. Such a term is unscientific in the extreme."

"And we wouldn't want that, would we?" said Kirk,

his sigh nearly subsumed by the opening of the lab doors. Spock followed him, until Kirk turned left before reaching the lift.

"Aren't you coming, Captain?"

"You go ahead, Spock. Help Giotto out with the search. I need to think." He took his time returning to the officers' lounge, taking the intraship ladders rather than the turbolift. It felt good to stretch, to do something kinetic, and besides, let the suspects stew a while longer.

He reached the officers' lounge to find the Nadorian party divided by gender, lined up upon opposite walls of the room, and looking none too happy about it. In the center of the room stood two small, hastily erected booths. Not that anything so crude as an actual hands-on body search had been required of their guests, but being isolated from the rest mitigated the embarrassment of a personal search, and, Kirk had found in the past, increased the chances that a guilty party might let something slip—an anxious glance, a gesture, a nervous twitch, that might give something away to a discerning observer.

This time, however, his experience proved no match for the facts. Chief Giotto stood outside the booth Kirk assumed had been assigned to the males, holding a tricorder and speaking in low tones to Spock, who nodded as if Giotto had been discussing the temperature of the room. They were joined after a moment by Lieutenant Sinclair, who obviously been assigned the task of supervising the women's examination. He recalled that Sinclair had done well on the security portion of her rotating assignment roster.

After a moment's further consultation the trio approached Kirk, who retreated with them to the far side of the chamber. "Besides the method by which the princes were singled out for attack, our search has elicited literally nothing, Captain," said Spock. "None of the members of the Nadorian entourage can conclusively be proven to have planted the transmitter on the princes, nor can any one of them be proven not to have planted it."

Kirk nodded, almost absently. He had been afraid of that. He glanced briefly at Giotto, who nodded his agreement with Spock.

"Then we haven't accomplished nothing," said Lieutenant Sinclair, smoothing back a lock of her honey-colored hair, "we've accomplished less than nothing." Then she seemed to have caught herself, and looked up at her superior officers. "Sorry, sirs," she murmured, quickly.

"Never be afraid to give me the facts, Lieutenant," said Kirk, "no matter how glum they might seem." Despite the situation, he managed a small smile. "We don't slay messengers aboard this ship."

"Yes, sir," replied Sinclair, a slight flush coming to her cheeks.

"Besides, Sinclair, that's not entirely true," said Giotto. "I'm sure the captain is aware that by the exhaustive investigation he's put the suspects through, he's reestablished, in their minds, his desire to put this matter to rest, and the lengths to which he's willing to go."

"Aye, sir," said Sinclair.

"I only hope that's enough," said Kirk. "I'd be happy to let whoever's behind this get away with it if it would just stop his attempts. But I don't think— Yes, Commissioner?"

Commissioner Roget had neared them, waiting at a

sufficient distance to avoid the appearance of eaves-dropping—a safe orbit, thought Kirk, dryly.

"Captain," said Roget, his voice lowering in proportion to his nearness to Kirk, "while I realize the ticklishness of the situation, I have to point out that Their Serene Highnesses' party is growing extremely restless."

"Has it escaped their notice that we're investigating an attack on the persons of 'Their Serene Highnesses'?" asked Kirk, with more anger than he had intended.

"Certainly not," said Roget, in a mollifying tone. "But I wonder if there is anything more to be learned in your investigation. Several of the party have already begun protests through the proper diplomatic channels. Which," he added, with a wry twist to his mouth, "is greatly facilitated by the fact that the conduit of such protests is confined in the same room with them."

"I see your point," said Kirk, conciliatorily. He turned to Spock and Giotto. "Is there anything else we can learn?"

Spock shook his head. "Any such measures we might take would be locking the barn door after the equines have been stolen—if I am using the colloquialism correctly."

"You are, sir," said Giotto, suppressing a smile. "Captain, I agree with Mr. Spock, there's no reason why we shouldn't let these people go."

"You have something in mind?" asked Kirk.

"Let's put it this way: We should give them a lot of line," said Giotto, "but that doesn't mean we can't reel them back in if we need to."

"I understand," said Kirk, nodding slowly. He turned and walked toward the Nadorian party, the *Enterprise* staff and Commissioner Roget trailing in his wake.

"You have my most abject apologies for the prolonged delay," he said. "As citizens of Nador, I trust you will understand my zealousness to apprehend anyone who might wish to do harm to Princes Abon and Delor."

"We may leave?" asked Counselor Hanor, who had a tendency to cut to the heart of the matter.

"You may," said Kirk. "Of course, I do retain the right to recall any of you at any time, should new evidence be discovered."

"Do you always deal so high-handedly with citizens of a sovereign planet, Captain?" asked Counselor Docos.

"I do when murder is attempted aboard my ship, Counselor." When Docos made no reply to that, Kirk stood to one side and swept a hand toward the doorway. "Again, I apologize for the inconvenience, and hope—"

"What of the princes?" asked Pataal, in a voice that sounded very much like that of a child.

Kirk nodded, and went to the wall intercom. "Kirk to bridge. Any word from McCoy?"

"No, sir." Kirk, expecting Uhura to answer, didn't recognize Lieutenant Palmer's voice at first. Then he realized that hours had passed, and another shift had taken their posts. He shook his head; it felt like years. *"Shall I try sickbay?"*

"Negative, I don't want to—" From somewhere behind him came a muffled gasp; he always assumed it had come from Pataal, but never found out with any degree of certainty. The doorway of the lounge had opened, and someone entered.

"Bones?" The doctor was almost unrecognizable; he seemed to have aged a decade or more. He walked with a slight shuffle, and his eyes were smears of dirty blue, with masses of wrinkles under them. He wore a clean, new tunic whose crisp faultlessness only emphasized how tired he looked. McCoy spoke very rarely about his past; still it seemed to Kirk that at this moment McCoy must very much resemble his father. And he remembered a fact he often forgot: Despite his youthful demeanor, Leonard McCoy was no longer a young man. "Bones, what is it? Are the princes—?"

"Their Serene Highnesses are resting peacefully," said McCoy. His voice sounded like a recording of it, played through several layers of subspace static.

"They—they live?" asked Regent Lonal. His recent authoritativeness seemed to be ebbing away.

McCoy looked at Kirk, who nodded. McCoy took a deep breath before he spoke. In that moment, Kirk would have given a great deal for the abilities of a class-A telepath.

"They do," he said. The Nadorian party changed little in their demeanor; a pair of eyes closed here, a chest rose and fell there. Still, it was as if the tension of a coming storm had broken with the first clap of thunder. Whatever happened after, at least they knew.

"And their condition?" asked Hanor, slowly, her manner not betraying which answer she wanted to hear.

"Oh, how are they?" shouted Pataal, pushing to the front of the crowd. "Are they crippled, or—?"

"I had to separate them," said McCoy, dully, as if he himself still hadn't fully comprehended what he had had to do.

For an instant, the room was totally silent, as devoid of sound or of the potential for sound as any interstellar gulf Kirk had ever flown.

"The negotiations . . ." said Counselor Docos, hesitantly.

"The tribes . . ." said Counselor Hanor, emphatically. Her ugly face was without expression. She suddenly seemed like one of the statues her planet's past had produced, lifelike, but not alive.

"The handover," said Sylvan Roget, more loudly than any of them. "Captain, will this adversely affect the handover?"

"I don't see how it can not affect the handover, Commissioner—but, of course, the health of the princes must come first."

"They must be transferred to Nador," said Regent Lonal, rapidly and in a low voice; it was a moment before Kirk realized the official was talking to himself.

"Like hell!" said McCoy. He had fallen into a silence that seemed almost a comatose state. Everyone in the room was surprised to hear him speak, especially in the fiery voice he reserved to deal with things he deemed beneath his contempt. "Those boys are staying right where they are," he said, his eyes sweeping across the crowd. "If they get through the next twenty-four hours they might have a fighting chance at a full recovery. But no one is moving them. Is that clear?" For some reason, he looked at Kirk, who held his hands at chest height, palms out. There were certain fights he could pick with McCoy with a fair chance of winning, but he knew this wasn't one of them. Nor, if McCoy felt this strongly about it, did he see any need to.

"They will need security," said Securitrix Llora, the sharpness in her voice a challenge.

"We'll work it out," said Chief Giotto, evenly, not picking up the gauntlet. "Security details can consist half of your men, half of ours."

"That would be acceptable," said Llora, slowly. "I don't like the idea of your gun-booted troops messing up my sickbay," said McCoy, "but you've got a point. We will work it out, yes."

Kirk released his breath; for McCoy, this was a major concession.

The party began to drift slowly to the doorway, the long night beginning to catch up to them now that its strain had been dissipated. Kirk stood by the doorway, bidding farewells to the few members of the entourage who met his eyes. He took special care to see if Securitrix Llora would look at him, and if so, what her gaze would say. She did meet Kirk's gaze. Her eyes were so dark that they seemed almost not to reflect light.

That look told Kirk nothing; it was as if she had paid no attention to him at all.

With the Nadorian party gone, Kirk turned to take one last look at the room before sealing it off.

There he saw a young woman, sobbing to herself, more from exhaustion and relief than grief.

"Please," said the Lady Pataal, approaching McCoy, hands outstretched. "May I see them?" She stood before McCoy, extended her hands beseechingly, and began to sink to her knees.

"Here, we'll have none of that," said McCoy, an undercurrent of sympathy beneath his gruffness. Despite his obvious exhaustion, he stooped and, gripping the girl by her upper arms, lifted her back to a standing position. "You can have a brief glimpse of them," he said, in a low, soothing voice, "but just a brief one, understand? They'll be asleep anyway."

"Thank you," she sobbed, smiling at the same time.

Barrows walked up to Pataal and put a comforting hand on her shoulder. "I'll go with her."

"Are you sure it's safe to allow a visit?" asked Kirk after the two women left.

"Between Giotto's people and Tonia, it'll be fine, I'm sure, Jim," replied McCoy, wiping a hand across his eyes. "Don't worry," he said, looking at Kirk, "I'm not going to take any chances with their health—not after what I just pulled them back from."

"Are you all right, Bones?"

"Fine," said McCoy, with an unconvincing nod. "I just need a little rest. Can't pull those all-nighters like I used to."

"Who can?"

McCoy nodded and smiled, but made no motion to leave.

"Is everything all right, Bones?"

"I'm beginning to become a little concerned about the princes' recovery, especially after such a complex operation. Some of their readings are a little off, and I'd rather be safe than sorry." McCoy absently scratched the replacement tissue over the wound in his forehead. "Nadorians are humanoid, of course, but they're not actually human, any more than Vulcans. I'm running an analysis of the Nadorian genome and their DNA through the medical computer, just to make sure I'm not overlooking anything. But a genome analysis will take some time, even with our computers."

"Can't you ask the palace physician for that?"

"I did. But in such a delicate situation, I'd rather depend on my own data." Kirk nodded; in matters like this it was best to give the doctor his head. McCoy turned to leave, but Kirk placed a hand on his shoulder.

"Go a little easy on yourself, Doctor. You've saved two lives today, you've earned a little rest."

Despite his exhaustion, he managed a grin. "Are you writing prescriptions now, Captain?"

"Consider it an order, if you like," replied Kirk,

matching the grin. McCoy shuffled out, navigating, Kirk would have bet, more on instinct than will.

Suddenly, Kirk's own limbs began to feel leaden. He realized that it wasn't sudden at all, just the effects of the accumulated tension built up over the last few hours, having come to no resolution. He closed his eyes, squeezed the bridge of his nose, then rolled his head around.

"Are you well, Captain?"

"Spock." Kirk hadn't realized the first officer was watching him—another example of his fatigue. It was a safe bet to assume that Spock was always watching everyone. "Just . . . tired."

"Understandable." At Spock's side hung his tricorder, with its deadly addition. "With your permission, Captain, I should like to utilize the services of Engineer Scott when alpha shift begins."

He had heard that tone in Spock's voice before. "A plan?"

"A theory. Perhaps nothing more."

Kirk left the lounge with him and they made their way to the turbolift. It was like walking through water. "Use anyone you need. And keep me posted. This has turned out to be one sweet mess—if you understand the colloquialism."

"I do." The lift opened on deck five and Kirk disembarked, virtually dragging himself to his quarters, feeling, as his father would have said, like three days of bad—

He realized suddenly that he hadn't heard from Peter for hours, his nephew's presence on the ship driven entirely from his mind by more pressing concerns. He realized that, in a way, it was a compliment to the boy, the tacit assumption that he no longer needed a baby-sitter, or a chaperone. Still, he should call him.

He peeled off his shirt, which felt as though it had been grafted to him, and sat in his desk chair, by the wall intercom. "Kirk to Peter Kirk."

No answer. Of course, it was late. But the damage had been done, so . . .

"Kirk to Peter Kirk. Peter, are you there?"

No answer. "Kirk to bridge."

"Palmer here, sir."

"Has anyone reported seeing my nephew in the last few hours?"

"Let me check, sir. . . . No, Captain, no report. Shall I institute a shipwide search?"

"I'm sure that won't be necessary, thank you. Kirk out."

Kirk's fatigue left him as though it had never been. He put back on his shirt, left his quarters, took the lift to the guest deck, and overrode the security lock when there was no answer.

The room assigned to Peter was nearly undisturbed, the bed unused. Kirk looked around the chamber keenly; there was something gone that should be here, something missing that ought to be obvious.

Something, that is, besides Peter. Peter Kirk was gone, as surely as if he had crumbled to dust and been swept into space.

Chapter Nine

"HERE YOU ARE, SIR," said Commander Scott, pointing to a screen diagnostic of the transporter system. "The lad beamed down to the planet at 2135 hours."

"That was after the attack," said Kirk, as the realization hit him.

"Aye," replied Scotty, stifling a yawn. He respected Jim Kirk as he did few other people in the galaxy, and not just because of his rank; he would have charged a Klingon armada for him—and, come to think of it, he had done that and a good deal worse—but he wondered if it had been really necessary to be called from a warm bunk, after hours spent making sure the *Enterprise* had been put back together correctly after the attack, just to read a bloody transporter diagnostic screen.

Then he remembered how he'd feel if his own newborn nephew—also, by some odd coincidence, christened Peter—were gone, his whereabouts unknown, on a planet whose conduct toward Federation citizens, let alone Starfleet personnel and their blood kin, was chancy at best.

"I'm sure the lad's fine, Captain," said Scotty, heartily.

"Captain." The conference room doors parted to reveal Chief Giotto and Lieutenant Sinclair, neither looking too much the worse for having been disturbed in the middle of the night. But, Scotty was certain, like himself, they hadn't been in bed long when Kirk's summons came. Giotto and Sinclair approached Kirk, Sinclair placing a small bundle on the table before him.

"What's this?"

"It appears to be the uniform issued to your nephew when he came aboard, Captain," said Giotto. "A tricorder scan reveals millions of cells left behind corresponding to his DNA."

"But what we didn't find, sir—" Sinclair began to say.

"Were the clothes he wore onto the ship, the clothing he had worn on the planet!" said Kirk, the realization coming to him in the sudden, intuitive rush Scotty had seen so often.

"Exactly, sir," said Giotto. Scotty noticed that Sinclair seemed disappointed that she hadn't had the privilege of explaining this to Kirk. Well, he had been young once.

"So wherever he was going on Nador, he didn't want to be connected with Starfleet. He wanted to be able to blend in with the citizenry, for whatever purpose he had in mind."

"Aye, that seems reasonable," said Scotty.

"But to return planetside with the tensions in this society . . . that doesn't seem reasonable at all," said Kirk, thinking furiously, not looking at any of them, but staring intently into space.

"*Captain.*" Lieutenant Palmer's face appeared on the three-sided viewer set in the center of the table. "*I have Commissioner Roget.*"

"Put him through." Palmer's face faded, to be replaced by Roget's. The silver-haired statesman had tried to compose himself, despite being disturbed in the middle of the night, but his confusion was still quite evident.

"Captain?" asked Roget.

"My nephew has beamed down to the planet," said Kirk. "Have you had any contact with him?"

"Your nephew? Peter? I—no, no we haven't." Despite obviously having been roused from a deep sleep, Roget grasped the situation immediately. *"Shall I issue a memo to Nadorian security?"*

"No, I—yes, yes you'd better." Scotty saw a rare conflicted emotion play over Kirk's features, and he wondered if Kirk's momentary hesitation to involve planetside security was due to the possible political complications of Peter's status, not only as a Federation citizen, but as the nephew of a starship captain, or some other, security-related reason.

"Very well, Captain. I'll put a few unofficial feelers out too, if you don't mind."

"Whatever you can do would be greatly appreciated," said Kirk, fervently. From somewhere off the screen came a murmured voice. Roget turned to heed it for a moment, then looked back at Kirk.

"After all these years, my wife still forgets that diplomats don't have regular hours. She sends her wishes that your nephew will be found soon, and well. I'll be in touch the moment I have anything to report."

"Thank you, Commissioner, Kirk ou—"

"One last matter, Captain," said Roget.

"Yes, Commissioner?" Kirk sighed, but Scotty saw him shake himself almost imperceptibly and face the screen, his interest renewed. Scotty had heard something else in Roget's voice, an undercurrent that he didn't like, and figured Kirk had picked up on it as well.

"I was going to wait until morning to report this, but . . . well, I've not been able to keep from the citizenry the fact that the princes have been separated."

"I didn't think you would be, given the fact that many people already knew it," replied Kirk. "How are they taking it?"

"Some of them are taking it quite badly—there are rumors of civil unrest, of riots, looting mobs . . ."

"Don't they know Their Serene Highnesses are alive and well?"

Roget smiled faintly, cynically, one man of the world to another. *"Some of them don't care, Captain. Some people only want a chance to spread chaos. Others, more sincere but no more rational, see it as an omen of social breakdown or as a portent of religious chaos."*

"I've encountered a few of those, yes," said Kirk. "Please keep me apprised of the situation, and tell the Federation citizens we'll make every effort to guarantee their well-being."

"Thank you, Captain, I'm sure they'll appreciate it."

"In the meantime, you might counsel Regent Lonal to release the whole truth about the princes to the Nadorians. Mobs live on gossip and innuendo."

"I will do that, Captain. Good night."

Kirk sat for a few seconds, drumming his fingers on the arm of his chair, restlessly. Finally, he rose stiffly from the chair, sighing, exhibiting a fatigue Scotty had rarely seen in him.

Then he turned to the three-sided screen again and called the bridge. "I'll be in my quarters, Scotty."

"Aye, sir," he said. "Pleasant dreams."

"At this point, I'll settle for no dreams," said Kirk with a tired smile. "Thank you for all your help, Scotty."

"Anything I can do t'help, sir, just ask." Scotty knew Jim Kirk didn't ask for help unless there was no other way. Scotty was that way himself, and so was determined to give Kirk whatever help he could.

"May I approach them, Doctor?" asked the Lady Pataal.

"I'm afraid not," said McCoy. "The princes are in a sterile field, it's best not to chance compromising that."

Pataal nodded and swallowed, her eyes blinking back tears as she watched the two unmoving forms on the sickbay biobeds. "They have never slept alone before."

"They're not alone, Pataal," replied Yeoman Barrows, squeezing the girl's hand reassuringly. "Dr. McCoy or Nurse Chapel will never be far away, in case there's some kind of emergency, or—"

"No, I mean they have never slept separated before. In different beds."

To Tonia Barrows, who had grown up with a full complement of siblings of both genders, sleeping in bed with your brother not six feet away hardly constituted being "alone." Yet after trying to view the situation from Pataal's perspective, she knew what her friend meant.

"They are not moving," said Pataal, anxiously. "Are they all right?"

"They're fine," said Nurse Chapel, glancing at the medical scanners over the twins. "Dr. McCoy has them medicated and immobilized so they won't roll over on their backs and disturb their wounds before the physiostimulator can heal them. See? Look closely enough and you can see them breathing."

"Your Mr. Spock said Dr. McCoy was an excellent physician."

"Mr. Spock said that?" Chapel smiled, and it seemed to Barrows that the nurse particularly savored the possessive adjective Pataal had used. "Well, he's right." She reached out and patted Pataal's free hand, smiling. "But you'd better keep that to yourself, all right?"

"Very well," nodded Pataal, thoroughly confused. "May I stay and watch them for a few more . . ."

"Pataal," called Barrows, softly.

"What?" Pataal's eyes jerked open. "Are the princes—?"

"They're fine, but you almost passed out on your feet," said Barrows, putting a hand around Pataal's back and guiding her to the doorway. "You'd better get back to the palace and get some sleep."

Upon hearing the word "palace," Pataal gasped, as if hearing a familiar word used in an obscene context. "The palace? Oh, Tonia, I can't return there! With Abon and Delor—with Their Serene Highnesses absent, the place will be either as empty as a mausoleum or so full of royal lackeys, jockeying for position in their absences, that I won't be able to sleep." She looked at Tonia, trying not to appear too desperate. "Please, may I stay with you? If it's too much trouble, you needn't bother, but—"

"We're not supposed to have guests without the approval of the watch officer," replied Barrows, as they headed down the hallway, "but I'm sure it'll be okay."

"Your room is very . . . nice," Pataal said, as they entered Barrows's quarters.

"It's probably a little smaller than the room you're

used to, but it'll be fine," said Barrows. She spun the closet on its axis, rotating it into the wall, revealing a chest of drawers surmounted by a beauty table. "Here," she said, handing Pataal a pair of pajamas, "I think these will fit you."

"I feel like a real member of Starfleet," said Pataal with a grin.

"It's good to see you smile," said Barrows, brushing her hair.

"Sometimes I wish I were in your Starfleet," said Pataal, a little more plaintively. "Sometimes I wish I were anywhere but on Nador."

Barrows listened carefully. This was something Leonard had mentioned, a clue as to her emotional state. "Nador seemed like a lovely place."

"Oh, it is. It is my home and I love it. But . . . sometimes, my life can be very difficult." She blushed immediately, and shook her head. "I know what you're thinking, 'How can her life be hard?' Many people on my planet envy me, I assure you. By most people's standards, my life isn't difficult, no, but it can be, sometimes."

"Well," said Barrows, cautiously, "I imagine it's difficult, being—with two men, isn't it?"

"I could hardly be with just one of them, could I?" asked Pataal, reasonably. "That would be impossible. Though . . . not anymore." Her voice started to thicken, and she started to blink back tears. Barrows hurried to her, sitting next to her on the bed.

"But they're twins. Isn't it almost like there's just one of them?"

"Oh, no," said Pataal, shaking her head. "They are very different. They have always been, ever since they were little. I even find their appearance normal. It was when I saw them up in the sickbay that they seemed strange to me, for the first time in my life. I enjoyed dancing with them," she said, keeping down the faint shudder in her voice, "you saw how graceful they are— were."

"They're remarkable," said Barrows, noncommittally. The girl seemed to want to talk. The best thing was to let her talk without getting too distraught, Leonard had said.

"Of course, they didn't always get along so well," said Pataal, stifling a capacious, unladylike yawn.

"Here, stretch out," said Barrows. "That's it. What do you mean?"

"They would fight often," said Pataal, her voice growing fainter.

"About dancing?" asked Barrows.

"About everything. Matters of state, treaties, land disputes between the tribes, everything."

"Well how did they get to be so popular, if they couldn't make up their minds?"

"I helped them make up their minds." Pataal smiled, her voice sounding as if it were coming from very far away. "When we were alone, I would often ask them about their day, and help them to decide, help them realize what was best."

Behind every great man, Barrows thought, then was immediately thankful she hadn't said that aloud.

"Now, Tonia, tell me about your Dr. McCoy," said Pataal, her eyes opening slightly.

"He's not mine," said Barrows, dryly. "He's his own man, that's for sure."

"But do you love him?" Pataal murmured, her voice almost inaudible.

"I don't know. How do you know when you're in love?"

"I was in love with my princes," said Pataal, faintly. Her eyes flickered open, and she sat up, big tears rolling down her face.

"You still can be, honey," said Barrows, going to her, hugging her.

"Can I?" Her voice came in hiccups between sobs. "Things will never be the same again, Tonia. Never."

"No," said Barrows, helplessly. "No, they won't."

They rocked back and forth for a while, until Pataal's grip loosened around Barrows. Barrows laid the sleeping girl down, gently, then tiptoed across to her couch, where she lay for a long time before sleep came.

"I assure you, Admiral Fitzgerald, I am fully aware of the gravity of the situation," said Captain Kirk to the small viewscreen in his quarters. He refrained from sighing; a call from a skittish Starfleet admiral was not his favorite way to begin the day, especially after a night like the one before.

"I'm sure you are, Captain," said Admiral Fitzgerald, sounding rather the opposite, *"but the request for this communication came directly from the Federation Council, which has received a report that is severely critical of your handling of this matter."*

"Let me guess," said Kirk, this time allowing himself the sigh. "From Counselor Docos, Counselor Hanor, or Regent Lonal?"

"The source of the report was not revealed even to me," replied Fitzgerald, *"but the Council was most emphatic that your mission on Nador not be side-tracked by planetary politics."* Fitzgerald seemed tense, and looked as though he needed sleep. His mane of fair hair, which he was normally as vain as any beauty queen about, seemed somewhat mussed. Kirk, who had

known him for several years, since before he had ascended to the admiralty, recalled when his hair had been jet black.

"Nor is that my desire, Admiral, I assure you," said Kirk, evenly. "Unfortunately, the *Enterprise* crew seem to be the only persons in this whole affair who don't care about the politics of the planet—or, rather, didn't. When the rulers of the planet were nearly killed while my guests, you can imagine that my interest in Nadorian politics was suddenly rather accelerated."

"I understand, Captain," replied Fitzgerald, sympathetically, *"but you must do everything you can to make sure the handover goes off without a hitch—despite the myriad ways it can go astray."*

"I assure you, my crew and I are attempting to do just that, sir."

"Good. How are the princes?"

"According to Dr. McCoy's reports, recovering slowly but surely. The fact that they are still young men counts for a lot, I'm told."

"And there's no chance they can be beamed back to the Royal Palace? Regent Lonal has issued several official requests for their return and protests that they haven't been. According to a report received by the Council, the absence of the princes from the planet is a major thorn in the side of the people."

"I'm sure it is, Admiral, but Dr. McCoy has been quite adamant about the fact that the princes are to remain aboard the *Enterprise* until their recovery progresses. And, given the fact that the attempt to kill them came from Nador, I feel better having them aboard."

"Except that the attack that nearly killed them came while they were aboard your ship," said Fitzgerald.

"Sir, I have not forgotten that," replied Kirk, icily.

"See that you don't, Kirk. And Captain," said Fitzgerald, after a few seconds, in a much gentler tone, *"best of luck in finding your nephew. Please let me know if I can be of any help."*

"Thank you, sir."

"Not at all. Fitzgerald out."

Kirk sat deep in thought for a few seconds after Fitzgerald's image had faded from the screen, then tapped a button on his desk. "Kirk to Spock."

"Spock here," came the imperturbable voice of the Vulcan.

"Any progress on that transmitter?"

"None to speak of, Captain. Lieutenant DeSalle and I are attempting to reconstruct its circuitry, but it is an effort akin to assembling a Tholian sand sculpture in absolute darkness, in a high-velocity wind."

"As long as you have something to occupy you," said Kirk, dryly. "Keep me posted. Kirk out." He sat for a moment, then thumbed the intercom button again. "Kirk to sickbay."

"McCoy here."

"Bones, any—"

"No change in their condition in the last seventeen minutes, Jim. They're resting comfortably, but I've still got them pretty heavily sedated." His voice lowered a little, a sure sign of worry. *"The real complications will come when they awaken. They'll need physical therapy, psychological counseling—"*

"I'm sure you're up to it, Doctor. Keep me posted. Kirk out."

Kirk sat for a few seconds, replaying the last conversation in his mind. He shouldn't have been so short with Bones; his life hadn't been any too pleasant these days, either. He reached for the intercom button . . .

"Bridge to captain," said Uhura's voice over the speaker, suddenly, just as her face appeared on the screen. *"I have a transmission—"*

"An emergency?"

"No, sir, quite the opposite, in fact. It came in on a Federation frequency so low I almost missed it."

Kirk tried and failed to mask his irritation at what seemed to be a trivial issue at best. "Its content, Lieutenant? Does it require my attention?"

"I'm not sure, sir." Her fingers flashed over the console before her expertly. *"It seems only to be a set of numbers—geographic coordinates, I think—and a single word: 'Peter.'"*

"Captain, it's obviously some kind of trap," said Giotto, summoned hastily from his office.

"The coordinates?" asked Kirk, now seated in his chair on the bridge.

"Sir," said Chekov from Spock's post, "the coordinates seem to be in one of the older sections of the capital city."

"No way of tracing the transmission, Uhura?"

"No, sir. It vanished as soon as I received it. They must have been monitoring for reception."

"Of course." Kirk nodded. He rose and paced the bridge rapidly. Giotto was right, but still . . . this was something he could act on, take action against.

"Uhura, tell ship's stores to prepare clothing in the native Nadorian fashion, three—no, four sets." He cocked a brow at Chekov. "Feel like a little stroll, Chekov?"

"Yes, sir," responded Chekov, enthusiastically.

"Giotto, get one of your best people and prepare for a landing party."

"Captain," said Giotto, helplessly, "every instinct I have tells me this is a—"

"Trap, I know. Have I ever told you about my experience with the *Kobayashi Maru* test?"

"No, sir, but—"

"Perhaps later. See you in transporter room two."

Giotto headed for the turbolift, still grumbling under his breath.

"Mr. Sulu," said Kirk, on his way to the lift, "you have the conn."

It felt a little odd going on a landing party without Spock or McCoy, but they both had urgent tasks of their own. Besides, Giotto was an excellent officer, and—

The doors of transporter room one opened to admit Chief Giotto and Lieutenant Sinclair. Kirk caught Giotto's eye and motioned to him to approach. In a low tone of voice, he asked, "That's your choice, Chief? A little young, don't you think?"

"Sinclair's got more experience than you'd think, Captain. Besides, she's done a lot of research into the planet and their customs."

"We may need an experienced hand in combat more than we need a tour guide," replied Kirk, tersely.

Giotto looked at Kirk, as if not quite understanding what he saw. Or rather, what he heard. "Captain," he said respectfully, "you left the choice of personnel up to me. Sinclair was my choice. If you're going to question my decisions—"

Kirk took a deep breath, glanced at Sinclair, and shook his head. "All right, Chief. It's just that they seem so damn young."

"And we seem so damn old?" asked Giotto with a grin.

"I didn't say that," said Kirk. He turned to Sinclair, who looked away, with a false nonchalance. "Welcome to the party, Lieutenant. Keep your head down and follow my orders."

"Yes, sir," said Sinclair. She couldn't conceal the thrill in her voice, an emotion Kirk remembered from his early landing parties. Had he ever been that young?

The Nadorian native garb—shirts, leggings, and a kind of long overcoat for the men, a sort of hooded serape for Sinclair—fit well.

"Communicators on security mode," said Kirk, as they took their places on the transporter pad. He flipped a switch on his own, deactivating the audio signal, should the ship try to reach them. As he did so, one of McCoy's medtechs gave each of them a precautionary hypospray inoculation. "Mr. Kyle," said Kirk, "do you have a reading on those coordinates?"

"Yes, sir, it's an open-air park."

"Put us down on the other side of the park, opposite the location indicated by the coordinates." He glanced at Giotto and shrugged. "Just in case. Energize, Mr. Kyle."

Though they could see buildings on a nearby horizon as they materialized on Nador, the park was obviously quite large. They beamed down amid a grove of strangely stunted trees that seemed to oddly complement the few structures of the park, which had been designed in the same sweeping style Kirk had admired earlier. It was early evening; every few yards stanchions had been placed, supporting lit globes that increased in brightness as the natural light dimmed.

Kirk took a deep breath; the air was slightly sweet, from the scents of native flowers and grasses, no doubt. As they left the copse of trees, Kirk saw a few people:

couples of various ages strolling, the older couples holding hands, the younger couples unable to keep their hands off each other; children running in circles, playing a game whose abstruse rules escaped Kirk, trying to pack in as much fun as possible before being called in for the night; a few lone figures out for solitary strolls.

"The coordinates you received are about one hundred yards in that direction, Captain," said Chekov, pointing.

"Not too fast," said Kirk, "we're just locals out for an evening stroll."

"Looks like some other people had the same idea," said Sinclair, tilting her squarish jaw toward a gathering some distance away.

It was a sizable group of people, Kirk realized; as the landing party neared the group, he could hear voices, first a lone voice saying something with passion, but indistinguishable at this distance, then a chorus of voices responding, then a smaller, less organized chorus on the heels of the first. Some sort of open-air theater, or a concert, or—?

Whoever they were, they seemed to be standing at the base of some sort of huge, thick column that seemed to support nothing. He could see figures limned by flickering light, and caught a whiff of smoke—a fire, then. But not the sweet, heady scent of burning wood, something else. Fabric, that was it.

The illumination of the light globes paled to insignificance beside the brightness of the blaze. As they neared the crowd, Kirk realized the shape that had seemed like a thick column from a distance was actually a huge statue of Princes Abon and Delor, conjoined back-to-back. It was a new piece, very recently unveiled, based on how smooth and clean the rock was.

It was competent enough in its rendition of the twin monarchs, but with none of the lifelike stylization that characterized the older statuary in the palace.

At the base of a statue was a flat open-air rink of what Kirk assumed was a native stone, with a dais set into it for public assemblies. At the dais, Kirk could see one man, dressed in a robe of burnt orange and blue, holding something aloft that caused the shadows to shift and rotate when he swung it, the way the sun moved the hand of a sundial. The hoots of the crowd that followed were at once triumphant and indignant.

Kirk did not gasp, but felt his jaw tighten. Over his head the man in the robe was holding aloft the banner of the United Federation of Planets, and it was aflame.

The reason for the conflicting responses of the crowd became clear now: most of the crowd were Nadorian citizens, angry at the Federation for, they felt, having virtually kidnapped and severely mutilating their rulers. The response to their cheers came from, Kirk assumed, a group of Federation citizens living on Nador.

"The coordinates for the meeting are on the other side of the crowd, Captain," said Chekov. He didn't have to worry about whispering to avoid eavesdroppers. Kirk hardly heard him over the noise of the mob.

Kirk nodded his acknowledgment. "Better give them a wide berth," he replied, "for both our sakes. Phasers on stun, just in case."

Giotto and Sinclair each nodded once, sharply. Seeing the Federation's flag burned by a howling mob didn't set well with them, either.

But to give in to his anger would have jeopardized the mission, and possibly Peter. Kirk gestured for the landing party to fan out. They would not only be less conspicuous, but less likely to get picked off if it was a

trap. They flowed around the mob, whose components—the Nadorians and the Federation citizens—
seemed on the verge of attacking each other, like a
snake consuming its own tail. It occurred to Kirk that
there were almost certainly Nadorian security officers
watching the crowd, in mufti. With that in mind, he gestured for his crew to disperse even farther from the
crowd. It wouldn't do for them to be recognized by any
of Securitrix Llora's troops.

They were upwind from the smoke of the burning
Federation banner, which was at least a small blessing.
Not far away was another copse of trees, set roughly in
a circle, branches grasping at the darkening sky like
many-fingered hands.

There were light globes situated around the knot of
trees, but the trunks were thick enough and the branches intertwined sufficiently that a large portion of the
illumination was blocked from the inside. As Kirk
neared the trees, he thought he saw a single figure
standing in their center, as if the trees had grown around
him to imprison him. Or had he caused the trees to grow
around him, to protect him?

Kirk shook his head. *Now I'm thinking like McCoy.*
He made a surreptitious gesture, commanding the rest
of the landing party to stay back, and entered the circle
of trees, trying very hard not to look like a man trying
very hard to be nonchalant.

He got as close to the dark figure as a stranger could,
and leaned against a twisted bole, as though mildly
fatigued from his walk.

"A fine night," he said, noncommittally.

"Indeed," came a dim voice, after a few seconds. The
subsequent silence stretched on so long, Kirk wondered
if he would have to speak again. Then: "A night to think

of old friends, friends from far away. Perhaps even see them."

"Depending on the cost, yes," said Kirk, trying to keep his tone enigmatic. "What do you think about that?"

"I think you will remain still," said the other, his voice suddenly steely. His left arm rose, the pale light glinting feebly off the barrel of a Nadorian controlled force beam.

Kirk pitched himself backward over the twisted bole, somersaulting to the ground, hearing the whine of the force beam rip through the tree's trunk, filling the air with the odor of hot sap. Glancing around from his position as he drew his phaser, Kirk saw some of the other trees seem to move as the people hidden behind them made their presences known.

Kirk crouched and began to move backward, turning to sneak a glance in that direction. He saw another figure moving toward him, already drawing a bead on him.

From the darkness beyond the trees grew a long, thin finger of angry red radiance. The phaser beam struck Kirk's would-be assailant in his back; he went down, landing on a group of bushes.

The night was suddenly illuminated by a web of energy beams, the scarlet of the Federation phasers crisscrossing with the cool blue of the Nadorian controlled force beams, aimed with such precision that it seemed obvious their wielders wore some kind of night-vision gear. Kirk crouched behind a tree, peering out every few seconds to fire from behind either side of the tree, knowing the best thing he could do was wait for the landing party to catch up with him.

Behind him and to his left, furtive footfalls crushed grass. Without time to bring his phaser around, Kirk pivoted and brought his free hand up, clenched into a fist, aimed low.

The figure gave a low moan of pain and crumpled next to Kirk. He yanked the figure closer, pulled the hood of his robe back, and saw the face, bordered by gold, of Lieutenant Sinclair.

"Dammit, Sinclair," Kirk said, keeping his voice low, "don't you know the protocol for approaching friendly personnel in a combat situation?"

"Sorry, sir," she grunted, getting the wind back in her. "I won't forget next time."

"If there is one." The opposition—Kirk judged there to be about six of them, counting the first—had halted their approach, crouching behind trees as they dodged phaser fire, responding every few seconds with their own.

Kirk heard a low whistle from some distance away on the right. He lifted his head and peered carefully into the darkness. A human silhouette lifted a hand in a pre-arranged gesture Kirk recognized.

"Either Giotto or Chekov is to the right of us," said Kirk to Sinclair. "It's time to take the offensive."

"How exactly do we do that, sir?" asked Sinclair, with no trace of irony.

"Like this." Kirk gave a low whistle, which Sinclair recognized and made preparations for. Kirk, meanwhile, produced a canister from the depths of his robe and tossed it into the middle of the trees.

"Hold your breath!" he shouted. The canister arced to the ground, where it exploded, releasing a thick cloud into the night air.

Their assailants continued to advance through the gas.

"They're probably wearing gas masks," said Sinclair, her tone baffled.

"I hope so," whispered Kirk, with a grim smile. "I gave them enough warning."

"Sir?" But Kirk's only reply was to fling another object, this one a small, silver sphere that followed nearly the same path as the canister—

—then exploded soundlessly into a miniature nova. In an instant the copse of trees became a study in harsh black and white.

Not that Kirk could appreciate its stark beauty; his eyes were closed, as were Sinclair's. But the eyes of their assailants were wide open. They had been prepared for the gas attack, but were taken by total surprise by the blinding flare.

Kirk tapped Sinclair's arm and they charged forward. The flare had expended its brilliance in an instant, and their attackers were reeling unsteadily, as though drunk.

Chekov and Giotto also emerged from behind trees, charging their opponents, firing phasers as they came. The gas swirled around the landing party, but the injections they had received immunizing them to the nerve-deadening abilities of the gas before they had beamed down functioned exactly as planned.

A couple of their attackers must have heard them coming and fired their weapons blindly. Kirk straightarmed Sinclair, taking her out of the line of fire, then gave the first assailant a martial-arts chop that quickly rendered him *hors de combat*. He wheeled, preparing to attack the second, but found him lying at Giotto's feet.

"Didn't mean to hog your fun, Captain," he said, slyly.

"Plenty for everyone, Chief," responded Kirk. Not far away, Sinclair got groggily to her feet. Kirk approached her, but she waved away any assistance. "Sorry, Lieutenant, but—"

"I understand, sir," she said, shaking her head. Kirk hoped she wasn't getting used to being decked by superior officers.

"Captain, look!" said Chekov, pointing off.

Kirk followed his line of sight, just in time to see the tall statue of Their Serene Highnesses topple over, severed at the base by someone's weapon. Its descent was accompanied by a fearsome screech of sundered metal, and the panicked cries of many of the populace as they tried to dodge it.

The double-faced statue hit the ground with a sick thud, bouncing like a felled tree and calling up a cloud of dust that obscured the whole scene.

"Giotto, you and Sinclair get over there, see if anyone's hurt!"

"Aye, Captain," said Sinclair, dashing off to join Giotto, who was already on his way.

"What about them, Captain?" asked Chekov, indicating their assailants.

"Make sure they're disarmed, then revive them for questioning," said Kirk, tersely. He bent to the nearest member of their team, carrying out his own instructions. He pulled back the person's hood.

This time he did gasp. He was staring at the face of Chief Securitrix Llora.

Chapter Ten

"WE ARE AWAITING an explanation, Captain Kirk," said Regent Lonal.

"And so am I, Regent Lonal," replied Kirk. *The best defense is a good offense,* he thought, grimly.

Around them, in the throne room of the Royal Palace, interested parties coughed nervously, shuffled their feet, and tried to pretend that their interest in the proceedings was motivated solely by concern for the throne and the good of the people of the planet Nador.

It was almost as if the interrogation following the attack upon the princes aboard the *Enterprise* had been resumed here. Regent Lonal, seated in his official seat to one side of the two-sided throne normally occupied by Their Serene Highnesses, tried to act as though he was worthy of the power he wielded in the absence of Princes Abon and Delor. Counselors Docos and Hanor hovered at either side of the gathering, Docos unimposing but constantly watchful, Hanor looking more magnificently than ever like a gargoyle belonging on the rain gutter of some old Earth church. Commissioner Roget's presence seemed to lend a dignity to the proceedings, though his manner was one of a father who was deeply disappointed in the conduct of his charges. The Lady Pataal hovered in the background, her manner less effusive than usual, dark smudges under her almond eyes making her look older than her years.

And, to one side of Regent Lonal, Chief Securitrix Llora, standing stock-still, yet conveying the impression that she not only could erupt into indignant action at any minute, but would. Her dark eyes never left Kirk; in other circumstances, he would have been flattered.

"You are awaiting an explanation from *us?"* asked Lonal. There was something about his manner that bothered Kirk, something about his choice of words . . . well, it couldn't be more important than the matter at hand.

"I am," said Kirk, taking a few steps forward. The rest of the security party had beamed back aboard the *Enterprise,* at Kirk's orders. Giotto wanted to accompany Kirk, "just in case," he had said, gravely, one hand on his phaser, but Kirk had sent him on his way. Best to handle this alone.

"I would like to know," said Kirk, his tone one of considerable understatement, "why a matter concerning the security and well-being of a Federation citizen— who has been reported to your office as missing—was kept from me, and was attended to by palace security?"

Regent Lonal began to speak, but was cut off by an icy tone from Chief Securitrix Llora, who had not even looked at him. Lonal took this with a sniff of indignation, but suffered the palace's chief security officer to continue. "As noted earlier, Captain," she said, her voice precise and cutting as one of McCoy's exoscalpels, "the Federation citizen Peter Kirk was wanted for questioning regarding his association with the rioters who broke into the palace. While we agreed to let you have custody of the young man, in the interest of peaceful relations with the Federation, we regarded our interest in Peter Kirk as having established prior jurisdiction. Thus, when we received a message as to his whereabouts—"

"That's what I want to know," said Kirk, pouncing on the disclosure. "How did you know where to go?"

"My security office maintains an open line of communication, upon which any information concerning matters pertaining to security may be left—anonymously, of course."

"Of course," said Kirk, with a poisonous smile. "And you learned of Peter's alleged whereabouts through this network?"

"Just a moment, Captain Kirk," said Regent Lonal, "it is you who are being questioned here. Did your ship receive a similar communiqué regarding the location of your nephew?"

"Yes," said Kirk with an impatient nod. "Yes, we did. And we—"

"And you did not think it imperative to notify us?"

"The regent will understand," said Kirk, with a contriteness he did not feel, "if my concern for not only a Federation citizen but a blood relation of mine temporarily took precedence over my duties as a diplomat."

"Of course," said Lonal, blandly.

"It seems obvious," continued Kirk, "that some agency was responsible for notifying both our parties of the alleged whereabouts of my nephew, in an attempt set us against one another, to create another diplomatic incident—a firefight which could have counted both a Nadorian high palace official"—he gestured at Llora, who did not acknowledge it—"and a Federation captain in its casualties. I submit that when we find who was behind notifying both our offices of the alleged whereabouts of my nephew, we will find the party who secreted a transmitter on the princes, enabling them to be attacked while they were aboard the *Enterprise*. If we do not bring all our resources to bear upon this matter, such disputes may become the cause for severing diplomatic ties between Nador and the Federation—which is exactly what our mutual foes wish."

"And may still achieve," said Counselor Docos. It was as if one of the chairs had spoken. All eyes turned to him. Most had even forgotten he was there.

"What do you mean, Counselor?" asked Counselor Hanor.

"There were casualties caused by the toppling of the statue of Their Serene Highnesses—an unfortunate piece of symbolism," he said, never one to let the obvious go unsaid. "Should any of those casualties worsen into fatalities . . ." His voice trailed off, apparently not wishing to state two obvious facts in the same breath.

"My men were ordered to set their weapons only on stun," said Kirk, firmly. "Such a setting is not powerful enough to sever a massive statue. It must have been one of the Nadorian weapons that caused the statue to collapse. Such a determination could easily be made by scientific examination—"

"In such incidents, it is of little moment to attribute fault," said Commissioner Roget. "It would be most unfortunate if an incident, motivated by rabble-rousers, were the cause of a rift in Nadorian-Federation relations."

"Perhaps even enough to delay the handover?" asked Lonal.

"No one is talking about that, Regent Lonal," said

Roget, slowly. "The Federation does not consider that an option."

"Such an option would doubtless endanger more than diplomatic relations," said Kirk. "It would place the lives of the Federation citizens in Nador in severe jeopardy." He turned to Llora. "What measures are you taking to ensure their safety?"

"All reasonable measures have been taken to preserve the safety of Federation nationals," said Llora, as if reading from a press download. "The Nadorian people take seriously their responsibility as hosts—more so, Captain, than you do, I think."

"Securitrix, silence!" said Lonal with a hiss.

"No, let her speak," said Kirk, taking a step forward. "What do you mean?"

"Many of our people say you are holding Their Serene Highnesses hostage to ensure the desired outcome to the decision of the Nadorian people concerning the handover—desired by you, of course."

Kirk tamped down his temper, shrugged, and smiled—the last expression he knew they would expect to see on his face. "Do you deny that, given the nature of the princes' wounds, they can best be cared for on the *Enterprise?*"

"No, but—"

"Indeed, is not the medical care on the *Enterprise* far better than any they could receive on your planet?" He shifted his gaze quickly to Regent Lonal. "Meaning no offense, sir." Lonal had barely managed a formal nod before Kirk spoke again. "I understand your desire to have your monarchs returned home. But my chief surgeon is the monarch of his medical facility, and in those matters, his dictates are not subject to question, not even by his captain." Kirk made a helpless shrug, and saw that a few of the members of the inquisition managed a faint smile.

"Perhaps this, Regent Lonal," said Kirk, while the current was still flowing in his favor. "A planetwide address by Their Serene Highnesses to the Nadorian people, from the *Enterprise*. Would that allay your people's fears as to the condition of the monarchs?"

Counselors Docos and Hanor quickly approached Lonal as if drawn by magnetism. For several seconds three voices rose and fell as each fought for supremacy. Finally, Counselors Docos and Hanor stood away from Regent Lonal, who faced Kirk with great dignity. "Such an address to the Nadorian people would be well received, Captain," he said. "How may we facilitate this?"

"I'll have my chief engineer contact you," replied Kirk. "Between you, you can work out a proper date and time for the address."

"We look forward to hearing from him," said Lonal with an imperious nod. Kirk tipped his head in agreement, still wondering what it was about Lonal that was rubbing him the wrong way. His appearance? His conduct? No, nothing like that. At least, no more so than usual. Then what . . . ?

No matter. The meeting was breaking up; Kirk made a few gestures and nodded. Lonal rose from his seat as some of the other members of the audience stayed to speak with one another.

Trying not to make it look like he was hurrying, Kirk ran after Chief Securitrix Llora, and tapped her gently on the shoulder. Though she must have heard Kirk's advance across the stone floor of the throne room—Kirk had made no secret about his approach—she nonetheless wheeled as if taken by surprise. Kirk found his right wrist caught in a grip whose constricting force seemed to be that of a crushing vine, rather than that of a human being. Kirk briefly wondered what else those hands were capable of, but dismissed that thought under the category of wishes he'd probably never see granted.

"Yes?" asked Llora, coldly.

"I simply wished to apologize for this entire matter," said Kirk, trying to ignore his wrist—an easier matter than it seemed, as he was losing all feeling in it. "You can count on the full cooperation of my ship's security forces with yours from here on."

"That is wise," she said, flatly. The pressure on Kirk's wrist did not cease.

Around them, other members of the assemblage had finished their own conversations and were watching Kirk and Llora, drawn by some atavistic human instinct that told them some disturbance was nigh.

Kirk hid a grimace as the pressure on his wrist increased.

At the corner of Kirk's vision, he saw Commissioner Roget start to approach. Kirk shook his head back and forth, once, in two barely perceptible motions, his eyes not leaving Llora's.

Other members of the palace entourage watched this with interest, as if it were a sporting event or a friendly wager, but with small smirks upon their faces, telling the most perceptive where their allegiance lay.

Kirk could no longer feel his right hand; it was as though his arm ended at his wrist, the aftermath of an amputation. All he could see were two dark eyes, seeming as huge as lakes.

To fight force with force was his first instinct, and it would even have been justified, but clumsy, and lacking finesse. Also, engaging Llora in hand-to-hand combat and upping the situation a notch or two would put him no nearer a solution.

He leaned backward slightly, as though trying to pull free. Llora pulled that much harder.

Kirk reached for his belt with his left hand. Quickly withdrawing a small metal device, he brought it up just within Llora's field of vision, bringing his thumb down over its familiar contours. Llora, her gaze locked with Kirk's, finally seemed to realize what he was doing. With a perceptible start, her skin paled, her eyes widened. "No weapons!" she cried.

She released Kirk's wrist, and was thrown suddenly backward by the effort of her own pulling to retain her balance.

"You'll forgive me if I don't extend a hand to help you up," said Kirk, dryly.

"You used a weapon!" snarled Llora, trying to salvage what small triumph she could.

"You consider this a weapon?" asked Kirk, blandly. He extended his left hand, and flicked the metal box slightly, bringing it back to his face. "Kirk to *Enterprise*," he said. "Await my report." He clicked the communicator shut, transferred it to his right hand, and put it away, taking care not to drop it from his nearly numb fingers. *Showing off would serve me right,* he thought.

Llora sprang lithely to her feet, like a felled cat newly wary of prey that unexpectedly fought back. "I thought that to be a weapon!"

"And I thought I was making an overture of cooperation," said Kirk, deliberately letting his right hand swing free. "I guess we we both need more experience in these matters. Commissioner Roget," said Kirk, turning to the ambassador, "may I speak to you aboard the

Enterprise?" At Roget's nod, Kirk turned to Regent Lonal, nodded once, withdrew his communicator— with his right hand—and contacted his ship.

Upon materialization, Kirk immediately seized his right wrist in his left hand, massaging it vigorously.

"Are you all right, sir?" asked Kyle from the transporter controls.

"Never better," said Kirk cheerfully.

"You'd better have Dr. McCoy look at that," said Roget, as Kirk peeled his right sleeve back. "I think her fingernails broke the skin."

"That's what happens when you try to tame wild animals," said Kirk, leading the way out of the transporter room. "Do you mind a quiet drink in my quarters?"

"I rarely mind a quiet drink anywhere," replied Roget, with a straight face.

"You may be captain material," said Kirk with a smile. "Deck five."

"You might want to use that as a disinfectant," commented Roget, some minutes later. He was sitting on the other side of the desk from Kirk, two amber glasses between them.

"I prefer to begin disinfecting procedures from the inside out," said Kirk, clinking his glass against Roget's, then putting its contents where they would do the most good.

Roget smiled, refilling Kirk's glass. "It's too bad we don't have a post for a ship's diplomat," said Kirk. "You'd fit in around here."

"Janine would kill me," said Roget with a chuckle, "then get off by invoking diplomatic immunity. She's quite looking forward to retirement." He sampled the contents of his glass and nodded approvingly. "What was it you wanted to ask me, Captain?"

"We saw Nadorian nationals down there burning the Federation flag," said Kirk. "And as much as that puts a knot in my stomach, I'd rather see that than blood in the streets. But is vandalism like that just letting off steam, or is it a symptom of real danger to Federation citizens? How bad is the situation down there?"

"About halfway between where you'd like it to be and where Lonal says it is. I've heard reports of Federation citizens getting shoved around a little, but no real damage has been done to them. The Nadorian people are pretty levelheaded as a rule, Captain. I don't think you need to worry about individuals being lynched by mobs."

"What worries me," said Kirk, slowly, "is what happens when the Federation citizens decide they need to fight back. When it becomes mob versus mob, even the most level heads have a tendency to get caved in."

"I'll certainly keep you notified of the circumstances."

"Providing you know the truth," said Kirk, bluntly. "The Federation's representative is the last person whom they'll give the unvarnished truth to."

"I haven't survived this long in the diplomacy game because I'm such a charming dinner companion, Captain," replied Roget. "I have a few sources of information the Nadorian government knows nothing about." His voice softened. "We'll find your nephew."

"It's not so much that he can't take care of himself, all things being equal," said Kirk, rising and pacing his cabin, thinking of the lessons his father had taught him and Sam, and that Sam had passed on to Peter, "it's that there's more than just a simple criminal conspiracy here. There's some motive we haven't begun to see yet, and when we do, we'll have a larger, clearer view of this puzzle."

"Something that goes deeper than upsetting the throne of Nador?" asked Roget, dubiously. "That would seem to be a pretty ambitious goal in and of itself, Captain."

Kirk seated himself again and peered at a lighting fixture through the amber contents of his glass. "I think the political intrigue is important to whoever's behind this," he said, at length, "and we can't discount the possibility that the throne itself might have been offered to one of the coconspirators as a bribe."

"Such as . . . ?"

"Throughout that recent spat in the throne room, I had the feeling there was something wrong with Regent Lonal—"

"'Wrong'? Do you think he's ill, or—"

"Nothing like that," said Kirk, slowly. "Just something different, out of place about his aspect, his way of dealing with the rest of us. Then it hit me—he kept using the pronoun 'we.'"

Roget waited a moment, as if there might be more. When he responded, his tone was disappointed. "There were many people present," he said. "And?"

"And that's it," said Kirk with a disarming shrug. "Not much, I grant you, but it finally occurred to me . . . I don't think he was referring to the Nadorian people, I think he may have been referring, almost subconsciously, to himself—using the royal 'we.'"

"You mean he intends to keep the throne?" Roget's tone was incredulous, yet its surprise was not entirely convincing, as if the same idea had occurred to him.

"Why not? If the riots continue, Regent Lonal will have no choice but to declare martial law, which will only further aggravate the rioters, which means Regent Lonal will have to assume more powers to preserve the peace." Kirk drained his glass and spread his hands, in seeming helplessness. "I know it sounds fantastic, but many a would-be usurper has taken such steps to a throne."

"But the princes would never allow—"

"Not as long as they lived," said Kirk, his voice almost a whisper.

"You've given me much to think about, Captain," said Roget, rising. "I do thank you, but I wish I felt more grateful."

"I quite understand, Commissioner," said Kirk, ruefully. "Let me escort you back to the transporter room. I've kept you from that lovely wife of yours long enough. Please give her my apologies."

After seeing the commissioner off, Kirk paced the corridors of the ship restlessly—causing no end of consternation to crew members engaged in legitimate pursuits, both ship-related and personal—then returned to his quarters. His system was contrary enough that the alcohol he had imbibed was acting as a stimulant rather than a depressant, at least for the present.

After a few minutes of pretending to read various departmental reports, Kirk swung to face his console. "Kirk to bridge."

"Lieutenant Palmer here, sir, how can I help you?"

"Status, Lieutenant?"

"All systems normal, sir."

"Any reports from Dr. McCoy or Mr. Spock?"

"No, sir. Shall I patch you through to them?"

"No need for that. Don't even tell them I was asking. But keep me posted on anything unusual. Kirk out."

"Good night, sir."

Kirk lay back on his bunk and shook his head, hoping Palmer's salutation would prove prophetic. He lay there for several minutes, courting sleep, which proved an elusive mistress. He rose and turned on the cabin lights, shaking his head. McCoy had given him certain prescriptions to use in a situation like this, but he didn't like to rely on chemicals. He turned to the row of books at the head of his bed, and selected one, an anthology of seafaring stories Spock had given him. He had just cracked the volume, his fingers caressing the leather bindings, looking for a story he hadn't read, when his cabin speaker sounded. *"Palmer to Captain Kirk."*

Kirk was at the console before the first syllable had faded. "Kirk here, Lieutenant."

"Sir, I apologize for disturbing you. This seems extremely trivial, but—"

"What is it, Lieutenant?"

"Sir, earlier this evening we received a very low-gain transmission, on an old Federation frequency. Since it seemed to contain nothing urgent, it was filed for the science officer's inspection."

"What was it?" asked Kirk, his interest now thoroughly piqued.

"You said to keep you abreast of anything unusual, so—"

"What was it, Lieutenant?" asked Kirk, keeping his voice level.

"I'm sending it through, sir." After a moment's silence, a short series of mechanical tones emitted from the speaker, underlain by a great deal of static. Kirk listened intently to it, once, then twice. It was a code, a nonverbal code he had learned when at the Academy. . . .

He played the message a third time, jotting down the letters the message had coded as he dredged them from his memory. Then he looked at the message, thumbed the console, and said, "Palmer, have Spock, McCoy, and Uhura meet me on the bridge. Immediately."

Then he turned to look at the message again, at two words which read: JAM. OKAY.

"No, sir," Uhura was saying, seven minutes later. "There's no way of telling anything about the signal's origin, other than what we know from examining the signal itself. Its very simplicity works against its being thoroughly analyzed."

"Nor is there any way to precisely determine the message's point of origin," said Spock, looking up from his scanner. "Given the *Enterprise*'s position in orbit about the planet at the time the message was received, we were within range of transmitters on fully one-third of the planet."

"Including the capital city," mused Kirk.

"What's so mysterious about this signal anyway, Jim?" asked McCoy. He and Uhura looked understandably rumpled, having been disturbed in the middle of the night, while Spock, as usual, looked as though he had been waiting for Kirk's summons. "Is it from Peter?" asked McCoy, anxiously. At Kirk's nod, McCoy turned to Spock. "Human intuition," he said, proudly.

"In more precise terminology, a guess," said Spock.

"Whatever it was, he's right," said Kirk.

"How can you be so certain, Captain?" asked Spock. "The message might support the interpretation as reading 'J. AM OKAY,' but absent any definitive proof—"

"Are you certain of the message's spacing?" Kirk asked Uhura, ignoring Spock for the moment.

"Sir?"

"Are you sure the message does read 'JAM. OKAY' and not, for example, 'J. AM OKAY'?"

Uhura nodded. "I see." She flipped switches on her console and listened to the message again as a graphic scan of it raced across her screen. She listened to it twice, then turned to Kirk. "Yes, sir, it definitely reads 'JAM. OKAY.'"

"Thank you, Lieutenant," said Kirk. "In that case, it is from Peter." He surveyed the faces of his senior staff and Uhura, and smiled. "As an infant, Peter couldn't say the name 'James,' so he called me 'Uncle Jam.' Still does, once in a great while when we're reminiscing. He's telling me that he's all right. He can't say anything else, but he's all right."

"Does anyone else know of this nickname?" asked Spock, dubiously.

"No one," said Kirk, firmly.

"Unless—" Spock began.

"I know," nodded Kirk, solemnly. "Unless he's been captured and it's been forced out of him. But if that were the case, wouldn't his captors have requested a meeting of some sort?"

"Logical," conceded Spock, "but they also know you would be extremely wary of any such lure, given your last experience planetside, which the guilty parties in this matter are doubtless aware of by this time."

"This first communication may be just a way of setting you up for more," said McCoy. "If it really is from Peter, what the devil is he doing on Nador?"

"Probably trying to get to the bottom of this mess," said Kirk. "Probably in over his head, as usual."

"If that's true," said McCoy, stifling a yawn, "we'll probably hear from him again, and soon, asking for help."

"We can only hope," said Kirk.

"Captain," said Spock, "I find the timing of the message somewhat suspicious, coming as soon as it did after the false message intended to pit you and the Nadorian security forces against each other."

"I considered that, too," said Kirk, "but it may be that Peter, wherever he is on Nador, knows of that altercation. Citizens were injured by it, it made the news, and a sharp boy like Peter could have put two and two together. Plus, if this second message were a forgery, wouldn't it have tried to draw us into another trap?"

"It may be that that assumption is what the plotters are counting on," said Spock, "to lend credence to their next communiqué."

"That may be," replied Kirk, "but until the authenticity of this message has been disproved, I will assume this is a genuine, if somewhat truncated, note from my nephew."

"That is an exact reversal of the usual method of establishing a proof," said Spock.

"That's the way we Kirks sometimes do things." He looked at the three of them, and Lieutenant Palmer, who was standing not far away. "Not a word of this to anyone without my express permission. Understood?"

"Aye, Captain," came four replies.

"Good," said Kirk, briskly. "Spock, any progress with that transmitter?"

"Lieutenant DeSalle and I have made some progress in its restoration, sir, but full success is some distance away."

"Keep on it. Bones, the twins?"

"Healing nicely, so far," said McCoy. "I'm beginning physical therapy with them tomorrow—assuming I can keep my eyes open."

"In that case, you may return to your quarters, with my thanks and apologies. Unless," he eyed them slyly, "you care to join me in a nightcap."

None of them did. Just as well. Kirk returned to his quarters, his mind racing, his heart lighter than it had been in days, and fell asleep in minutes.

"This is remarkable," said Prince Delor.

"It is like looking into a mirror," said Prince Abon.

"From any other set of twins I'd call that a cliché," replied Dr. McCoy, "but from you two—well, there's a first time for everything."

The relative youth of the twins had aided greatly in their recovery, McCoy knew, and the increase in their strength and vital signs was certainly encouraging. But McCoy also knew that the twins, like any person who had been on the receiving end of a life-changing condition, whether massive disfigurement, spinal-cord damage, or loss of sensory input, had not yet fully come to grips with the permanent change in their status. And when they did, that would be the first real danger to their recovery.

The twins had slept for hours after the operation, and had seemingly taken the news of their separation in stride. But McCoy knew better, knew that it hadn't really sunk home yet; he could only hope he was there when it did.

For royals, the princes made pretty good patients. They had taken a shine to Nurse Chapel, whom they flattered endlessly in vain attempts to wangle special privileges. Only occasionally, when they demanded something they couldn't have—such as returning home or even news of how their kingdom was faring under Regent Lonal—did they become moody or truculent. And on those rare occasions, Nurse Chapel was able to jog them back to normal spirits, not by catering to them, but by treating them exactly the same as she would any other patient.

It's the novelty of that that worked, McCoy thought. *Probably the first time anyone talked to these boys like they were normal.*

Then it occurred to him that this was the first time in their lives that they *were* normal—or at least, within hailing distance of that state.

They had been confined to bed for the first couple of days after the operation, giving their systems a chance to recover, to take up the work caused when they were finally weaned off sterilite. They had wanted to get on their feet right away, of course, but McCoy had firmly vetoed that, feeling the twins needed a chance to get slowly accustomed to their new physical status.

When they were able to get out of bed, McCoy had produced a couple of wheelchairs partially controlled by thought impulses—some of the younger officers referred to them as "Pikes," a term he took extreme exception to—thinking the chairs would serve a dual purpose, not only helping them to get used to the revised structure of their bodies, but enabling their spinal nerves to grow accustomed to transmitting along new neural passageways to take the place of those severed in the operation.

"Surely not a mirror," said Delor. "No mirror I have ever viewed distorted my features that much."

Abon was dumbstruck for a moment, then broke out laughing. McCoy even got a chuckle out of that, more from his own surprise at Abon's reaction than a sharing of Delor's joke. McCoy wasn't at all sure Delor had been joking.

In fact, though, McCoy and Chapel had both noted small differences in the twins that enabled them to be told apart. Such differences were small, but subtle. Abon had a minute but distinguishable cleft in his chin, while Delor's mouth was just a trifle wider than his brother's. McCoy wondered if anyone had noted such discrepancies before, since no one person had ever been able to see the twins face-to-face at the same time.

"All right now, we're going to try a little work on the parallel beams," said McCoy, preceding Abon, Delor, and Chapel into a medical lab on the other side of his office. He tapped buttons on the console set into one of two facing tubular structures that each held two lenses. Once activated, two rays of solid light, modified tractor beams, shot out from the lenses, to meet seamlessly in the middle. "Who's first?" he asked, cheerily.

"You wish me to balance on beams of light?" asked Delor, dubiously.

"It does not seem safe," added Abon.

"It's perfectly safe," said McCoy. "Here, I'll show you." He stepped between the two beams of light, gripped them, his palms facing down, and pushed his feet off the floor a few inches. "There, you see?"

"I see, but I am not convinced," said Abon and Delor simultaneously. The twins turned to each other and grinned at their impromptu chorus.

"Believe me, it's safe," said McCoy. "It's been used for years, by hundreds of thousands of people. I wouldn't let you use it if it weren't safe." From somewhere behind him came a kind of muffled snort. "Something funny, Nurse Chapel?" said McCoy, not turning.

"No, Doctor," replied Chapel, through clenched lips.

From McCoy's office, the entry tone sounded, and Chapel, thanking whatever force sent them a visitor, ran to answer it.

"All right, who's first?" asked McCoy, rhetorically. "You," he said, pointing to Abon. "Give it a try, Your Highness."

"I don't think I'm ready," said Abon, all humor gone from his voice.

"Of course you are, come on," said McCoy, chidingly. He wheeled Abon to one of the tubular structures, between the parallel beams of light. "There, give them a feel. I've reduced the gravity to seventy-five percent of Nadorian normal, just to give you a head start."

Abon gingerly reached up and touched the beam of light on his right, the fingers of his hand splayed as if passing them through a spray of water. He had obviously expected his hand to go right through it, despite McCoy's example, but his hand tightened about the beam and remained there, despite any pressure he could bring to bear.

"There, you see?" said McCoy encouragingly, from the side. "It's not going anywhere. Now get your left hand up there." Abon did so, grasping both beams tightly. "Good, good. Now get your feet underneath you on the floor and just stand up. We'll take it easy for today, that's all you have to do."

Abon's expression did not share the ease that McCoy's voice conveyed, but the cleft in his chin narrowed as his jaw clenched. McCoy took that as a sign that he resolved to do his best. He gripped the beams even more tightly, and pushed up, hearing the faint hum of the wheelchair as it moved a few inches back.

"Oh, hello, Pataal," said Nurse Chapel, as the girl entered McCoy's office. "Captain Kirk said you might be dropping by."

Pataal nodded, nervously, clearly uncomfortable in this chamber of strange devices. "I would like to see Their Serene Highnesses, if I may," she said, tentatively.

"I'm sure you would," replied Chapel, brightly. "Please, this way."

"I have brought them a gift," said Pataal, her voice a little brighter. "A box of their favorite sweets from the palace chef."

"I'm sure they'll appreciate that," replied Chapel.

"Good, good," said McCoy to Abon. "Now get your arms under you. Don't lock your elbows, that'll lift you off the floor."

"I am trying, Doctor," replied the prince slowly, between exhaled breaths.

"Don't look at your hands, look at your feet. That's what you need to see. Just a little lower, and—"

With a cry that betrayed more horror than any he had felt during the assault that placed him here, Prince Abon's left arm went out from under him and he fell to the floor.

"Don't struggle," said McCoy, running to his patient. "I'm right here—"

"Abon!" shouted Delor, on seeing his twin collapse like a rag doll. He gripped the arms of his wheelchair, pushing himself forward.

"No, dammit, stay where you are!" shouted McCoy. "You're not ready to—" True enough, Delor likewise fell to the floor.

A shriek shattered the air; McCoy turned to see the Lady Pataal standing there, an expression of pure terror on that part of her face that wasn't covered by her hands. She started to run forward, dropping the box of sweets.

"Nurse, get her out of here!" thundered McCoy.

"Woman, leave us!" shouted Prince Delor.

"But my princes—"

"Are you deaf? Leave!" shouted Abon, his tone equal parts reprimand and self-loathing.

Despite himself, McCoy watched as Chapel pulled

her back, and the doors to the therapy room hissed shut, like the door of a prison, crushing the box of sweets between them.

"Dammit," said McCoy fervently, surveying the two young men who lay writhing on the floor before him. Days ago they had been conjoined, but healthy, happy, and capable of facing the world on its own terms. Now—well, he had to do what he did, he only hoped they could forgive him. "Gravity at twenty-five percent," he called, moving to Abon, who was closer, and flailing like an overturned crab.

"I'm so sorry," said Nurse Chapel. "I shouldn't have let you in without Dr. McCoy's permission."

"They ordered me out," said Pataal, not hearing Chapel. "They did not want to see me." Tears began to grow in the corners of her eyes, which shifted from side to side nervously, surveying this place where her princes had been changed into something new and bizarre.

"They're very proud men," said Chapel.

"Then how can I help them?" asked Pataal, her voice agonized. "How can you help someone you care for if he refuses to let you?"

"You poor thing," said Chapel, suddenly, as her voice broke. She grabbed Pataal and hugged her, as Pataal wondered why her new friend the nurse was crying, too.

Chapter Eleven

IT WASN'T AS THOUGH Captain James T. Kirk didn't like showing off the *U.S.S. Enterprise.* On the contrary, he loved to display the *Enterprise* like a proud parent showing off a beautiful child, telling visitors what his ship could do, the power she—and by extension, he—could command, the nearly incalculable speeds she could achieve, the energies she was capable of bending to her use. He took special pleasure in giving tours of the ship, revealing little-known trivia about her past missions and the total number of parsecs she had traveled, all the while conveying to friends that the *Enterprise* was an excellent ally to have on your side and, to foes, that she was an opponent to be dreaded.

But he hated having events on his ship happen without his express permission; it was like freeloaders coming and living in your house without your permission.

Not that he regarded Their Serene Highnesses, Princes Abon and Delor, as anything akin to freeloaders. The attack that had laid them low had been delivered while he was their host; he regarded that as an insult someone would pay for when this whole business was resolved, hopefully very soon.

No, Kirk saved his disdain for the technicians—seemingly hundreds of them, though the actual number was quite small, and constantly under the supervision of Chief Giotto and Lieutenant Sinclair—that had been assigned to the supervision and production of the planetwide broadcast of Their Serene Highnesses to the people of Nador.

"Admiral," Kirk had said earlier to Admiral Fitzgerald, in his most persuasive tone, "I assure you, my engineer and his technicians are quite capable of supervising the dissemination of a simple holographic wave transmission."

"I'm sure they are, Captain," Fitzgerald had replied, wearily, *"but the issue here is more than just accomplishing the actual transmission, it's a chance to mend some fences, to show the Nadorian people that we regard them as allies."*

"But sir, the security measures alone—"

"Are well within the capabilities of Security Chief Giotto," Fitzgerald had cut in acidly. *"I informed Regent Lonal that the Nadorians coming aboard will be subject to the most stringent security, to avoid anything unexpected."* His tone had left volumes unsaid, and though Kirk had hated to have to take it, he couldn't deny Fitzgerald's concerns. *"This is our chance to make amends to them, Captain. I suggest you take advantage of it."*

"Understood, sir," Kirk had said, well aware that the definition in a Starfleet admiral's lexicon of the word "suggest" was far different from his.

"Any word on your nephew?" Fitzgerald had asked, in a gentler voice.

Kirk had shaken his head. His knowledge—or what he felt was his knowledge—of Peter's status was best kept to only the five who knew of it. "Not yet. The Nadorian authorities claim to be searching for him, but I'd feel better if we could stage an investigation of our own."

"Certainly, Captain," Fitzgerald had said, *"if you can secure the permission of the Nadorian government."*

"I am attempting to secure just such permissions even as we speak."

"Good luck with that, I'm sure the boy will turn up safe and sound. Fitzgerald out."

"This is all your fault," Kirk now said to McCoy over a quick drink. Aside from the hurried conference last night, he hadn't had many chances to see Bones since the princes had been attacked, and none socially.

"Me? What did I do?"

"You won't release the princes from sickbay," Kirk reminded him, pointedly.

"Oh, that. No, Jim, they're not ready. But with the security measures you've taken, I doubt you'll have any problems."

"Famous last words," said Kirk, draining his glass. "Whose idea was this broadcast, anyway?"

"Do you really want me to remind you?" replied McCoy.

"No," said Kirk, his reply followed immediately by a chiming sound. "Come," he called, and the door to his quarters slid open to reveal his science officer. "Spock, how are the preparations coming?"

"All personnel and equipment native to the planet have been examined quite thoroughly by a system implemented by Chief Giotto and myself," replied Spock. "I anticipate no breaches of security, Captain." He didn't add the words "this time," but it was as if he had. Kirk knew the Vulcan to be irritated at the security lapse that had allowed the princes to be attacked. *Not,* he thought wryly, *that he would ever admit it.*

Kirk nodded. "And have you and DeSalle made any headway on the transmitter?"

"Only in the negative sense. We have tried many combinations of wiring and circuitry, which have not worked."

"Well, that's progress of a sort," said McCoy. "I'm sure you'll get lucky eventually."

"As you must surely be aware by now, Doctor, I prefer not to rely on that commodity, particularly in situations like this, when it has been in short supply."

"You're right there," said Kirk. "How much longer until the broadcast?"

"Thirty-one minutes, twenty-three seconds."

"I suppose we'd better get down there," said Kirk. He stood by the door of his cabin and motioned the others through. "After you, gentlemen."

Pataal answered the door chime of Yeoman Tonia Barrows's quarters, assuming it would be some friend or professional acquaintance of hers—perhaps that nice Dr. McCoy, to whom Pataal had not yet had a chance to apologize for interrupting his session with Their Serene Highnesses. But when the door opened, it revealed Prince Abon, in his wheeled-chair conveyance. For the first time since Pataal had known him, the smile on his face was uncertain.

"Best wishes, my lady," said Prince Abon. He nodded, his manner somehow contriving to give it the grace of a full bow. "May I come in?"

"I am just preparing for the broadcast, Your Highness," said Pataal, uncertainly.

"I won't be long," replied Prince Abon, commanding the chair forward. "And even if I am, there can hardly be a broadcast without both princes, can there?"

"I suppose not, my prince," said Pataal. She sat on the edge of the bed, her smile quivering like the wings of a butterfly.

"I simply wished to say," said Abon, "that since my brother and I have—what is the proper term?—attained our physical independence from each other, there will be a great deal of changes in our relationship."

"I am certain you and he will have much to discuss," replied Pataal, her voice sounding hollow.

"No, I meant the relationship between you and me," said Abon. "When things were as they were, the arrangement among the three of us was acceptable to all."

"It is so no longer?"

"I am not yet sure, but no, it may not be," said Abon. He spread his hands to indicate not only the wheelchair but, thought Pataal, himself. "When my brother and I were conjoined, we were forced to share almost everything. Now that we are apart . . ." He rolled his wheelchair forward a few feet closer to Pataal and took one of her hands in his. "Our lives will be very different." He looked up at Pataal. "My lady, do I make myself clear?"

"I fear not, Your Highness," Pataal said, though in truth she felt exactly the opposite.

"I wish you to be mine," said Abon, gently but firmly. "And mine alone."

"I see."

"Make no answer now," said Abon, releasing her hand and withdrawing a few feet. "But know how I feel and what I wish. I hope it is also what you wish and feel, as well."

"You have made your wishes known," said a voice from behind Pataal, "as have I." To most ears it would seem that Prince Abon was still speaking, but she knew better.

"As so you have, Prince Delor," said Pataal, wishing, at that instant, that she had never been conceived.

Prince Delor's wheelchair motored smoothly out from behind the partition in Tonia's quarters. He gave his brother the most cursory of glances, speaking to the Lady Pataal. "Despite the difference between my brother and myself, we are quite agreed on one point. Our lives will indeed be very different now that we are separated." He pivoted before Pataal and, placing an index finger under her chin, lifted her head until their eyes made contact. "You have a decision to make, my lady, and sooner than any of us might wish." Delor wheeled toward the doorway, but was intercepted by Prince Abon.

"Look at me, Delor," said Abon. His words were a request but his tone made it a demand. "For once, you can."

"What would you have me say, brother?" asked Delor. "That our lives were less complicated when we were an aberration?"

"That is the difference between us, Delor," replied Abon, his hands tightening upon the arms of his chair. "I saw us as unique."

"And we are neither any longer, are we?" asked Delor. Pivoting his chair neatly around Abon's, he sped through the doorway, turning right. Abon remained behind for a moment, looked at the Lady Pataal, then hummed through the doorway, and to the left.

Pataal tried to rise on wobbly feet. Instead she collapsed to the bed, wishing she knew how to increase the temperature in Tonia's cabin. She was suddenly very cold.

Kirk walked among the group assembled in the cargo hold, trying not to look as though he distrusted most of the assembled audience from Nador. He assumed at least a few of those assembled felt exactly the same about him.

But one of them, he felt, was the prime mover behind the assaults, not only on Princes Abon and Delor, but on his ship. He could live with not being universally loved, and had, in fact, given many persons in the galaxy reason to feel exactly the opposite about him. He was also sure that the futility of wishing for universal acceptance was one point every one of the Nadorian politicians gathered here could agree on—well, most of them, anyway. He was uncertain about Regent Lonal. But he could not tolerate an attack upon his ship, and he was determined that whoever was behind such an action would pay, and dearly.

"Counselor Docos, so good to see you," said Kirk with a smile, exchanging with the Abonian representative a Nadorian two-handed grip, the equivalent of a handshake. The surprise on Docos's face made the effort worthwhile. "Counselor Hanor, likewise a pleasure. That's a lovely gown." Her gown was in fact an exact duplicate of the gown she had worn the last time Kirk had seen her, but what the hell, a fact was a fact.

Nodding and waving to a few others, Kirk made for the cargo-bay control center. Slightly raised above floor level and couched behind a shield of transparent aluminum, this point in the cargo hold, usually used to supervise the loading and storage of large items, afforded an excellent vantage of the entire structure.

"How's it going, Scotty?" asked Kirk.

"I'll be grateful when this night is over, sir," said Scotty, fervently. Kirk almost smiled; if Scotty, questioned about any situation in which he did not control every variable, had replied that all was shipshape or that there was nothing to worry about, Kirk would have known something was wrong.

"Are the transmission teams deployed?"

"Aye, sir." Scotty pointed to a team of holograph technicians who would oversee the transmission of the princes' address to the planet surface. "All their equipment was gone over within a micrometer. Nothing was smuggled aboard by them, or the rest of the Nadorian natives." Scotty's dour countenance briefly cracked into a rare smile. "But you can bet some of those bigwigs'll be registerin' complaints with Commissioner Roget."

Kirk laughed tightly. "I'm beginning to think I wouldn't know how to act if an encounter with the Nadorian government didn't end in a diplomatic complaint."

"I'd know how t'act," said Scotty, fervently.

They heard a small beep, an indication that whoever wanted to enter the control center had passed the retinal scan. "Chief Giotto," Kirk said, "how's it going out there?"

"Not bad, sir," replied Giotto, slowly. For the cautious security chief, this was high praise. "We had to find some temporary homes for a lot of cargo—some of Commissioner Roget's possessions among them—but we cleared the area in time."

"It was one of the most secure places on the ship with enough space to handle this many people," said Kirk with a nod. "But I was referring to the security situation."

"Everyone passed through scanners and no one objected—well, not strenuously anyway. It's always possible to kill a man with your bare hands or an available prop if someone wants to badly enough, but I'll stake my rank on the fact that there's no powered weapons or explosives down there that we don't know about."

"And your personnel?"

"Deployed throughout the crowd, sir," said Giotto, spreading a hand to indicate the entire hold of visitors. "Some making themselves obvious, like Lieutenant Sinclair, who the Nadorians know about. Others not so obvious—serving drinks and whatnot."

"Seems secure enough," said Kirk with a nod. "It's, what, ten minutes until the transmission? I'll see you later."

Leaving the control center, Kirk made his way across the cargo hold, whose temporary decor, largely wall hangings in the colors and designs of the royal families, satisfactorily hid its drab, functional origins.

Passing through the cargo hold to its main hatch, only Kirk's skills at navigating a crowd prevented him from colliding with a young woman who seemed to be watching nothing but the floor. When she looked up at him, it took him a moment to recognize the face of the Lady Pataal. Her face, normally so young and pretty, seemed to be bearing the weight of a thousand worlds. Furrows were just visible in what little makeup she wore; she had been crying.

"Captain, oh, I'm so sorry," she said, her voice throaty, confirming Kirk's deduction as to her emotional state.

"My lady," said Kirk, gently, "is everything all right?"

"Oh, yes, yes, of course." She attempted a smile, which looked even sadder than the expression she had formerly worn. "It's just . . . all the excitement, I suppose. It can be very exhausting."

"Yes, it can," replied Kirk with a smile. He stepped slightly closer to her and lowered his voice. "If you want to talk about anything, feel free—"

To his astonishment, she seemed almost repelled by the simple conciliatory gesture he had made, taking one of her hands in his. She snatched it back as though Kirk were about to extrude acid on it.

"Thank you, but . . . it's nothing." She practically dashed for the main hatch, her actions giving the lie to her words.

Before Kirk could make a move to follow, he heard a blast of trumpets from the sound system, the fanfare for the Nadorian planetary anthem, which he was beginning to know far better than he had ever wanted to.

A hatch leading to one of the cargo-hold lifts opened and Their Serene Highnesses, Princes Abon and Delor, entered, still confined to the wheelchairs McCoy had put them in, but looking quite well otherwise. The crowd, some of whom had been sitting at small tables set up for the occasion, rose spontaneously to their feet in a roar of approval and a round of applause. The crowd craned their necks to see their monarchs, not so much from loyalty, Kirk thought, cynically, as from a desire to see how grotesquely they had been maimed at the hands of the Federation. *Sorry to disappoint you,* thought Kirk, allowing himself the brief satisfaction of private malice. He also noted nearly all of the assembled crowd immediately sharing some sentiment with a nearby partner, doubtless expressing their astonishment and concern at seeing the princes physically separated for the first time in their lives, a sentiment of which Kirk was more understanding.

Escorted by some footmen who had beamed up from the palace, the princes rolled to a central, low dais that had been draped in the Nadorian flag—*and the* Enterprise *is showing the Nadorian colors far more respect than their planet has shown the Federation banner,* thought Kirk—and maneuvered into position behind it, waiting for the applause to subside.

The princes did look good, Kirk decided, grinning to himself, in retrospect, at the private joke that McCoy's treatments would kill either the disease or the patient. But there was something uneasy about them, something wrong. Kirk watched them for a few moments before he realized what it was: the princes had not once made eye contact with each other. Scanning the scene more closely, Kirk noted Chief Securitrix Llora in the shadows of the lift the princes had come from, scouring the crowd with her gaze. But that couldn't have been the reason for the monarchs' unease with each other. Recalling the distraught state of the Lady Pataal, Kirk thought he'd found the cause, if not yet the specific reason.

Regent Lonal came forward, shaking hands and bowing to the princes, which they took in good grace, saying something to him that made him beam with approval. *Keep your friends close and your enemies closer,* thought Kirk, and wondered into which category Lonal fit.

Then, since they were being hosted by a Federation starship, Commissioner Roget came forward and made a few gracious remarks. Automatically watching the crowd for any suspicious signs, Kirk saw Mrs. Roget applauding her husband, while nodding encouragingly. It wouldn't be the first time a politician had taken cues from a spouse offstage.

" . . . and Their Serene Highnesses have informed

me," Kirk realized Roget was saying, "that they are most grateful to the efforts and the hospitality of the captain of the *U.S.S. Enterprise,* Captain James Tiberius Kirk." He had been making his way to the main hatch, but turned just in time to see nearly every eye in the room turn toward him as a fresh round of applause sprang up. Kirk noted that most of the applause was coming from *Enterprise* personnel. Some of the Nadorian entourage were barely applauding at all, and some, like Llora, had defiantly crossed her hands across her chest.

"Our loyal subjects, and valued allies," said Abon. There was a brief pause, then Prince Delor took up the conversational thread. Kirk frowned slightly. Before their surgery, one had followed up on the other's thoughts almost instantly. Well, perhaps this was the result of the separation. If so, it was a small price to pay for having saved their lives.

"We wish you to know how much we have valued your thoughts and prayers during these trying times. We are convinced that the reason for our presence here today is those good wishes by Nadorian citizens."

"As well as the surgical skills of Dr. Leonard H. McCoy," said Abon. Kirk wasn't sure—was Delor taken by surprise by Abon's remark? At any rate, some of the starship personnel applauded this statement, which Kirk was only too happy to join in on, both for the doctor's sake and for the higher cause of good relations between the Federation and the Nadorian government. Kirk didn't actually see McCoy anywhere around, and wondered briefly where the doctor had stowed himself. "We are different than you have known us, yes, but we are still your princes, and our wish for the continued prosperity and safety of the planet Nador and her people is still one."

"But foremost in our minds has always been the welfare of the Nadorian people," said Delor, seeming to try to jerk the presentation back on track. "To this end, we have for long days and nights pondered the issue of joining the United Federation of Planets and what that would mean for the future of Nador."

"And it is our decision, and our most heartfelt recommendation to Counselor Docos, Counselor Hanor, and the full assemblage of the Nadorian Planetary Council—" Kirk caught a brief glimpse, on one of the portable viewscreens posted throughout the hold, first of the counselors' momentary shock on seeing their images broadcast all around their planet, then at their own shock at seeing that their shock had been broadcast. He hoped (not charitably, but not unfairly) that Counselor Hanor's face wasn't being broadcast on too many large screens. "—that Nador join the Federation for the good of her people and the confusion of her enemies."

This time Kirk led the applause, and was prepared to see his own face, smiling and nodding, on the viewscreens across the hold and across Nador. He wondered if Peter was watching. Such a decision would still need to be seconded by the Nadorian people, Kirk knew, but such a ringing endorsement from the planet's rulers could hardly fail to influence the opinion of the public, as well.

Kirk was motioned to the dais by Commissioner Roget, who had, through the medium of one of his aides at the embassy, produced a bottle (thoroughly scanned by Giotto's staff) of Nadorian wine from the year the princes were born. Glasses were filled and toasts were raised to the people of Nador, to the people of the Federation, to Their Serene Highnesses, to Commissioner Roget, and to Captain Kirk, which, Kirk noted with a smile he kept to himself, even Llora had to partake of.

To many of those assembled and across the planet Nador itself, it might have seemed like something of an anticlimax, with those behind the movement who assaulted the princes still at large, but Kirk knew how truly rare such moments actually were in life, and was just glad that this decision, at least, had been made known to the citizenry, who would be making the actual choice.

There remained in the ceremony several acts, but Kirk pulled out during the presentation of a bust of themselves—separated, of course—to the princes by representatives of the children of the planet Nador, and headed for the turbolift.

"Well, you must be feeling pretty good," he heard McCoy say as he emerged onto the bridge. "You'll get your handover ceremony, and the princes are still hale and hearty."

"I'll congratulate myself when we've caught the people who tried to scuttle the handover," Kirk said, gravely. "Mr. Sulu, scanners on maximum range."

"Aye, sir," replied Sulu.

"And by the way, what are you doing here, Bones?" Kirk asked. "Shouldn't you be playing mother hen with your royal charges?"

"Roget and I discussed that," said McCoy. "He thought that to have a Federation doctor hovering over them would show a certain kind of paternalism that would be bad for interplanetary relations—"

"So the good doctor decided to assist me here on the bridge," said Spock, from his bridge post. His tone left no doubt that though Vulcans might not be able to bluff, they were quite comfortable with the concept of sarcasm.

"I'm certain you missed our little chats," said McCoy, with a taunting smile Spock did not rise to.

"You'd better reschedule, Doctor," said Kirk, keeping his eyes on the viewscreen. "We're liable to get pretty busy up here."

"What's the matter, Jim?"

"Doctor," said Spock, "it cannot have escaped even you that every public appearance of Their Serene Highnesses since our arrival has been accompanied by some manner of disturbance or assault."

"And you're expecting this one to be no different?" asked McCoy, anxiously.

"We are," said Spock. "Such a public telecast as this would seem the perfect place to blacken another of the Federation's eyes."

"I've been caught twice by whoever's behind this," said Kirk, grimly, "and I don't intend to be asleep at the switch for a third time. Weapons status, Sulu?"

"Full complements of phasers and photon torpedoes ready, sir," said Sulu. "Shall I order phasers charged?"

"Negative. If we're being monitored, it might tip them off. Just have those weapons ready if we need them."

"Aye, sir."

"Well, I know when I'm not wanted," said McCoy, dryly. "I think I'll sneak down to the cargo hold, grab a glass of wine, and—Jim!"

McCoy's tone was so urgent that Kirk instantly jerked his gaze from the viewscreen to the doctor, to see the surgeon bending over Spock, who had suddenly and inexplicably collapsed to the deck.

Chapter Twelve

"I ASSURE YOU, DOCTOR," said Spock, from a bed in sickbay, "I am, as you would put it, 'fine.'"

"Shut up, Spock," replied McCoy, his bewilderment over what had happened to Spock eclipsing his pleasure at being able to have the Vulcan under his thumb. "Until I find out what's wrong with you, you're not going anywhere. You collapsed on the bridge, do you call that 'fine'?"

"My assessment was of my present condition," said Spock, lifting his head to indicate the diagnostic screen overhead. "As to what caused my temporary collapse, I have no idea."

"What did you feel, Spock?" Kirk asked.

"Who's the doctor here?" said McCoy to Kirk, acidly. "Well, Spock? What did you feel?"

"A momentary numbness," said Spock, "almost a sensation of coldness in my mind, if such a description could apply to tissue which is unable to register any such sensation. Not so much pain as a sudden absence of sensation, one might say."

"None of which is much help," said McCoy, almost to himself.

"My apologies, Doctor," said Spock, with every appearance of sincerity. "I assure you, this incident troubles me as much as it troubles you."

"I'm sure it does," said McCoy, absently. For years, Kirk knew, McCoy had harbored a dread of Spock needing medical attention of such magnitude that he would be unable to provide it. Occasions such as this brought those feelings to the surface.

"What can you do?" asked Kirk.

"I don't know if I can do anything," replied McCoy. "He's right, all his readings are textbook, for him. It's that momentary lapse on the bridge that bothers me."

"Wouldn't it have left some residual effect?"

"I don't know, Jim. I've gone over him with the cortical scanner, but those readings have to be compared to a cross section of readings, it's not a diagnosis that pops up in a few seconds. However—" He played a medical scanner over Spock, examining its readings thoughtfully. "—even a preliminary scan indicates that his encephalographic readings are way above his norm."

"A telepathic attack of some kind?" asked Spock.

"We can't rule it out. Even an illogical human like me," McCoy said, dryly, "knows better than to try to chalk what happened to you up to coincidence. Not with everything that's gone wrong the last few days."

"Bones, you're telling me that the faction that wants the princes dead has another weapon?"

"That's my best guess, Jim. But," he said, as Kirk opened his mouth, "I know you want more than a 'best guess,' so give me a little time."

"I'm not sure how much of that we have, Bones. Isn't there anything to indicate how the attack was launched? Anything to say where it might have come from, or—"

"Jim, right now there's nothing except our memories to show that Spock was ever out of commission at all. And I can't promise that I'll find anything that will, unless it occurs again."

"Most inefficient," murmured Spock, raising a brow.

Nurse Chapel entered. As always when Spock was present, her professional manner was at its most precise. Kirk assumed she thought that was how Spock would wish to be treated on an occasion such as this. "Mr. Spock's cortical scanner readings are being cross-referenced now, Doctor. I'll let you know as soon as they're ready." McCoy nodded, not looking at her.

Nodding crisply, she left, her gaze at the Vulcan lingering a second longer than professionalism demanded the only clue as to her feelings for him.

"Well, Spock," McCoy said, turning to his patient, "I'd like to keep you here for a few hours to see if anything turns up that—"

"Bridge to Captain Kirk," came Uhura's voice from the wall speaker.

"Kirk here."

"Captain," cut in Sulu, *"we've got something here—"*

"'Something,' Sulu? What is it, a missile, that cloaked ship, or—"

"None of those, sir, it seems to be some kind of . . . energy storm. Our scanners can't seem to figure it out."

"Red alert," said Kirk. "Raise shields, and Uhura, cut off the telecast to the planet. I'll be right there. Kirk out." He turned and faced his senior officers. "I'm going to need Spock on the bridge."

"Captain, are you sure that is the wisest course?" asked Spock. His voice was as level as ever, but Kirk could sense another level behind his even tone. He glanced at McCoy, whose gaze confirmed that he had heard it, too.

"Why not?" asked Kirk.

"Captain, as both science officer and first officer, I must function at peak efficiency, especially during situations such as this." He stopped, as if waiting for Kirk or McCoy to jump in. "I need not remind you that I collapsed on the bridge without warning, owing to a cause we have not ascertained. I must question your decision to place me at such a critical tactical position with these matters unresolved."

"Spock," said Kirk, coaxingly, "you said yourself you were fine."

"And I currently am. But I was not, minutes ago, and I may not be, minutes or even seconds from now."

Kirk looked at the Vulcan, uncertain what to say. He could order him to the bridge, and Spock would comply, but this wasn't a matter of testing his command. "Spock . . ." he said, uncertainly.

"Spock," said McCoy, interrupting Kirk, "the last thing I would have expected of you was malingering. I know you probably want to take a nice, long nap here, but I won't have it. The readouts say there's nothing wrong with you, and though there could be, to assume that there will be is simply . . . illogical."

For a long moment, McCoy and Spock locked eyes.

"Acknowledged," said Spock, swinging his legs over and rising.

"Be careful," said McCoy.

"I always am, Doctor," said Spock.

"I was talking to Jim!" Behind his back, Kirk winked

at McCoy, who managed to look very pleased with himself.

"What do you think happened to you?" asked Kirk, as they ran to the turbolift.

"Unknown, sir. But I recall the symptoms that occurred at its onset, and I shall report any such reoccurrence immediately."

"All right, Spock, but don't worry about it."

"Captain, I am incapable of worry. I simply point out—"

"Of course you are, Spock. My apologies." The lift doors hissed open and they entered the bridge. Sulu left the conn and returned to his position.

"Normal lighting," said Kirk, crisply. "Status?"

"The ship is under assault, Captain," said Spock, peering into the viewer at his station, "but with no discernible pattern behind it. We are being subjected to bursts of energy which seem dispensed at random, but frequent intervals."

"Maintain shields, Mr. Sulu. Uhura, did you kill the transmission to the planet?"

"Yes, sir, but the technicians weren't very happy about it."

"They'd be a lot less happy to see their rulers under attack on planetwide video. Screen on, Sulu, let's get a look at what's gnawing at us."

"Aye, sir." The viewscreen sprang to life, and they stared into the heart of the storm.

Literally, it seemed. Before them was a roiling mass, which seemed composed of random tendrils of pure color, swirling all about themselves, first in one pattern, then suddenly in another, with no interval. When Kirk looked right at the phenomenon, it tended to vanish. He found that he could view it best by looking not directly at it, but from the periphery of his vision.

"Analysis, Spock?"

"Little useful information to be determined by my equipment, Captain. The phenomenon varies in size from less than half a kilometer to more than five, with no pattern to its fluctuations. It seems composed of pure energy, though I can detect no power source, and cannot yet determine the composition of its energy."

"Is there any sign of how it's generated? Where it's coming from?"

"No, sir. It seems self-perpetuating, but conditions in this solar system are not currently conducive to the generation of such energy manifestations."

"Look out!" said Kirk, urgently. A portion of the roiling mass seemed to thicken, to become more opaque, then to almost lazily flick a tendril of energy at the *Enterprise*. The ship tilted from side to side as its internal stabilizers fought to keep her steady. "Damage report!"

"Deck five hit, Captain, the cargo hold," came Uhura's voice, from behind Kirk.

"Damage?" asked Kirk, quickly.

"No appreciable damage."

"Not this time," Kirk said grimly. "Uhura, give the order to evacuate the hold." *Damm it*, he thought, most of the anger directed at himself, *how do they know where the princes are? A spy, or*— He tore himself back to the more immediate matters.

"Shields down to eighty-five percent, Captain."

"All available power to shields, Sulu. Phasers on random spread and fire." From below the plain of the viewscreen, two rays of destructive force lanced out at the phenomenon.

"No damage, sir," said Spock.

"Has it withdrawn?"

"Negative."

"It's firing again, Captain."

"Fire photon torpedoes!" Two silver smears of light were briefly visible before being lost in the eerie luminescence that hovered before them. From inside the beautiful menace they could see the torpedoes briefly flare, then fade to useless darkness. A portion of the mass seemed to draw in upon itself before disgorging another bolt.

"No major damage, sir," said Uhura, "but we're getting plenty of calls from the cargo hold, and a few inquiries from the planet, as well."

"From the planet? I thought you cut off the telecast."

"Various sites on Nador are also under assault from the same phenomenon, Captain," cut in Spock.

"On the planet?" said Kirk, almost to himself. "Why—?"

"Unknown at this point, Captain. I have been unable to compile a list of targeted sites, and therefore unable to ascertain a pattern, if any, in their selection."

"Worry about the matter at hand. Uhura, tell them . . . we're doing everything we can."

"Aye, sir."

"Sir, it's firing again, starboard."

"All power to starboard shields," said Kirk. Despite the situation, he shook his head ruefully. "The Nadorians are going to think I'm one hell of a host."

"Strengthen gravity under the cargo loads to one hundred twenty-five percent Earth normal," said Giotto.

"Yes, sir," said the cargo-hold technician. "I think that'll keep the cargo bays from buckling."

"If only that were the worst of our worries," said Giotto, fervently. He tapped an intercom. "Giotto to Sinclair."

"Here, Chief," crackled Sinclair's voice. Through the bay window of the cargo-hold command center, Giotto could see her on the floor below, trying, like the rest of his detail, to keep their invited guests from panicking. Two-person teams attempted to prevent the guests from stampeding through the cargo hold to the only available hatches—with varying degrees of success—and Giotto's broadcast announcement that the hold was one of the most secure parts of the ship didn't seem to be getting much traction.

"I can increase gravity in the entire hold, Chief," said the technician. "That would keep them in their places."

"And it might panic them further," said Giotto. "Not to mention what that might do to the princes. Leave things as they are. The captain's orders were to get them out of here." Before he could hear the reply, he was out and into the hold, fighting his way through the crowd to the front of the room.

"Securitrix Llora!" he called, to the woman standing by Their Royal Highnesses. She and her forces had formed a cordon around the princes, and the other Nadorian dignitaries, preventing the panicking crowd from hurting them, thus far, but also preventing them from evacuating the hold.

"You must let us depart this hold!" shouted Llora, over the din of the mob.

"We're trying," replied Giotto, fervently.

Elsewhere on the floor of the hold, Sinclair could have given Chief Giotto a heartfelt debate as to the wisdom of that statement. It was all she could do to bust up clusters of panicked celebrators who were dashing from one side of the hold to the other, before they picked up too much momentum or too many members to be stopped, not unlike the bovine stampedes she had read about in the days of old Earth. Occasionally her hand gripped her phaser longingly, but to use that method of crowd control would not only be contrary to the intended goal of evacuating the hold, but would only place more unconscious people in harm's way; not an option. It might be possible to release the anesthetic gas the captain had used to seize the ship back from Khan's control via the intruder-control circuit, but it might not work quickly enough to prevent the same danger of innocent parties getting trampled. And again, that would get them no further to a full evacuation.

Then, over the thundering cacophony of the crowd, came a voice—no, two voices, almost exactly alike.

"Our loyal subjects," came the voice of Prince Delor, through one of the miniature microphones supplied to them for their planetary address, "we do implore you to stop this mindless action."

"Is this how you wish our new friends of the Federation to think of you?" said Prince Abon, similarly amplified. "As a people so primitive they cannot be replied upon in times of crisis?"

It took a few seconds, but slowly the words of their monarchs seemed to sink into the minds of the citizenry. They slowed, took a look around themselves, as if waking from a sleep, then stopped.

"Excellent," said one of the princes—Sinclair could no longer tell which was which. "Make an orderly line before the holds and prepare to exit—"

A fresh tremor shook the hold. A collective scream

rose from the crowd, and with an instinctive jerk of reflex fear, but they remained largely calm—

—save for a small knot of attendants on the far side of the hold who either didn't seem to have heard the announcement of Their Serene Highnesses, or didn't care. They continued to jolt across the hold, borne no longer by fear, or even the basic urge for survival, but by the sheer need to move.

Sinclair saw, with horror, a figure topple directly in the path of that surging wall of flesh: the Lady Pataal! To use her phaser would still only halt the outer perimeter of rioters, and leave them open to being trampled themselves. Sinclair vaulted a table and leaped before Pataal, covering the girl with her own body, in an attempt to stop the crowd.

She couldn't bear to watch the crowd advance, but she could feel the vibrations of them nearing through the hold floor; it wasn't going to work. She had begun to resign herself to this when there was a sudden sort of screeching noise, followed by the sudden cease of the crowd's advance.

Sinclair and Pataal looked up, timidly. Between them and the crowd, which had now fully halted and seemed to be weaving back and forth like a thick liquid in a bowl, were Princes Abon and Delor, the color only beginning to return to their deathly pale faces, their chests heaving, their mouths split in capacious mutual grins.

"Is this an adventure?" asked Delor.

"I think so," replied Abon, panting with excitement.

"We're hit again, Captain!" said Kyle from the bridge engineering post.

"Fire!" said Kirk, and saw phasers pass through the

gossamer mass of the thing like light through air. "Maneuver the ship between that thing and the cargo hold!"

"Trying, sir," replied Sulu, after a few seconds, "but those energy blasts seem to be able to curve—almost like tendrils of a plant or—"

"Kirk to engineering!" he shouted, into his chair console. "Scotty, how's our power?"

"Sinkin' by dribs and drabs, Captain! It wouldn't be bad if we could get a good punch off at that thing, but as it is, it's the death of a thousand cuts. Same with the hull damage. None of 'em are bad enough to hurt us much, but in total—"

"Understood," said Kirk, unceremoniously terminating the conversation. The ship rocked again, from, Kirk thought dryly, another "cut."

"Spock," Kirk said, "this thing appeared just after your seizure. Is it psionic in nature? Are you able to sense any kind of intelligence in it?"

Spock stared at the viewscreen intently for a few seconds then turned to Kirk, shaking his head. "Unsuccessful, Captain. I must usually make physical contact with an entity for a determination of that nature. However, given its conduct thus far, if forced to conjecture—"

"Consider than an order."

"Given that the manifestation has not modified its conduct, nor increased its attack, despite our inability to repel it, I would say it has thus far exhibited not true intelligence, only a facility for the imitation of intelligence, in the same manner that a pet performs a trick without understanding its true meaning, or a bird may mimic speech." The latter part of this was cut off by another thunderous crash, but Kirk caught his meaning.

Kirk shook his head. They couldn't take much more of this. But he had noticed something, if it was what he thought . . . "Mr. Sulu," he said, enunciating clearly, "drop shields."

"Sir?" From the unspoken reaction of the bridge crew, it seemed Sulu was not alone in his response.

"All power to sensors, focused entirely on that—whatever it is."

"Done, sir," replied Sulu. "What exactly is it that we're looking for?"

"Just before that thing fires, part of it grows darker, seems to coalesce, for some reason."

"Yes," said Spock. "Perhaps a manifestation of its energy discharge."

"Watch it, Sulu. . . . Ready photon torpedoes and phasers to fire on my—there!" He half-rose from his chair, clenched fist proffered toward the viewscreen. "In its lower starboard quadrant! Power to weapons! *Fire!*"

The *Enterprise* flung both types of energy weapons at the hovering spatial phenomena in the same moment. For an instant the weaponry seemed to simply pass through the darkening portion of the manifestation's cloudlike nature, unharmed.

Then the wavering ball of force seemed at first to grow thicker, more opaque, before it finally dissolved into wisps of drifting energy that soon dissolved into the surrounding void.

"Maintain sensors," said Kirk. "We want as much information on this thing as we can get."

"Whatever we had will have to suffice, Captain," said Spock, after a few seconds. "The manifestation has dissolved."

"Begin working on what you have, Spock. I want

answers." He swiveled and spoke to Uhura. "Damage report?"

"No appreciable damage, sir," said Uhura, after monitoring incoming reports for a few seconds. "Some minor hull damage, no fatalities."

"That's something," said Kirk, taking a deep breath. "Spock, what about the storms across Nador?"

"They dissolved approximately the same time as the storm which attacked us, Captain. I read minimal damage to property and no loss of life."

Kirk nodded, tapping a button on his chair's console. "Scotty, are you still in one piece down there?"

"We're fine, sir, now," came the voice of the engineer. *"It's not that we were bein' so badly hammered, but it was like bein' continually pummeled while you had yer hands tied behind yer back."*

"Work with Spock to determine exactly what that thing was. If it was a weapon, I want to know how it could target the cargo hold even through shields. And I want options, and anything you can give me on who's behind it. It may be our friends in the mysterious ship, but it may be another faction entirely. Understood?"

"Aye, sir."

Kirk glanced at his first officer, who nodded imperturbably.

"Bones?" Kirk said, a moment later. "Everything all right?"

"Compared to some of the shakings you've given us, this was a walk in the park, Jim."

"For us, perhaps. Have you seen the princes?"

"I'm down in the cargo hold now. They're fine. No damage done to their surgical incisions. I understand they even performed a bit of heroism down there." A chorus of low laughter, which sounded like that of the

princes, was heard from the background; leave it to McCoy to elicit humor from a situation like this.

"I'll look forward to hearing about it. Kirk out." He thought for a moment, then rose from his chair. "I'll be in the cargo hold," he told the bridge at large, and left.

Kirk used the brief trip in the turbolift to mentally gird his loins, expecting the assembled Nadorian higher-ups to phaser him a new orifice—or to at least give it the old Academy try. He was therefore pleasantly surprised, on entering the cargo hold—though he took great pains not to show it—to see Counselors Docos and Hanor seemingly playing tag-team with a beleaguered Regent Lonal.

"This is the work of the Abonians," said Counselor Hanor with a hiss, her outraged face nearly the color of her burnt-orange robes. Kirk wondered, idly, if anyone had ever told her she was never more magnificently ugly than when she was angry. "They wished Prince Delor slain, so Prince Abon can take the throne himself!"

"Woman, are you mad?" asked Counselor Docos. "Prince Abon was as much endangered as Prince Delor! Such a strategy is hardly worthy of the term!"

Kirk watched this for a few seconds, then turned to the rest of the brass and Their Serene Highnesses. They seemed to be chatting among themselves earnestly, perhaps on the verge of a disagreement. Nothing unusual there, though Kirk wondered if they were aware of the subject of the discussion Regent Lonal was having with the counselors, that each of the counselors was in essence trying to sell one of the princes down the river.

Kirk took a look around the hold. McCoy and his medical team were treating what few injuries had resulted from the attack. Giotto, Sinclair, and security teams were ushering attendees of the transmission to the transporter room for return to the planet. He approached Giotto and told him to fire up the cargo transporters; they weren't as elegant as the transporter rooms, but he didn't think the Nadorians would mind.

Turning back to the princes, Kirk prepared to pay his respects and tender more apologies. They were speaking quickly to Commissioner Roget, who looked little the worse for the experience. Mrs. Roget was seated nearby, speaking to the Lady Pataal, who seemed calm enough—Kirk gathered there was a story to be told from her disheveled manner—but who had a look in her eyes Kirk had seen before: the aspect of a person who realized she had a decision to make, but who had no idea what to decide.

"Captain!" came the voice of Abon—or was it Delor? Kirk turned and neared them, briefly acknowledging the look in Commissioner Roget's eyes without seeming to, an expression that was at once wary and a little tense. Kirk would normally have chalked this up to the evening's "entertainment," but he knew Roget well enough even after only a short time to know that whatever disturbed him went deeper than just the recent physical rigors he had endured.

"Your Highnesses," said Kirk, in his most mollifying tone, "please accept my apologies for this incident. Once this affair is over, I should appreciate the opportunity to show you that chaos doesn't erupt every time a planetary dignitary sets foot on the *Enterprise*."

"We are as aware as you of the forces which seek to dissolve the bonds between Nador and your Federation," began Abon.

"And we wish to see their dissolution as eagerly as do you," continued Delor, in that odd tag-team speech of theirs. "But now may not be the time to aggravate these forces anew." The princes looked around the room without seeming to, then back to Kirk. "May we speak to you alone?"

"Palmer," said Kirk, hours later, as he strode onto the bridge, "get me Admiral Fitzgerald at Starfleet Command, immediately." Kirk slumped into his chair, looking far more fatigued than Commissioner Roget, who followed him.

"Captain, it's nearly three A.M. at Starfleet Command," replied Palmer.

"Time is of the essence, Lieutenant," said Kirk, in a soft tone that said more than a frantic shout would have.

"Right away, sir," said Palmer.

"You seem as though you knew this was coming," said Kirk, to Roget.

"I have the advantage of knowing Their Royal Highnesses far better than you do, Captain," Roget said with a sigh, "though sometimes I wonder just how much of an advantage it really is. They had not told me in so many words what they wanted, but, yes, I believe I saw this coming. I only wish I'd had a chance to warn you."

"It's done," said Kirk with a shrug, the fatalism in his voice betraying how tired he was. "All we can do now is work with them."

"I have Admiral Fitzgerald, sir," came Palmer's voice.

"On screen." The viewscreen flashed to life, first showing the seal of Starfleet Command, then fading to Admiral Fitzgerald, behind a desk in a room Kirk did not recognize. The walls seemed to be filled with books and models of ships; probably his home. The admiral's usually crisp good looks seemed somewhat frayed, worn at the edges; his appearance gave every impression of a man who had been woken from a sound sleep. *Good,* thought Kirk, pettily.

"Captain Kirk," nodded Fitzgerald, evenly. *"It's quite late here, you know."*

"I am aware of that, sir," said Kirk, trying to give every impression that he cared, "but a situation has arisen that I knew you would want to be immediately notified of." He told the admiral of the most recent developments in the Nadorian situation, including the attack on them by the strange storm they had been unable to classify.

"But you said the princes do wish to join the Federation, did you not?" asked Fitzgerald. Some of the sleep had left his eyes; he leaned forward in his chair, his head cocked to one side, like a hound who had caught a scent.

"They do, sir," agreed Kirk, "but after tonight's disturbance, they have said that they wish the resulting vote and the handover ceremony to be delayed until the ringleaders behind the disruptive elements can be identified and captured." Fitzgerald's demeanor did not change for a few seconds after hearing this. It was as though Kirk's words had been delayed by subspace transmission.

"I see," said Fitzgerald, at length. *"Captain, here are Starfleet's orders . . ."*

"Gentlemen," Kirk said to Spock, McCoy and Giotto, "I am sorry to have awakened you at this hour—"

"You don't sound very damn sorry," said McCoy.

"But," continued Kirk, ignoring the doctor, "we have

something of a situation on our hands. Following the latest incident, Their Serene Highnesses have told me they wish to delay the vote and the following ceremony in which Nador will join the Federation."

"Sounds like the fix is in on the vote," commented Giotto, from behind a cup of coffee.

"If I understand your colloquialism correctly, Chief Giotto," said Spock, "I do not believe any manipulation of the balloting process would be necessary. This is the first time the native Nadorians have been given any say in a matter concerning their governance, so it stands to reason that they would follow the endorsement of their princes, since they are by and large a contented people."

"Yes, sir." Giotto nodded, with a quick glance at Kirk. Giotto, Kirk thought, never quite knew how to take Spock.

"Did the princes give any reason for wishing such a delay?" asked Spock.

"Probably waiting for whoever's behind this to get nabbed. I'd feel better knowing that someone who had targeted me was out of the picture," said McCoy.

"Of course," said Giotto, "they may just be fearful for their lives, and think this will placate whoever wants them dead. I'd like to think they were made of sterner stuff than that, but they've had their lives turned upside down several times now."

"It's also the fact that Nadorian citizens have constantly been placed at risk in these attacks," said Kirk. "The princes told me that was their main concern, and from what I've seen of them, I believe them."

"Yes, they're not worried about their own skins," said McCoy.

"At any rate," said Kirk, "Starfleet has categorically rejected any such delay. The voting will take place tomorrow, with the handover ceremony scheduled for two days after."

"It seems odd that Starfleet wouldn't give the Nadorians their head in this," said McCoy.

"Actually, it's not that they so much rejected any such delay, they placated the Nadorians by assuring them there would be no need for a delay—that all the rough spots would be ironed out by the time the handover ceremony comes around."

"In other words," said McCoy, "you've been ordered to sink or swim."

"After a fashion," said Kirk. "Gentlemen, I need ideas. We have to determine who is behind the movement trying to assassinate the princes, and pull their claws once and for all."

"That would be the most logical way to assure success," said Spock with a nod.

"We're all behind you, Captain, but we don't have much to work with," said Giotto.

"You're an old law-enforcement man, Chief," said Kirk. "You know that when you don't have anything to go on, you find something. If there's anything about this affair that you haven't told me, now's the time. For instance, Spock." Kirk thrust a finger at his first officer. "During our battle with that—storm or whatever it was, you said other sites on Nador were also under assault."

"Correct," said Spock. "These locales include the Nadorian Art Students' League, the Nadorian Heritage Museum, and the Royal Palace of Nador. While this does not categorically rule out the possibility of the storm being a weapon, it certainly makes it a very inefficient one."

"You see?" Kirk said to McCoy and Giotto. "That's

what we want. Spock, you and DeSalle were also working on the transmitter."

"That avenue of investigation is still under way," said Spock. "I shall tell Lieutenant DeSalle to redouble his efforts."

"You've always given me your best efforts in the past," said Kirk, standing as he surveyed them. "I need nothing less now. I'm tired of waiting for our faceless opponents to move, I intend to make them move, for a change."

Dismissed, they filtered out of the conference room into the crew taking their places on the first shift. Kirk drained his cup, then lowered it, to see McCoy waiting. "Yes, Bones?"

"I'm sure we'll find him, Jim."

"Peter? I didn't even mention him."

"You didn't have to." McCoy approached Kirk and squeezed his shoulder briefly. "We'll find him, that's all I'm saying."

"I hope I can trust that diagnosis," said Kirk.

"Dr. McCoy tells me he'll be sorry to lose you, Your Highnesses," said Kirk, heartily. "He says you were two of the best patients he's ever had."

"The doctor has his own unique ways of enforcing order in his sickbay," replied Prince Abon, dryly.

"Yes," said Delor, in the same tone, "I wonder if he is aware that your Starfleet is a signatory to the Galactic Treaty forbidding torture."

Despite the many pressures on his time, Kirk forced himself to keep pace with the princes as they slowly proceeded—let's face it, he thought, hobbled—down the corridors of the *Enterprise,* supported by exoskeletal braces that gauged how much support the wearer needed and adjusted servomotors accordingly. For a physician who had always staunchly advocated that a little bit of suffering never hurt anyone, McCoy was being awfully protective of Abon and Delor. Kirk liked it; it was a side of McCoy he didn't see too often. But even McCoy realized when it was time to leave well enough alone. He had opted not to accompany his patients on this trip, citing neglected business in sickbay.

"Don't lean against the wall, Abon," said Delor, peevishly, as the turbolift took them to the nearest transporter room. "Let your muscles strengthen themselves."

"Yes, Mother," replied Abon, acidly, pushing himself out from the railing around the lift and standing erect. And Kirk wondered, again, what their parents must have been like as well as what the twins' delivery must have been like for their poor mother.

"Now, are Your Serene Highnesses aware of the agenda?" asked Regent Lonal, for only the fourteenth or fifteenth time. A small contingent of palace personnel, including Llora, had beamed up to the ship in order to provide security and support—both physical as well as spiritual, Kirk supposed—when the princes made their return to their native world.

"'Your Serene Highnesses' are, Lonal," said Abon with a sigh. "We will transport down to the place of voting nearest the palace, which has been set up in one of the schools."

"Will not the children be inconvenienced by this?" asked Delor, practically.

"The day has been declared a holiday, Prince Delor. You will cast your votes first, and then the people will begin to vote," said Lonal, swiveling from Abon to Delor, as if on a pivot. The princes seemed to take a subtle but real pleasure in standing far apart in order to confound those who had before always been able to take both of them in with one glance. Kirk at first thought this rather petty; then he realized that if he had been forced to live with the same handicap as the princes had, all those years, he'd enjoy his newfound sense of singleness, too. With the experiences he had had, and the things he had seen, there were very few conditions he could categorize as "unimaginable," but being in the forced company of a person glued to your spine every day of your life, never to be alone or to enjoy a solitary moment, was something he could not imagine, and found himself not wishing to try.

"I wish to register the strongest possible protest to this," said Llora, in a low voice. "The princes cannot be properly protected in such a setting."

"We have scattered *Enterprise* security personnel throughout the crowd as well," interjected Kirk.

"Given your record of protecting Their Serene Highnesses, I do not find that fact reassuring," said Llora.

"Nevertheless," said Kirk offhandedly, "there it is." He would not let this woman bait him.

"I think we should go over the agenda one more time—" said Lonal.

"And I think we should get this over with," said Prince Delor, clumping his way onto the transporter pad. "Captain?"

"I wouldn't miss it," said Kirk, sincerely. He offered a hand to Prince Abon, who refused it, but graciously, and took his place with them on the transporter pad.

There was a moment of shimmering air, and Kirk found himself in what indeed gave every appearance of being an educational facility of some sort. The landing party stood in a huge central room off of which branched smaller rooms with walls that could be moved to either expand the central room or isolate the smaller chambers.

A full-throated roar, already in process, was the first thing Kirk heard as soon as they materialized. His first thought was that some kind of attack or threat had been mounted, but its tenor was different, higher. He soon realized it was only the clamor of an appreciative crowd, eager to see their princes again, and in a state in which they had never before beheld them live. The crowd stood behind carefully watched cordons, under the constantly watchful eyes of Llora's troops. It had been rumored that Their Serene Highnesses would make an appearance to begin the process of voting, but it had not been announced at which voting location the princes would appear, so the crowd's greeting had the added benefit of genuine surprise as well as spontaneity. Kirk noticed, without seeming to, a few familiar faces in the crowd as well; there was Chief Giotto, wearing an elementary sort of disguise and giving every air of enjoying himself thoroughly, as well as Sinclair, her blond hair darkened to brunette for this occasion, and others under Giotto's command.

"Friends and fellow citizens of Nador," said Abon, after the crowd quieted, "we do thank you for coming out to exercise this new right that has been granted you." (Kirk tried to analyze the logic of a right that could be granted, but shrugged it off, reminding himself not to mention it to Spock.)

"We are privileged to lead you into this new era of peace and opportunity," added Delor. "Now," he said, looking around, "how do we begin?"

The crowd laughed, but it was clear that the princes had little if any idea how the actual process of voting worked, though they were clear on the principle. A middle-aged man, whom Kirk supposed to be the principal of the school, shouldered aside other functionaries to near the princes, made a detour around Llora, whose gaze seemed to shoot through him like a phaser beam, to escort the princes to a cylindrical machine, slightly taller than the waist height of the average person, with a viewscreen and a small groove embedded in its surface.

Instruction, which was broadcast on a larger viewscreen that descended from the ceiling, explained how the voters brought up the information on the relevant issue, cast their votes, then pressed their thumbs into the small groove to identify themselves and register their votes.

"It is simple," said Prince Abon to the crowd, wobbling only slightly before the small cylinder.

"How did you vote, Your Highness?" shouted someone from the audience.

"That would normally be private," said Delor, "but I think all of Nador knows of our opinion."

"Then I shall vote that way, too!" cried another voice, which was immediately followed by a flood of assent.

"Fellow citizens, no!" said Abon with a laugh. "The point of voting is to fashion your own opinion!"

The crowd seemed to have a little trouble with this, noted Kirk, hiding a sympathetic grin. He had watched this scene play itself out again and again across many planets, as a culture took its first steps toward self-determination, sometimes with the blessing of its traditional rulers, sometimes without. It was always the same and always different, and he never tired of it.

"Now," said the factotum, to the audience, "citizens,

you may proceed." He opened the roped-off area that led to voting cylinders placed at intervals in the schoolroom.

For a long moment, nothing happened. The crowd, apparently unsure of what they were to do, stood back, waiting for someone else to make the first move.

Then the crowd seemed suddenly to part like a snow-drift before a spray of lava. A shriek came from nowhere and everywhere and a person, swathed in robes and carrying a bundle, shot at the princes as though propelled by full impulse power.

Kirk wasn't closest, but he was the first to see it. He shot forward, felt something strike his side and fall back, then found himself standing before the princes, phaser drawn—

—protecting Their Serene Highnesses from a young woman, her eyes a little wild with delight at seeing her rulers, and carrying a baby for them to bless. Kirk stood back as security troops came forward to envelop the woman. Massaging his side, which had been struck, Kirk looked around and saw Llora picking herself up from the floor, looking at him with loathing.

Kirk knew better by now than to risk offering her a hand. Had he seen Llora coming, he would have let her have the spotlight. He thought about saying something mollifying to her, but rejected the notion. She wouldn't have believed him anyway.

Investigation proved mother and child to be exactly who they appeared to be and utterly innocent of weapons and, with much nervous laughter, the voting process continued as the citizens filed forward to make their will known, first haltingly, a few at a time, then more and more rapidly, until the room was aswirl in the process of nascent democracy.

But it did not escape Kirk's notice that, as a cadre of

security personnel flurried about the princes, two people—gender and any identifying features swallowed by voluminous robes—detached themselves from the crowd, making haste without seeming to, and were gone before Kirk could order pursuit.

Kirk shook his head. There was only one way this would end.

"I must say, I found that invigorating," said Prince Abon. He sat on a bed in sickbay, removed his trousers (one leg at a time, Kirk noted), then took off the exoskeleton brace he had worn under them.

"Spiritually, perhaps," replied McCoy, hovering over the twins with a medical scanner, "but physically, it was exhausting. I shouldn't have let you boys overdo it like that." (Despite the situation, Kirk grinned. Only McCoy would call the rulers of an entire planet "boys" and make them like it.) "I think you two should stay here tonight."

"But, Doctor," said Delor, as he and Abon swapped a forlorn look, "the results of the vote will be in in a few hours."

"So?"

"It is our custom that when a new pronouncement is made to our people, the rulers do it from the palace," said Abon.

"Specifically, from a special balcony of the Royal Palace," said Delor. "Our subjects have been through trying times recently," he continued, with what Kirk thought to be magnificent understatement. "Those customs that can be preserved, should be."

"I don't know . . ." said McCoy, dubiously.

"Actually, Doctor," said Kirk, tapping McCoy on the arm and gesturing for him to follow, "let's talk."

* * *

Some hours later, a throng of people gathered below an ancient balcony in the southeast wall of the Royal Palace of Nador. For longer than the memory of anyone who had ever lived on the planet, native Nadorians had assembled there to hear announcements both joyous and sorrowful, proclamations of births, notices of deaths, of the results of battles, of marriages and executions.

The knot of loyal citizens that had gathered there today was one of the largest in recent memory. Many of the attendants simply wished a look at Their Serene Highnesses, following their surgical separation, not believing the rumors that Starfleet had turned the princes into pawns of the Federation, yet seeking reassurance anyway. Most, having voted to join the Federation, simply wished another look at the monarchs who had ruled over them most of their lifetimes before their way of life changed forever. A few wished to give their children a glimpse of their beloved rulers. Some simply wished to partake of the fair air on a warm night. At least a small percentage of those present were security personnel, owing their allegiances either to the planet Nador or to the Federation.

Others were present for their own reasons.

When the Hour of Announcement came, the bellows of a wind clock in a church next to the palace sounded a long, tremulous note, filled at once with longing and anticipation. Curtains hung across the balcony parted, revealing a retinue consisting of Regent Lonal, Counselors Hanor and Docos, the Lady Pataal, and, representing the Federation, Commissioner Roget and his wife. They stood in a semicircle, as if enclosing something. The audience craned its necks trying to see, but there was nothing there, nothing to be enclosed by the semicircle of Nadorian and Federation dignitaries. Their bafflement was understandable.

Then, as the fat, melodic breath of the last bellows faded, the air at the center of the semicircle of dignitaries seemed to flicker, to shimmer as if alive with starlight. Few in the crowd had ever traveled by a transporter of any design, but all of them had heard of the device, and most of them had seen what it looked like.

A high-pitched note, as if to counterpoint the fading hum of the bellows, was heard.

The shimmers of light began to resolve themselves, to reveal themselves to be two figures . . . men, perhaps.

Then a kind of rhythmic noise was heard, like the pulse beat of a huge, invisible man.

The twin shimmers of light, which had begun to coalesce in an orderly fashion, were suddenly shot through with harsh streaks. A discordant wail—or was it two?—was heard. The Lady Pataal started forward, her scream melding with the wails.

Then the twin shimmers of light imploded, leaving only two small, identical piles of smoldering matter.

Chapter Thirteen

"NADORIAN DNA," said Dr. McCoy, some seconds later, standing over the small mounds of what for all the world looked like some sort of goo scraped off the bottom of a petri dish. "It's the princes'." He sounded very old.

"Fan out," said Captain Kirk, phaser at the ready. "But be careful with the crowd. Spock?"

"Scanning, Captain," replied the first officer. The hum of the tricorder at least filled the air with something besides the shouts from the crowd below and the muted sobs of the Lady Pataal. After a few seconds Spock looked up from the device and faced Kirk. "I am reading residual energy emissions very much like those produced by deflector shields."

"Deflector shields?" asked Kirk. "But if it was activated while the princes were transporting down—"

"A massive disruption in the transporting process would result," Spock said, with a precise nod.

"Where did the energy emissions come from, Spock?" asked Kirk. "Can you trace them?"

"Yes, sir," said Spock. "This way."

They had beamed down a security force the instant the news had reached the *Enterprise;* the remnants of the transporter malfunction examined by McCoy were still steaming when they had materialized.

They made their way down one of the seemingly infinite number of stairways in the palace to a door leading to the ground. Outside, citizens were still in a state of shock; women were sobbing, men looked as though they wanted to sob. Few of the crowd paid any attention to the *Enterprise* crew, but the gazes of those who did held no love. If there were any Federation citizens in the knot of people, Kirk didn't notice them and they didn't call attention to themselves.

Spock led them into the church next to the palace; their entrance was blocked by a pair of massive wooden doors.

"Locked," said Spock.

"Not for long," said Kirk. He rapidly phasered the crack between the two doors, and a moment later, they swung open. At McCoy's disapproving glance, Kirk gave a fatalistic shrug.

The interior of the church was darker than the outside, probably owing to the lack of moonlight. A few candles tried to pierce the gloom, but seemed only to accentuate it. Motioning for silence, Kirk and his officers walked softly into the church, passing quickly through a kind of nave or anteroom into a larger, cathedral-like chamber. Pews were constructed concentrically, around a central fire pit that was not now lit. Some kind of religious symbolism, Kirk supposed.

He felt a light tap on his arm and turned to see McCoy pointing to one side. A mural showed what he took to be some kind of blessing of twin infants, conjoined at the spine. He nodded and returned to the job.

Spock pointed ahead and upward, and Kirk saw the flight of wooden stairs. The Vulcan led the way, his efficient, furtive progress reminding Kirk of nothing more than a huge cat. As they mounted the steps, Kirk noted in a thin coating of dust what might have been several overlapping sets of footsteps leading both up and down.

At the first landing Spock took a look at his tricorder, now on silent mode, shook his head, and led them past what seemed to be a floor of smaller rooms for individual instruction or meditation, then up another flight. Here the stairs gave onto a wide room that seemed to extend the entire breadth and width of the church— probably some a room used for social occasions or more informal meetings.

Spock pointed into the darkness, toward one of a number of small pools of moonlight leaking through windows spaced at regular intervals. There sat a small, rather absurd-looking machine that seemed to Kirk to be some kind of energy emitter jury-rigged to an emissions amplifier and a minute storage battery. A small light on the device's side flashed every few seconds; otherwise it seemed deactivated.

Spock scanned the device for possible traps cautiously, from a distance, but after a moment motioned Kirk and McCoy ahead.

"Handcrafted, but efficiently made," whispered Spock as his scanner played over the thing.

"Is it off?" asked Kirk.

"It is," said Spock with a nod. "It seems to have been built to function once, then to await further commands."

"Otherwise we'd also be piles of goo," said McCoy.

"Unlikely, Doctor. Mr. Scott's emergency systems

check after the initial malfunction revealed no further interruption—"

Though Spock hesitated briefly, Kirk motioned for him to continue, jerking a thumb behind them, into the vast darkness. Spock and McCoy nodded, and played along. Spock had heard the slight noises of an approach before Kirk had.

Despite their caution, whoever was out there had tumbled to their ruse. Kirk barely made out footsteps moving cautiously away, and motioned for Spock and McCoy to fan out. Spock headed for the stairs, while McCoy stood before the device they had found. It might yield information as to who had built it, in which case the intruder might try to destroy it, or perhaps it could somehow be used as a weapon.

Kirk crept further into the darkness, listening for any indication of motion, knowing that if he heard any footsteps, they wouldn't be Spock's; the Vulcan was too good at stealth maneuvers to give himself away that easily.

Straining to hear, Kirk heard more than he thought— thudding footfalls heading straight for him. He started to bring up his phaser, but too late. His quarry slammed into him, sending him sprawling. But Kirk had managed to get a grip on his assailant; he took the same ride Kirk did, but Kirk managed to wind up on top.

Kirk's free hand stabbed out and down. He felt the sting of contact as his fist landed on a jaw in the darkness and his opponent went slack. "I've got him!" he called.

The darkness of the chamber was partially repelled as Spock ignited his portable floodlight. Then, realizing it was set for more sensitive Vulcan eyes, he thumbed up the brightness, giving Kirk and McCoy a look at their captive.

"My God," said Kirk, his voice as emotionless—from shock, not discipline—as any Vulcan's ever could be.

"Jim?" asked McCoy. Kirk was never really sure what the question was. He suspected McCoy didn't know, either.

If Spock was shocked, he of course gave no sign. More likely he simply felt no comment was necessary or helpful.

They stared down at the barely stirring form of Peter Kirk.

Kirk pointed to Peter and McCoy bent over him, nodding. With his other hand, Kirk whipped out his communicator. "Kirk to *Enterprise*. Four to beam up immediate—"

"Stand where you are!" throbbed a new voice. "Hands empty and where I can see them!"

Kirk, Spock, and McCoy turned to face Llora and an entourage of security guards pointing far more Nadorian weapons at them than Kirk was comfortable with.

By the time they were led out of the church, a crowd had gathered at the doorway. Nadorian palace guards had been pressed into service to keep the crowd back, but they could do little about the mood of the people, which seemed on the verge of eruption. Though many hands pointed accusing fingers at Peter, none of them seemed to bear weapons. Kirk kept his phaser in hand, just in case.

"You have no right to keep him," said Kirk, speaking to Llora but keeping his eyes on the crowd. "Peter Kirk is a Federation citizen—"

"Who was found on what seems to be the site of the murder of Their Serene Highnesses," said Llora, coldly.

"That gives me the jurisdictional right to hold him for questioning, Captain."

There was nothing to be gained that way. "Nonetheless," said Kirk, switching tacks, "you can't really believe that Peter had anything to do with this."

"Truthfully?" Llora's voice lowered and she turned her back on the crowd so she and Kirk could converse. "It seems unlikely, to be sure. But there is a sizable gap between the unlikely and the impossible, Captain. And if I were to turn the suspect over to you, I do not relish to think of the consequences it would have on Nadorian society. Keeping the peace before was difficult enough. Now, with the current situation . . . with the princes dead . . ." Her voice trailed off for a moment, and her gaze lowered; Kirk almost risked putting a hand on her shoulder. Then her head snapped up and Kirk saw nothing in those eyes but cold professionalism. "Out of the question," she said.

"But think of Peter's safety, for that very reason," said Kirk. "How can you keep him safe when by now your entire planet thinks he was responsible for the deaths of your rulers?"

"That is my problem, Captain," replied Llora.

"If my nephew is hurt you can be sure of that," said Kirk, quietly.

"There is no need for this posturing, not from either of us," said Llora, after a long moment. "What has happened between us remains there. You have my word your nephew will be protected and well treated. You may visit him, provided you have cleared such visits through my office."

"At least let me be present when you question him."

She thought for a moment, then nodded. "Agreed."

Kirk had one more card to play; Roget was able to

get Llora to let McCoy examine the boy in his cell. Kirk stood by McCoy nervously as the physician played his instruments over the unconscious boy.

"Shouldn't he have regained consciousness by now?" asked Kirk.

"Ordinarily, yes," replied McCoy, "but my readings show he's been drugged to the gills, and for some time. He was just starting to fight it off when you gave him another sleeping pill, administered by way of his chin."

"I didn't know—"

"Of course you didn't," said McCoy. "But he'll be all right, Jim."

"Are you sure? I hit him pretty hard—"

"He's a Kirk," said McCoy, dryly. "His head comes with extra padding, remember?"

"But he'll be all right? Can't you give him something to bring him around?"

"What did I just say?"

"But, Bones," said Kirk, his voice lowering. "As long as you're going to—"

"Oh, all right." McCoy drew his hypospray from his medical kit, prepared an injection, and let fly. A few seconds later, the boy stirred slightly and groaned. "There, he's coming around." McCoy assembled his medical kit and called for the guard via the cell intercom. "I'll leave you two alone, Jim. For God's sake, don't smother him too much. This is why I never went into pediatrics."

Just before the cell door closed behind McCoy, Kirk met the physician's gaze. He nodded, once, then left.

Peter's eyes opened slowly, then narrowed, as if the light was too bright for them. "Uncle Jim?" he asked, slowly.

"Hello, Peter," said Kirk. "How do you feel?"

"Like death warmed over," he said, at length. He hitched himself up on one arm, stiffly, and wiggled his jaw with his right hand. "Did you hit me?" he asked.

"I'm afraid so," said Kirk, sheepishly.

"Dad said he could always take you, as long as you didn't connect with your right cross."

"He did." Kirk smiled, reminiscently. Then the present came flooding back. "You're in a great deal of trouble, Peter. You're accused of being complicit in the deaths of Princes Abon and Delor."

Peter's eyes, even though bleary, widened. "They're dead?"

"You were found at the site. Where did you go when you left the *Enterprise*—against my orders," he couldn't help adding.

"I sent you a message, didn't you get it?"

"We got it. But where did you go?"

"I was trying to scout out some connection to the rebels," said Peter. He looked off, as if into a shadowy tunnel, as the memories came crawling back. "I decided to ask some questions at a bar I know—where I'd seen some suspicious-looking characters hanging around, people who had made a lot of noise about not liking the idea of becoming part of the Federation."

The boy was resourceful, Kirk gave him that. "Did you learn anything?"

"I said a few things, and I asked some questions . . . maybe too many," he said, wincing as he touched his head. "The last clear memory I have is of taking a drink a guy bought me. And then—"

"You were here." Kirk shook his head. "Not much help."

"'Not much help'?" echoed Peter, incredulously. He jumped off the cot in his cell and staggered, obviously immediately wishing he hadn't. "You could go back there and—"

"Peter, think. If they chose you to be found where you were, it was almost certainly because they recognized you." He shook his head. "No, they'll be especially careful around strangers. Better to—"

The electronic lock of the cell door clicked open, allowing Spock to enter. "Peter," he said, evenly, "I trust you are well."

"Hello, Mr. Spock. I'll be better when I'm out of here."

"An event I should not look forward to anytime soon," replied Spock. Kirk saw Peter's eyes widen a little; it took a while to get used to Spock's bluntness where unpleasant facts were concerned.

"Anything at the church?" asked Kirk.

"Nothing that might serve as the springboard for an investigation, no, sir. The caretaker was more lax in his duties than he might be. He had not noticed any unauthorized entrants to the structure since the last services, three days ago."

Kirk nodded. "Peter could have been placed—or transported—there at any time since then."

"Correct. An analysis of the dust on the steps elicited no information as to who may have been responsible."

"We'll have to find another way to crack this particular nut," said Kirk. He walked to the cell door and buzzed the guard. "In the meantime, Peter—"

"You're *leaving* me here?"

"There's very little I can do about it, without creating an interplanetary incident."

"But, Uncle Jim—"

"Don't 'Uncle Jim' me. It doesn't become an adventurer like yourself to pout. Besides," he added, slyly, "at least I'll know where you are, for a change." The Nadorian guard opened the cell from without, looking the other way while Kirk and Peter hugged.

"The boy could be in grave danger," said Spock, without overture, as they headed out. The security center was a recent adjunct to the Nadorian Royal Palace, a modern complex that seemed rather incongruous when compared to the original palace architecture.

"I'm well aware of that, Mr. Spock," replied Kirk. He nodded to the officer in charge as he and Spock left the complex and began the walk down the hallway that connected the security center with the main body of the Royal Palace. "But to seize possession of Peter would be to create an incident which would finish the proposed Federation-Nadorian alliance."

"The proverbial straw on the camel's back," said Spock with a nod. "Still, are you convinced of the sincerity of Securitrix Llora's efforts to keep Peter safe?"

"I am," said Kirk, "but that doesn't mean I haven't taken measures of my own."

"The subcutaneous transponder?" asked Spock, softly.

"Exactly," nodded Kirk. "With that under his skin, McCoy can monitor his medical signs and we can pull him out of there if an emergency arises."

"Logical," murmured Spock. "Do you think that measure sufficient?"

"Not by itself, but I want to talk to Commissioner Roget to see if—" Kirk's comment was interrupted by the beeping of his communicator.

"It's Commissioner Roget, Captain," came Uhura's voice.

"Commissioner," said Kirk, "I was just about to call you—"

"Forgive me for interrupting, Captain," said Roget,

"but there's a small ceremony to install Regent Lonal as the planet's ruler. Can you attend?"

"If they want me there," said Kirk. "Spock and I are still in the palace. Lonal didn't waste any time, did he?"

"That's a matter of some discussion," replied Roget, tightly. *"We're in the royal chambers."*

The guard at the other end of the hall admitted them to the palace grounds proper, and Kirk and Spock made their way to the royal chambers, where Kirk was somewhat surprised to find Regent Lonal, Counselors Docos and Hanor, Commissioner and Mrs. Roget, and the Lady Pataal gathered. There was an aura of somberness over the assemblage, and the Lady Pataal was openly weeping.

Kirk and Spock took their places at the rear of the group as an elderly dignitary entered. Kirk had seen depictions of his robes in murals in the church in which they had discovered Peter. Kirk's eye was caught by Commissioner Roget, who moved through the small group to them.

"Thank you for coming," whispered Roget. "I wanted Starfleet to be represented here." A small technical crew was setting up equipment to transmit the ceremony, to the rest of the planet, Kirk assumed.

"Is not this ascent to power rather sudden on the regent's part?" asked Spock.

"Under the circumstances, he didn't want to wait for a proper mourning period," whispered Mrs. Roget, who had joined them. "He thought the people needed to know who was in charge."

"And their enemies, too, I'll bet," said Kirk. Regent Lonal sat before a huge portrait of Their Serene Highnesses, painted on the occasion of their coronation, Kirk surmised. A few seconds later, the transmitters hummed to life as Regent Lonal's image was projected around the planet.

"Citizens of Nador and our many allies," began Lonal. He leaned a little into the transmitter, his eyes sharp and self-confident. Gone was the man who seemed uncertain about not only the responsibilities of his job, but his capability to execute them. Kirk wondered if, once he had tasted power, Regent Lonal had decided he wanted to keep it. It wouldn't have been the first time.

"I join you in mourning our noble monarchs, Their Serene Highnesses, Princes Abon and Delor," Lonal said. "A proper day of mourning will be scheduled later, but I wished to leave in your minds no doubt of my resolve to carry on their work of unifying our people as your regent." The religious leader came forward and began to perform some some sort of ritual that Kirk gathered dealt with the transfer of royal power.

"The people have spoken," Lonal then continued, "and their wish to join the Federation will be granted, as Princes Abon and Delor also desired." Kirk glanced slowly across the royal chamber, having long ago learned that when important speeches were being made, more could be learned from the speech's reception than from the oration itself. He saw Counselors Docos and Hanor, at opposite ends of the royal dais, glaring alternately at each other, like two dogs who, having long drooled over a bone, found a third hound had snatched it from both of them, and at Regent Lonal, with an amalgam of undisguised envy and disdain.

"Let our enemies and the traitors among us know that Nador is a strong and united planet. Let them also know that whoever is responsible for the cowardly deaths of Their Serene Highnesses will be found and punished." Then Kirk saw the Lady Pataal, gazing at Lonal, sobbing quietly, her pretty eyes filled with tears. No, Kirk realized, she wasn't looking at Lonal, but at the portrait behind him, the image of the princes.

"And so I ask for your support and for your prayers in this, our most crucial hour." Lonal had risen from the throne during this last sentence and gestured to the transmitters. *A nice touch,* Kirk thought. The audience gave a smattering of applause, and the angle of the transmitters widened to include the audience, the realization of this causing Counselors Docos and Hanor to look like two children who had been caught raiding the cookie jar, before they joined in the applause with forced solemnity.

The hum of the transmitters ceased, and Lonal sank back into the throne, wiping perspiration with a sleeve of the royal robe in a gesture Kirk thought rather unregal. He nodded at Commissioner Roget and pointed across the hall, indicating he had business there first.

"Excuse me, my lady," said Kirk, courteously. The Lady Pataal had crumpled into one of the chairs that lined the walls of the royal chamber, her face in her hands. "I just wanted to express my—"

Kirk was interrupted by the sudden action of having his mouth crushed against the Lady Pataal's soft shoulder as she leaped to her feet. Putting her arms around Kirk, she began sobbing anew. "Thank you so much, Captain," she said, tearfully. "I wonder . . ." She stepped back from Kirk and sniffed heartily, causing Kirk to wish he had a handkerchief to give her. "I wonder if I might come with you back up to your big ship? I wish to speak to my friend, Yeoman Barrows."

"Of course. That is, if you have no business here."

She lowered her gaze and shook her head. "There is nothing for me here anymore."

"Don't make any hasty decisions," said Kirk, too late remembering how he had hated being told that. "Can you please wait a few minutes? Mr. Spock and I have some business with the commissioner."

"I will wait, yes." Kirk nodded his thanks and walked away, seeing her head lower like a flower with a broken stem. If he were ten years younger . . .

He returned to Roget, who was talking with his wife and Spock. From the Rogets' faces, he assumed nothing of import was being discussed; Spock's face was imperturbable whether discussing the annual yield of the sea ranches on a pelagic planet, or the consequences of a violation of General Order Seven.

"Pardon me, Mrs. Roget," Kirk said, smiling gallantly as he approached, "but we need to steal your husband for a few minutes."

Janine Roget nodded with a sympathetic smile and a nod. She seemed frayed, paler, like a fine, beautiful fabric that has been nearly worn through. "It's been one of those days, hasn't it?" she sighed. "I don't know that I'll be sorry to leave this place. And Captain," she said, as Kirk began to turn away, "I was very sorry to hear about your nephew. I'm sure it will all work out."

"Thank you very much." Kirk and Spock flanked Roget as they walked into one of the halls that protruded like spokes from the royal chamber. "It's funny your wife should mention my nephew," Kirk said.

"Janine's like that," said Roget, closing his eyes. The webwork of fine lines at the corners of his eyes and mouth seemed to have deepened; he looked tired and, for once, every year of his age. "She's been my secret weapon as an ambassador," he said with a smile. "This does concern your nephew, Captain?"

"It does, Commissioner. I certainly don't want to leave him in a Nadorian jail with the charges against him. Is there any way—?"

"That I can get him remanded to your custody?" The aquiline head shook from side to side. "I'd already put out some feelers in that direction, but with the circumstances being what they are, no one will hear of it. I can't say I blame them."

"Then you believe Captain Kirk's nephew is implicated in the regicide?" asked Spock.

"'Implicated,' Mr. Spock? Most certainly Peter Kirk is being used as a pawn, of course. But unfortunately, most of those who could secure his release or transfer are in no mood to do so."

"If anything happens to him . . ."

"I'm sure nothing will, Captain," said Roget. "I've already expressly reminded Llora through official channels that Peter Kirk is a Federation citizen and entitled to all rights and protections under Nadorian law— which is, I suppose, also Federation law now."

"As long as the agreement stands," said Kirk, quietly.

They had walked aimlessly through the palace halls, past the rows of statuary that seemed about to step down from their pedestals, to the outer perimeter of the palace. Not far beyond, the hall gave onto an open-air arch beyond which was a gate. Palace guards nervously walked back and forth on the palace side of the gate while on the other side roiled a mass of people who carried a banner: NO FEDERATION! KEEP NADOR FREE!

"Such sentiments, if widespread, could be deleterious to the enforcement of the handover agreement," said Spock, who sometimes had a gift for saying what everyone else was thinking.

Kirk's communicator beeped. *"It's Admiral Fitzgerald, Captain."*

"Tell him I'll respond in a few minutes, Lieutenant."

"He seems quite eager to talk to you, sir." Uhura's voice had a slight edge in it, which Kirk took as a warning.

"All right, tell him I'll be right—"

"I have an office here in the palace with a secure wave, Captain," said Roget. "It's at your disposal."

"Put the message through to Commissioner Roget's palace office in five minutes, Uhura. I trust the admiral can wait that long?"

"I hope so, sir," said Uhura, sounding not at all convinced.

Commissioner Roget's palace office, though fully equipped, showed few signs of heavy use. Kirk assumed Roget preferred his office in the Federation embassy. Still, the architecture, in the low, sloping style seen throughout the planet, was pleasing to the eye, and calming, something that could not be said for Admiral Fitzgerald's demeanor.

"Captain Kirk," said Fitzgerald, without prologue, *"Starfleet is extremely displeased over your handling of this matter."*

"I must confess the same, Admiral," said Kirk, who then almost visibly watched Fitzgerald deflate. "The deaths of Princes Abon and Delor were a severe blow to the people of Nador. However, I believe it is still possible to resolve this matter satisfactorily to all parties, and to bring the princes' killers to justice."

"Neither Starfleet Command nor the Federation Council shares your optimism," replied Fitzgerald. *"To*

that end, we are sending the U.S.S. Potemkin *to Nador immediately, with a full complement of Starfleet troops. They will be ready to put down the anarchy you seem to be unable to."*

"Admiral," said Kirk, choosing his words carefully, "if Starfleet troops set foot on this planet in any sizable quantity, I assure you they will be the *cause* of any such anarchy, not its antidote."

"Captain Kirk is correct, Admiral," said Roget. "The Nadorians are a proud people. To send such a contingent of troops would be to insult them grievously. In such an instance, they might even sever ties with the Federation entirely—"

"At which point the Nadorian Planetary Council would no doubt be quite amenable to opening negotiations with the Klingons," said Spock, quietly.

"The Potemkin *is scheduled to enter the Nadorian system in fifty hours,"* said Fitzgerald. *"I trust you will be able to resolve this without either anarchy or driving the Nadorians into the arms of the Klingons. Fitzgerald out."*

"Well," said Kirk, in the silence that followed, "I'd say we've got our work cut out for us, Spock."

"Indeed."

"Commissioner, thanks for your hospitality," said Kirk, as they left Roget's office. "I think," he added dryly.

Roget nodded and even managed a chuckle. "You know where to find me if I can help."

"Pataal?" called Kirk, his tone somewhat gentler as they passed into the royal chamber. "Are you ready to go?"

"Yes, Captain," she murmured. "Thank you, Mrs. Roget," she said, to the woman who had been keeping her company.

"Not at all, child. Good luck." The two hugged, and then Pataal stood between Kirk and Spock—not precisely in the proper spot, but the transporter would sort that out.

Kirk pulled out his communicator and flipped it open. "Energize."

"Pataal!" called Barrows to the girl, as they materialized on the transporter pad.

"Tonia, hello!" Pataal and Barrows embraced briefly and turned to go. Then the Nadorian swiftly ran back to Kirk.

"Captain, thank you again for all your kindness." Impulsively, the young girl leaned toward Kirk and kissed him on the cheek, then ran down the *Enterprise* corridor.

"No thorns without roses," said Kirk, with a smile. Spock cocked his head to one side, but otherwise made no reply.

"Tonia, it is so good of you to let me stay here," said Pataal.

"Not at all," said Barrows, softly. "You've been through a lot."

"I loved them," said Pataal, closing her eyes as the tears came again.

"And they loved you."

"But not equally," continued Pataal, as though Barrows had not spoken. "I loved them both, yes, but not . . . not the same."

"Oh?" Barrows leaned on her bed next to Pataal. She had learned enough of human psychology to tell that her friend wanted to talk, and she had learned from Leonard that in such cases it was best to let them.

"It feels odd saying that," said Pataal, after a long

silence. "It feels . . . disloyal, somehow. I was their consort, I was to have loved them both."

"Pataal, you can't turn love on and off like a circuit," replied Barrows, gently. "It's natural for people to love one and only one. Even some animals mate for life."

"I knew it when my first thoughts were of him after he died," Pataal murmured to herself, as if not looking at Barrows made it easier to speak. "I should have told him. Both of them told me."

"Pataal, please don't—"

"It was Abon!" she half-spoke, half-wept as she collapsed onto Barrows's bunk.

All Barrows knew to do in such situations was to let her cry herself out. That, and to make tea, and to wonder why such realizations always came too late.

"Doctor," said Nurse Chapel, as McCoy was leaving sickbay.

"Can't it wait, Christine? I have a meeting with the captain."

"Those readings you wanted," said Chapel, indicating a computer monitor. "You wanted to know as soon as the results were determined."

"Yes, thanks . . ." McCoy's voice trailed off as he scanned the screen quickly.

Then his eyes widened, he stopped, and began to examine the results much more slowly, before lifting his gaze to Chapel. "Did you read this?"

"I . . . I couldn't help but glance at it—to make sure the data was properly categorized . . ."

"It's all right, Nurse," said McCoy. "But keep this to yourself." He exited at a substantially accelerated rate.

* * *

"Gentlemen," said Captain Kirk, with a softness that did not hide his urgency, "I need answers."

"The Nadorians will certainly see a garrison of Federation troops as an occupation army," said McCoy.

"Precisely," said Kirk, "but the only way to forestall that, aside from forbidding the *Potemkin* to land—which I have no intention of doing—is to corral the dissident elements before they arrive, which will be in approximately forty-eight hours."

"Forty-seven hours, fifty-five minutes, and eleven seconds," said Spock.

"Why do you give him a chance to do that?" asked McCoy, peevishly.

"Unless you have a prescription that'll help, Doctor—" began Kirk.

"As a matter of fact," said McCoy, after a few seconds' silence, "I just might." He rose from the briefing room table and headed for the door. "Come with me to sickbay, Jim." Kirk nodded and began to follow, then McCoy stopped and turned. "You, too, Spock."

"Certainly, Doctor," said Spock.

"You said you wanted answers," said McCoy, in the medical lab in sickbay a few minutes later. "Well, I don't know if this will do any good, but . . ."

"Bones, what is it?" asked Kirk.

"It's this." He tapped a button on the console of the medical computer, and on the wall viewscreen appeared what seemed to Kirk to be a map of two overlapping, intermingling lines, a great many points on those lines coded in different colors.

But to Spock it seemed far more. He examined the screen for a few seconds, then turned to McCoy, both brows raised. "Remarkable," he said.

"Spock, what is it?"

"Dr. McCoy is the medical expert, Captain, not myself—"

"Will somebody please tell me what's going on?"

"I told you," said McCoy, speaking slowly, as if feeling his way through unfamiliar terrain, "I was doing a computer analysis of the Nadorian genome and the princes' DNA. This is the results of that analysis, cross-referenced with the princes' DNA and a readout of the princes' spinal column before the operation which separated them."

"Which explains the two overlapping lines," said Kirk. "Their spinal nerves?"

"That's right. But, Jim, what you can see on this scan, the highlighted points, are where the princes' DNA contradicts their spinal scan."

"'Contradicts'?" Kirk paused. A cold feeling was forming in his stomach, a harbinger that he had learned, from bitter experience, was always the bearer of unpleasant news and was never wrong. "But if their spinal scan is contradicted by their DNA, that means—"

"It means the princes were born separated, like any normal set of twins," said McCoy. "It means they were conjoined surgically, after birth!"

Chapter Fourteen

"MY GOD, BONES," said Kirk, softly, as the enormity of what McCoy had said sank in. To admire the conjoined princes for their grace, to respect them for making a full life under conditions that other men would find totally untenable—these sentiments were all perfectly admirable when you thought they were a response to conditions that a freakish whim of nature had dictated, a seemingly random caprice of fate that one could do nothing about, and could only learn to cope with.

But to realize that someone had deliberately planned this juxtaposition . . . that a mind had planned, of its own free will, to join two healthy infants together without their knowledge or consent, to have purposefully and coldly determined that the two should be denied a normal life . . . This was evidence of such malice that it drove the coldness in Kirk's stomach throughout his entire body, made him want to strike out and destroy whoever had done this until—

"But how? Why—?"

"There's no way of telling without an investigation, Jim," said McCoy. "The operation had to have been done not long after their births, with only a few key people aware of the truth. And the surgical technique was superb. If not for a few readings that were slightly off, I never would have seen it. Whoever conjoined them, I wouldn't mind studying under him for a while."

"He was a butcher," said Kirk. "Who else would have deliberately done that to two children, condemned them to a life like that . . . ?"

"Captain," said Spock, "your characterization is founded in emotion. We have no idea why the royal twins were so conjoined. Doctor, has your examination made you aware of any reason why such a surgical procedure should have been performed?"

"Not immediately, no. There are differences between the Earth-standard physique and the Nadorian system, of course, and the answer may lie there. But there's no guarantee that any of this will help you, Jim."

"It explains a great deal about the twins' relationship, though," Kirk said, musingly. The anger was seeping away now, to be replaced by a certain deliberate coldness.

"True," said Spock. "Their impatience with each other, their argumentative nature—I would think it comes from the memory, long since forgotten, naturally, of their not being joined when they were first born."

"It makes sense," said McCoy with a nod.

"But, Bones—could you have told that the twins were conjoined after birth from their official records?"

"No, Jim," McCoy said slowly. "The official records have been altered to conceal any evidence of the princes' true birth state."

"Then . . . they were never told."

"No." McCoy's voice trailed off, then he shook his head. "I have no idea if this helps you, Jim."

"You never know," said Kirk, blandly, at which point Spock and McCoy exchanged a glance. They had heard that tone before.

"Captain, this is most kind of you," said Lonal. "We had always regretted not having a chance to receive the full tour of your magnificent ship before."

"It was a regret of mine, too," lied Kirk. The change in Regent—no, *Prince* Lonal was even more pronounced now that he had officially been made Nador's ruler. *It's easy to seem confident when your word is the final authority,* Kirk thought. It had been a simple matter to persuade Lonal to tour the *Enterprise,* leaving his security guard in the transporter room—after all, weren't they all part of the Federation?

"And here," said Kirk, ushering Prince Lonal into his cabin, "I have a fine Saurian brandy I hoped Your Highness would give me an opinion on." Lonal smiled beneficently. It was the term "Your Highness" that did it, Kirk was sure.

"We should be delighted," he smiled.

Kirk saw that Lonal got the most comfortable chair behind his desk, then took the bottle of brandy from a secret compartment in one of the cabinets in his quarters. Kirk was sure Lonal did not see him surreptitiously press a button on the side of his viewscreen console.

"What shall we toast to?" asked Lonal, lifting his glass to the light. Kirk wasn't sure if by "we" Lonal included him, but figured the assumption wasn't too big a risk.

"There are so many things," said Kirk, sitting across the desk from Lonal. "How did the Earth writer, Lewis Carroll, put it? 'Of shoes, and ships and sealing wax, of cabbages and kings.'"

"'Cabbages'?" asked Lonal.

"A kind of Earth vegetable. Large, leafy, used in cooked dishes. I know," said Kirk, as if seized by sudden inspiration, "kings." He stood and raised his glass. "Let us toast the monarchy of the planet Nador." Prince Lonal remained seating, beaming from ear to ear.

"Captain," he said, at last, "I don't think I could—"

"Let us toast," continued Kirk, "the memory of Their Serene Highnesses, Princes Abon and Delor."

"Oh. Of course." Lonal raised his glass halfheartedly toward Kirk's, then lowered it and drank, guzzling the brandy far too quickly to properly enjoy it, Kirk noted.

"Interesting thing," said Kirk, as he paced around the cabin, "what Dr. McCoy found when operating on the princes."

"Captain," said Lonal, "must we speak of the two departed monarchs? Their memory is so still fresh in my mind that—"

"Of course." Kirk nodded sympathetically. "As I was saying," he continued immediately, "McCoy found that they had not been born conjoined, but had rather been conjoined *after* they were born." He raised his glass, drank, and lowered it slowly, peering at Lonal over the rim. "Remarkable, don't you think?"

"Quite impossible," said Lonal, gulping another mouthful of the brandy. Kirk shook his head sadly. He could have saved the good stuff and given him Scotch from the dispenser. "The princes were born conjoined, Captain. I was present at their delivery, which took days. Their poor mother was in agony, I well recall her screams." He shuddered, the unpleasant memory necessitating another gulp of brandy.

"That's your final word on the matter?" asked Kirk.

Lonal looked up from his glass and stared at Kirk, for the first time realizing something else was up. "What do you mean? Captain, do you doubt the word of Nador's monarch?"

"Not at all," said Kirk. "But shouldn't you put that in the plural?" He reached to one side and touched the button on his door controls.

The cabin door slid open. Kirk didn't look at who was standing there—or rather, who he hoped was standing there—he was watching Prince Lonal.

His scrutiny was well rewarded. Lonal half-rose from his chair, then thudded back into it as if the gravity in the room had been suddenly tripled. But not even increased gravity could have accounted for the expression on his face, which looked something like a minnow confronted with a shark. He dropped his glass, which fell to the carpeted floor, spilling its contents. At that, Kirk winced.

But he said: "Please, Your Serene Highnesses, come in."

Prince Abon and Prince Delor entered Kirk's cabin, nodding to Kirk and examining their surroundings, their expressions somehow contriving in the same moment to thank Kirk for the invitation and to appropriate the room as their own domain. It was a maneuver that only the truly noble, no matter their station of birth, could bring off. Even the Starfleet jumpsuits and slight disguises they were now stripping off could not hide their bearing, though Kirk thought he detected in their manner, beneath the gravity of the situation, a certain delight at for once not being mirror images of each other.

None of which described Prince Lonal at this moment—*if the honorific still applies,* thought Kirk, idly. His manner, his demeanor, were anything but graceful or noble; it seemed as though the old Lonal had returned, the man who was uncertain of his standing, the man who was used to having his every decision questioned, second-guessed, and then often overruled.

In that moment, Kirk almost felt sorry for him.

"Well, Regent Lonal," said Delor, putting a faint but discernible emphasis on the second word, "is this how you greet your monarchs?"

Lonal jumped like a little girl caught playing at her mother's makeup table. "Your Serene Highnesses," he said. "I rejoice to see you both—alive." Kirk gave him credit for not stammering, while at the same time realizing that Lonal's astonishment was quite genuine. He wasn't that good an actor. Anton Karidian hadn't been that good an actor.

"We are certain you do," replied Abon, "and hope our absence has not weighed too heavily on our subjects."

Lonal's mouth opened and closed twice, looking for all the world like a fish gasping for air. "How . . . ?" he finally said.

"A ruse," said Kirk, matter-of-factly, bowing slightly as he indicated chairs for the princes.

"But . . . your own doctor said the bodies destroyed in the malfunction of your transporter contained the princes' DNA."

"He didn't say they were bodies." Kirk smiled, though not in a good way. "Dr. McCoy was able to whip up a sample of organic matter from the skin-replacement samples in sickbay, laced with the princes' DNA."

"Why . . . ?" asked Lonal, at which point Kirk lost even more respect for him; certainly that answer was obvious.

"We thought the person who wanted the princes dead would be in a more vulnerable position if he thought his efforts to kill the princes had succeeded." Kirk leaned over his desk and gently poked Lonal in the chest, sending him back into his chair. "If you don't want to be included in the list of suspects, *Regent* Lonal, you'd better tell us what you know about Their Serene Highnesses' birth, and quickly."

"They—were not born conjoined," said Lonal. He still hadn't quite managed to catch his breath. Kirk glanced quickly at the princes; at Lonal's admission their eyes narrowed and their lips tightened, but they otherwise showed no reaction. McCoy had told the princes of his findings—Kirk knew the physician would consign to a special circle of hell doctors who kept vital medical information from those whose lives it affected "because they'd be better off not knowing"— but this was the first active admission of the fact they had heard from anyone in a firsthand position to know.

"We already know that," said Kirk, his voice cold. "But why were they conjoined?"

"Because—" Lonal's tongue darted out of his mouth like a serpent after a fly, in a futile attempt to moisten his lips.

At that instant, Kirk's console sounded. Kirk ignored it, keeping his eyes on Lonal, who seemed to be on the edge of a stroke. *"Spock to Captain,"* came a voice from the console. *"Captain, please respond."* Cursing the gods of timing, Kirk hammered a console button angrily.

"Kirk here," he snapped.

"Captain, the energy storm we encountered earlier has returned."

"Red alert. Sound battle stations. I'll be right there."

On the wall of his cabin, the red-alert panel began flashing, nearly, Kirk thought, in time to Lonal's pulse.

"You two get to sickbay," Kirk told the princes, as if they were the lowliest ensigns in Starfleet. The two exchanged a glance, filled with equal parts dread and awe at this new adventure, and nodded, rising and beginning to again don their disguises with an air better attributed to Huck Finn and Tom Sawyer.

"What about him?" Abon pointed to Lonal, who seemed to be having trouble breathing.

"No!" said Lonal, suddenly finding some spine, and using it to straighten to his full height. "No, you must return me to Nador!" Muscles coursed in his face for a few seconds. "My people need me!" he finally shrieked.

"No one's leaving this ship," said Kirk, grimly. He reached over and grabbed the collar of Lonal's robe, handing him over to Delor. "You two are awarded battlefield commissions. Take him to sickbay. Make sure he doesn't contact anyone on the planet."

"Yes, sir!" echoed the twins, utterly delighted at their newfound responsibility. From somewhere, Kirk found a smile. *I was young once.*

Spock rose from the center chair as soon as Kirk's feet hit the bridge. "Status?"

"As before, the storm seems to have coalesced with no noticeable indications," said Spock, now at his station.

"Normal lighting," said Kirk, seating himself. The viewscreen had already been activated. The morass of energy hovered before them in space, eternally whirling with some internal fury of its own that could never be sated, only expressed in destruction. It was like staring at the halo of energy from a dying star or at a nebula, always different, yet always the same. Yet it seemed somehow bigger this time; its edges were off the screen.

"Normal magnification," said Kirk.

"That is normal magnification, sir," replied Sulu.

"The manifestation's size—if not its mass—is appreciable larger than during our last encounter, Captain, by at least one hundred and fifty percent."

The thing neared them slowly, tendrils of energy flicking from it, like a cat twitching its whiskers as it approached prey.

"Shields on maximum," said Kirk.

"Aye, sir," said Chekov.

"Spock," said Kirk, without taking his eyes from the screen, "are other like storms appearing over the planet, as they did last time?"

"I scanned for that immediately, Captain," replied the science officer, "and have found other manifestations across the planet. Some of them over the same sites as the last time, some over entirely new sites, such as the Royal Art Museum."

"Have those storms grown in size, like this one?"

"I read an average size increase of one hundred and forty-five percent, yes, sir," he replied. "Sir," Spock continued, in the same tone of deadly calm, "the storm is attacking."

A tendril of energy flicked lazily from the cloud's center, a second later the *Enterprise* shook.

"Shields to ninety-five percent," said Sulu.

"Shield update in ten-percent increments," said Kirk. "Spock, I asked you and Scotty to put your heads together for options on how to fight that thing. Well?"

"We have developed a method of temporarily increasing phaser power, Captain," said Spock.

"Let's try it out," said Kirk, grimly. "Target the darker portion of it as it gets ready to discharge . . . *there! Fire!*"

A stream of energy leaped onto the viewscreen, targeting the thicker part of the energy cloud precisely. For a few seconds that area grew slightly less opaque, then coalesced to its original texture.

"Its new strength seems to make it more resilient to attack," said Spock, in a tone that was almost admiring.

"Captain," said Sulu, "I'm reading another patch of the manifestation darkening."

"Target and fire," said Kirk.

"Which one, sir?" asked Chekov. "There are five."

True enough, now five darkened regions appeared on the storm's mass, darkening and fading alternately, as if daring the *Enterprise* to hit them.

"Fascinating," said Spock, inevitably.

"Target all of them. Fire," said Kirk, and a moment later, five quick phaser blasts shot out, just too late to strike the darkened patches of the cloud before they faded.

"Shields down to eighty percent," said Sulu, as the ship quivered.

"All power to aft shields. Rotate the ship so the aft hull is closest to that thing," Kirk said. "Opinions, Spock?"

"I shall have to revise my previous estimate of the manifestation's intelligence, Captain. It seems possessed of the capacity to learn from its previous experience."

"Options, then?"

"Mr. Scott and I have also developed a manner of rotating the shield power, so any given area of the ship can be covered at each nanosecond. It is virtually as effective as full shields."

"Give it a try," said Kirk, as a new tremor shook the ship. "And forward current readings on that thing down to engineering. Scotty may be able to make use of them."

"Aye, sir."

"Sir, it's firing again," said Sulu. "With seven dark patches this time."

"Target a spread of phasers and photon torpedoes," said Kirk, "and fire."

The shuddering of the ship almost obscured the voice from Kirk's console. *"McCoy to Kirk."*

"We're a little busy up here, Doctor," said Kirk, with no trace of irony.

"Jim, I picked up the readings Spock sent down to Scotty. Take a look at the records I just sent Spock."

"What was that?" The last part of McCoy's speech had been obscured by a sound Kirk desperately hoped wasn't hull plates buckling. "Spock, prepare an anti-matter charge if there's no other—"

"Captain," sounded Spock's measured tones, over the din, "I suggest you see this."

"What in hell—?" But Kirk pulled his way to Spock's station and looked at the readings on his console. "That looks like the energy field of the storm! Spock, we need—"

"But it is not, Captain," said Spock. He tapped more buttons and a second, identical pattern appeared beneath the first one. He then manipulated the two over one another; they were a perfect fit.

"What is this?" asked Kirk, pointing to the first one.

"That's what I've been trying to tell you," came McCoy's voice. *"It's the* twins' *encephalogram reading—*before *they were separated."*

"But how could that—?" The *Enterprise* shook again, as if possessed of a seizure. "Bones, get up here right away—and bring Lonal with you. Sulu, all power to shields . . . !"

Lonal wasn't enjoying his tour of the ship nearly as much now. He took one look at the roiling mass of chaos on the viewscreen and nearly fainted.

"You were going to tell us why the princes were conjoined," said Kirk. "Does it have something to do with that?" He thrust a finger at the viewscreen; Lonal literally hid his eyes from the sight.

"They were naught but hours old," said Lonal, getting a grip on himself, "when a small storm—like that one," he waved a hand in the direction of the viewscreen, but did not look at it, "was created somehow. The scientists said it had something to do with their pure bloodlines . . ."

"And to the history of psionic abilities historically attributed to the Nadorian people," said Spock. "The twins' abilities were mutually destructive?"

"Yes," cried Lonal, clinging to the arm of Kirk's chair. "It was determined that the only way to quell them was to mingle their nervous systems—what better way to do that than to conjoin them?"

"And condemn them to a life as aberrations," said Kirk, grimly. He shook his head; now wasn't the time. "You're saying the twins' psionic abilities are doing this, without their even being aware of it?"

"It does correlate with the history of the Nadorian people, Captain, and the princes' pure bloodlines. Unfortunately, such 'purity' of bloodlines has historically resulted in minor genetic imperfections being intensely magnified."

"Bones, can you—" Kirk had to wait for the ship to stop shaking. "Can you somehow link the twins' minds together?"

"Already working on a neural link," nodded McCoy. "That'll take the heat off for a little while."

"Then go," said Kirk, jerking a thumb to the lift. "And take this with you."

"I suppose I can put him to work sweeping up," grumbled McCoy, dragging Lonal with him.

"Spock," said Kirk, "how far away is that thing?"

"Five hundred kilometers," replied Spock. "It seems to be readying another assault."

"Shields at thirty percent," said Sulu.

"Sulu, deploy a fusillade of photon torpedoes, set to explode at two hundred meters."

"Aye, sir, two hundred meters."

"It's discharging," said Spock. "Such a barrier will absorb only a portion of the blast."

"It'll buy us a little time. Fire."

The ship shook a little less this time, as the barrier of exploding torpedoes diffused some of the storm's attack.

"Ready another round, Sulu."

"Torpedo room reports no more ready, sir," said Sulu.

"Bones," said Kirk, making no attempt to keep the urgency from his voice, "if you're going to do anything, it better be now."

"Understood, Jim. C'mere, Your Highness."

"It tingles," said one of the princes, presumably in reply to whatever action McCoy had taken.

"Mine itches," said the other prince—right now, Kirk didn't have the wherewithal to tell them apart over the intercom.

"They better do more than that," said McCoy.

"Sir," said Spock, "the storm is readying another assault."

"All power to shields," said Kirk, in a tone of resignation.

On the viewscreen, several dark spots on the surface of the energy manifestation coalesced. Below them, energy flashed like blood pulsing below living skin. . . .

"Here it comes," said Kirk.

Then the flashes dimmed and the storm began to fade, the dark spots being the last to go.

"The manifestation has dissipated, Captain," said Spock.

"Secure from red alert," said Kirk, leaping from his chair. "Sulu, you have the conn. Spock, with me."

"Most interesting," murmured Spock, examining the metallic patches fastened to the backs of the necks of Their Serene Highnesses.

"Thank you," said McCoy, clearly uneasy at receiving an unalloyed comment from Spock. Kirk kept his grin to himself. Bones would replay Spock's remarks a thousand times in his head, causing himself more worry than if Spock had simply insulted him. Whether Spock had intended to do so would remain unknown; McCoy would never give him the satisfaction of asking.

"These neural links are normally used to facilitate the repair of nerve damage, but I reprogrammed them to do just the opposite of what they're usually used for, to intercept brain impulses rather than relay them."

"Good job, Bones. How long will they work?"

McCoy's smile faded to a frown. "That's another matter, Jim. I can't be certain; maybe a few hours, maybe a few days. Since there's nothing really wrong with the princes, eventually their neural impulses will find their way back to the proper paths."

"Then you'd better—"

"I'm already trying to develop other methods."

"Is there any kind of operation that might work?"

Kirk glanced at the princes, and saw their expressions fall. "Other than reconjoining them, of course."

McCoy shook his head. "Not a one, Jim. The brain is the trickiest organ in the body, and we don't know one-half as much as I'd need to know to operate without turning them into breathing vegetables. And as for reconjoining them . . . don't even think about it. They're still recovering from being separated. An operation like that would kill them for sure."

Kirk nodded, and turned to Lonal, who had been lurking in a corner of sickbay, trying to remain unnoticed.

"Regent Lonal," said Kirk, "do you have anything else you'd care to share with us?"

"I have told you everything I know," he said, summoning up all the dignity of a man trying to bluff on a pair of twos. "You will return me to the palace immediately."

"That would not be advisable, Captain," said Spock. "Should the conspirators learn that the princes are still alive—"

"Thank you, Spock," said Kirk, dryly. "Regent Lonal, I'm afraid you're going to have to remain our guest for a while yet."

"I will not! You have no right to keep me here!"

"Technically, you're right," said Kirk. He seemed to think for a moment, then nodded. "Very well, you may return to the palace."

"I should hope so," said Lonal, huffily.

"But you do realize that once you set foot back on Nador, we can no longer help you."

"Help?" Lonal's tone was contemptuous, but Kirk thought he heard a sliver of uncertainty in it. "Why would I need your help?"

"The conspirators think they have been successful in murdering the princes," said Kirk with a shrug, on his way to the sickbay door. "And if they're working their way down the chain, well . . ." His voice trailed off, but he suspended his hands in the air resignedly.

"You mean . . . *my* life may be in danger?"

"Perhaps," said Kirk, "but 'uneasy lies the head' and all that." Kirk resumed his progress toward the door. "Coming, Regent—?"

"I am not," said Lonal, emphatically. He had withdrawn to the farthest wall, spread-eagled against the instruments there. "I demand sanctuary!"

Kirk smiled. "I thought you might."

Chapter Fifteen

"ARE YOU SURE this will work, Spock?"

"The efficacy of the device is not in question, Captain. It does function. Rather, it is the outcome of the mission it makes possible which is open to question."

Kirk examined the polyglot device Spock had presented to him. It was slightly smaller than a human index finger. Its original surface was studded with microcircuits that gave it a jury-rigged look. "It seems a little large to have been concealed on the chair the princes sat in."

"This version is admittedly larger than the original," said Spock, "owing largely to the fact that much of the circuitry has been retroengineered, and is therefore doubtless not as space-efficient as the original model."

"But it will work?"

"Undoubtedly, sir. When activated, it will broadcast the same frequency which the missile that assaulted the princes was designed to follow."

Kirk hefted the object in his hand and swiveled to face Uhura. "And you can trace the frequency,

Lieutenant? Enable us to send a landing party back to its source?"

"I'm sure I can, sir," said Uhura, "but why would they keep that frequency open, after all this time? Why should its operators respond?" These were good questions, so Kirk looked inquiringly at Spock.

"Remember, Lieutenant," said Spock, "the manufacturers of this device believe it destroyed in the attack on the princes. They therefore have no reason not to believe the frequency is available for further utilization. And if the frequency had eluded detection in the past, there is no reason for them to discard a tool which has proven useful."

"Especially if they've gotten careless in the wake of the princes' deaths," said Kirk. "Our opponents have accomplished at least one of their major objectives."

"Precisely," said Spock, whose thoughts, Kirk was sure, paralleled his. But he kept this to himself; of the *Enterprise* crew, only he, Spock, McCoy, Chapel, and Scotty knew the princes were still alive

"I admit it's something of a long shot," said Kirk, tapping a button on his chair arm, "but it's the only horse we've got. Chief Giotto, Kirk here. I need a couple of people for a landing party that might get a little rough."

"Glad to be of service, sir," crackled back Giotto's voice.

"Meet me in transporter room three. Kirk out." He rose from the conn and looked at the crew members at the helm. "Mr. Sulu, Mr. Chekov? Feel like stretching your legs?"

"Yes, sir," said Sulu, fervently.

"Absolutely, Captain," said Chekov.

"Lieutenant Uhura, you've got the conn."

"Yes, sir," came Uhura's emphatic reply.

"Spock, you're with me," Kirk said, heading for the turbolift. "Let's go, gentlemen." As though he'd have to ask them twice.

In sickbay, Abon and Delor faced each other over a surgical cart they had turned into a makeshift card table. "Another game?" asked Abon.

"No." Delor shrugged, irritably. He rose and paced the room, still conscious of his newfound freedom of being able to move as he, and he alone, desired. "I wish we could leave this place."

"What we wish matters little," said Abon. "For the first time in our lives," he added, slowly. After a lifetime of rather pampered treatment, fully acknowledging that someone wanted you dead was not the easiest fact to grasp. But Kirk had ordered them to stay put, disallowing them any outside activity, even if disguised. He referred to their single sortie to bedevil Regent Lonal—who had finally returned to Nador, after doubling his security guard, determined to enjoy his short reign as much as possible—as a one-time (and quite enjoyable) exception.

"Much is new, these days," said Delor with a nod, sitting down again. "The fact that we may view each other, face-to-face, for instance."

"The separation has brought us both good and ill," said Abon. "The storms, for instance."

"This has occurred to me, yes," said Delor, after a few seconds.

"Our newfound freedom endangers others. I had not thought that would be the case."

"There is little we can do about it," replied Delor. He looked up, to find his brother staring at him and looking, for once, not at all like himself. "Is there?"

"There may be," said Abon, his words slow and measured. "If the storms come from our *mutual* psionic potential, then . . ." He looked down. "If there were only one of us . . ."

"I don't like that idea very much," said Delor.

"Nor do I," said Abon. "But if our continued existence endangers our planet, our subjects—" He waved a hand around him. "—even this mighty starship, can we be responsible for that?"

"How would we decide," asked Delor, idly. "Cast lots? Draw straws?" He reached out and grasped the deck of cards before him. "Cut the cards?" He shuffled the deck Dr. McCoy had given them and looked at the king of spades, smiling mirthlessly. "Or perhaps we could return—" His voice trailed off, the thought unspoken.

"I don't know," said Abon, tonelessly. "But there must be a solution."

"We don't need to think about it now," replied Delor, dealing the cards.

"Perhaps not, but we will need to think about it soon," said Abon, trying to ignore the tingling on the back of his neck.

"You've got it, Scotty?" asked Kirk.

"Aye, sir," said Mr. Scott, dutifully. "When Uhura's established contact, I'll beam you down t'the reception point—" Kirk started to speak and Scotty nodded patiently. "—after makin' sure our friends on the other end haven't planted any nasty surprises like that gizmo that scuttled the princes' transmission beam. Though," he said, after a moment's consideration, "that did make it easier t'explain the faked transporter malfunction."

"I'll tell them you were impressed by their thought-fulness," said Kirk, strapping on phaser and communicator. The door hissed open and Chief Giotto and Lieutenant Sinclair entered and took their places on the pad. "Phasers on stun. Welcome, Lieutenant, always room for one more at the party."

"I'll save you a dance, sir," she grinned, smoothing back a lock of blond hair. From Giotto's expression he thought the security chief seemed about to dress Sinclair down for what Giotto, who was rather spit-and-polish, doubtless considered insolence, but Kirk met his gaze and shook his head slightly. He approved of free spirits, as long as they knew when to rein back, and Sinclair's youth had not blinded Kirk to the fact that she performed with expertise beyond her years.

"Are ye ready, Uhura?" asked Scotty, into the intercom in the transporter console.

"When you are, Scotty," came Uhura's voice. Scotty looked at Kirk intently, head cocked slightly to one side.

"Transmit," Kirk said.

It all happened too quickly to voice: the activated transmission to somewhere on Nador that was quickly received, Uhura's signal to Scotty, then Scotty's quick, skilled manipulation of the beam. The transporter room blurred before Kirk's vision.

When things became clear again, he found himself breathing heavy, rather dank air, heard the smallest sounds echoing back immediately. A cave, then, possibly with a spring or underground river nearby. What little light there was seemed to come from far off, around a bend in the tunnel. "Spock?" he whispered.

"Approximately five meters underground," came the first officer's soft reply, as he consulted his tricorder.

The Vulcan was still a blur to Kirk; Spock's eyes were adjusting much more quickly. "The mouth of the cave is in that direction," Spock continued, pointing toward the faint smear of light.

"Then we'll go this way," said Kirk, heading deeper into the darkness. Spock joined him at point, with Sulu and Chekov in the middle, and Giotto and Sinclair bringing up the rear.

"I detect no life signs," said Spock, softly, "though it is possible that diverse ores in the cavern's structure may be interfering with my tricorder; they would doubtless pose an obstacle to an effective scan."

"A good place for a hideout," said Kirk.

"Or an ambush," added Sulu.

Suddenly, something skittered into the middle of their group, something thrown from not far away. A small, metallic object, to judge by the racket it made. . . .

"Scatter!" The six dove, as behind them came a gush of light and heat. *A flare of some sort,* thought Kirk. *They're not sure who they're up against yet.* And whoever had thrown the flare had made a crucial error. Since it was thrown into the middle of the group, they were able to face away from it, their eyes shielded from the worst effects of the splash of light.

In the brief burst of luminescence, Kirk saw a wider alcove farther back in the cave, probably their base.

"Maneuver five!" he called, and immediately the landing party formed two rows of three members, the front row with its backs to the second row. They drew phasers and sprayed fire in all directions, knowing that whoever they hit, it wouldn't be one of their own.

Immediately, return fire came in the form of familiar controlled force beams. In the strobing light of the conflicting fire, Kirk tapped Spock, who was to his back, on the shoulder and the two of them broke from the party, crawling rapidly on their hands and knees, while the remainder of their group continued to lay down covering fire.

The flashes from the phasers began to dim as they put some distance between them; Kirk's eyes were acclimating to the darkness, and he and Spock made for the wider alcove he had spied earlier.

Rounding a curve in the cave, Kirk and Spock rose to full height and crept along, their backs hugging the cavern wall. Ahead, Kirk could hear—and began to see—faint forms skittering through the darkness, making more noise than they needed to. Were they that careless, or—?

Kirk suddenly wheeled and laid down a hail of phaser fire, aimed at the other side of the cave. In the brief illumination of his salvo, he saw furtive forms there, crumpling as the phaser 1 bursts struck them. He had been right: the noise made had been an attempt to distract Kirk and Spock from an attack from behind.

Scrabbling across the cave, Kirk grabbed the weapons his targets had dropped. He tossed one to Spock, who caught it nimbly and nodded.

Kirk remained silent now, and still, waiting for any other enemies concealed deeper in the cave to make themselves known. After a few seconds, only silence came from the depths. But Kirk wasn't convinced.

Hearing a soft footfall behind him, Kirk swiveled, Starfleet phaser in one hand, Nadorian weapon in the other. But it was only the rest of the landing party, making their way to him and Spock.

"Any progress, sir?" hissed Giotto.

"We think there are more of them holed up back

there," whispered Kirk. "I could be wrong, but it's not a chance I'm willing to take."

"We could toss a couple of gas grenades down there, sir," said Sulu.

"They could attack under cover of the gas," replied Kirk. "I am open to suggestions."

"We have a couple of allies in this situation, sir," said Giotto, slyly, "whether they're aware of it or not."

Minutes later, in the depths of the cave, five people hugged the rock walls, nearly motionless, waiting for the intruders to advance or retreat. Given that the intruders were Federation, they were both cowards and imperialists, eager to conquer and mold other, peaceful civilizations to their will. The only certainty was that they would not remain still. If they chose to advance, they would be caught in a crossfire. If they retreated, the lurkers would catch up to them and shoot them from behind. It was nearly foolproof.

Just then, they heard rapid footsteps and noises that seemed to come from the throats of animals. But no; as the sounds grew louder, they were human, but muffled, as if wounded.

The footsteps grew louder now, and faster. The layer of dust the intruders' invasion had stirred up was pierced by Nadorian weaponry.

One lurker, to whom the others seemed to look, made a number of gestures. These motions had never been called anything so formal as an official code, but those who saw him knew what they meant:

The Federation people are fleeing, when they round the corner, merge our fire with that of our brothers!

Those not close enough to make out the gestures saw them repeated as they were passed along.

The footfalls became louder, as did the wail of the force beams that followed them. Finally, fleeing human forms could be made out through the floating dust. At last the lurkers drew their weapons and fired. The fleeing forms fell, and the lurkers emerged from the crevices and crags of the cave walls, the better to see their prey.

Or what they thought was their prey. "Wait!" called their leader. He saw more clearly now forms with their hands bound to their sides, their mouths gagged; only their legs had remained unbound.

And he recognized the forms.

"These are our people! Scatter, before—!"

Too late. From out of the darkness came phaser fire, felling the lurkers easily. Some managed to turn and flee, but not very far, nor for very long.

"Good thinking, Chief," said Kirk, as they neared the unconscious quarry.

"It's economical, if nothing else, sir," said Giotto. "The only people in the crossfire are your enemies."

"They don't seem to have sustained any long-range ill effects, Captain," said Chekov. "Fortunately for them, their allies weren't shooting to kill."

"That earns them some consideration, I guess," said Kirk. "Bind the legs of our bait, we don't want them running out on us. Then remove the gags of their friends. I want to have a little talk with them."

"I will tell you nothing—" said the leader, some minutes later.

"Except your name, rank, and serial number, I know." Kirk sighed.

"We are in no formal army!" shouted another, who looked to be one of the youngest members of the group. "We—"

Whatever he was about to say had been severely truncated. The eldest member, who seemed to be the leader, had managed, despite having his legs bound, to pull back and kick the younger man with both heels. "Hey, none of that!" said Sinclair, pulling them apart.

"We know all we need to know about who you are," said Kirk, leaning against an outcropping of rock. He turned his head and called off, "Spock?"

"I believe you are correct, Captain," said the science officer. He approached the landing party and their captives from farther back in the cavern, brandishing a flashlight, which they could now use in safety. "If you'll come this way?"

"Yes, I think we're in the right place," said Kirk with a nod, surveying the contents of the cavern. A few cots, some cooking utensils, and some dried foods indicated that the area had been used as living quarters, but the Nadorian flag hanging on a cavern wall—as well as the Federation flag hanging on the facing wall, besmirched with stains Kirk refused to recognize—identified the cavern's inhabitants as pro-Nadorian terrorists. If further proof of their intent were needed, next to the defiled Federation flag was a similarly defaced banner bearing the likenesses of Princes Abon and Delor.

"They also have large caches of literature," said Spock, "extolling the virtues of all true Nadorians and the vices of those of extraplanetary origin. A sizable list, in both cases."

Kirk played the beam of his own flashlight over the faces of their captives. "I recognize some of them. They were in the crowds of anti-Federation protesters."

"Protesting is our right!" rasped one of the prisoners. "We have done nothing illegal!"

"The presence of this transmitter would seem to give

the lie to that statement," said Spock. The beam of his light fell over a small, powerful piece of machinery on a table against a far wall.

"Tuned to the frequency we beamed in on?" asked Kirk.

"Indeed, Captain."

"Well," said Kirk, blandly, "it seems you boys have some explaining to do."

"We will tell you nothing!" said their leader, vehemently.

"Suit yourself," said Kirk with a shrug, reaching for his communicator. "But if you won't talk to me, I'm sure Chief Securitrix Llora will be able to loosen your tongues, wouldn't you say, Spock?"

"I am confident these gentlemen will be literally begging to speak when the Chief Securitrix is through with them—providing they are able."

"Now, just a minute," the leader said. "You can't turn us over to her."

"On second thought, I think that's exactly the proper thing to do," said Kirk. "The planetary government doubtless has jurisdiction over you anyway, wouldn't you say, Mr. Spock?"

"Doubtless," said Spock, with a nod.

"Kirk to *Enterprise*," said Kirk, into his communicator, "scan and transport us directly to palace security at—"

"Wait!" shouted the leader, no longer so sure of himself.

"*Enterprise*, hold," said Kirk, closing his communicator. "Well? Give us a name, now."

"We don't know anyone by name! They contact us when they want us!"

"How?"

"By coded transmission! I swear to you I'm telling the truth!"

"Spock?"

"His respiratory levels and pulse are up, Captain," said the Vulcan, examining the readings on his tricorder. "But that could be due to emotional duress, rather than falsification." He broke off for a moment, his eyebrows slanting downward, making him look more than ever like the personification of Satan. "This is curious, these readings indicate—"

"What, Spock?"

Spock swiveled, pointing to a crate of equipment against a far cavern wall. "A device, Captain," he said, calmly, "an explosive device, I believe, activated by repeated tricorder scans, and set to explode in seven— six—five—"

"Kirk to *Enterprise!* Six to beam up, *NOW*—!"

Kirk was never sure if he heard the explosion or not; he knew only that when he materialized aboard the *Enterprise,* the first thing he noticed was that his ears were ringing.

The second was the smell of charred flesh. He turned rapidly, examining the landing party, himself last, for signs of damage. This all happened in what seemed like less than a second. Then he looked down, and saw the seared remnants of a man laying twisted and smoking on the transporter pad.

He ran for the transporter console, but Spock had beaten him to it. Tying in to the bridge controls, Spock initiated a scan of the area they had just beamed up from. After a few seconds, he turned from the console, shaking his head.

"No survivors, Captain."

Kirk nodded glumly and turned to the landing party.

"Good job, all of you. Report to sickbay. I don't want Starfleet to accuse me of having returned any of its merchandise damaged." He even managed a smile, which the others returned, however faintly, before trooping out.

"Well done, Scotty," said Kirk, clapping the engineer on the shoulder.

"Thank you, sir. I thought you might be in need of a quick exit."

"Anything to be determined from this one?" asked Kirk, holding his hand before his nose as he approached what was left of the still-smoldering body on the pad.

"After a brief initial examination, I would reply in the negative," said Spock. "But I will have the remains shipped to sickbay for a thorough autopsy."

Kirk nodded, suddenly conscious of his own weariness. It was as though the rigors of the last few minutes had caught up to him. "I'll be in my quarters."

Some minutes later, freshly showered and uniformed (though as efficient as the sonic showers aboard the *Enterprise* were, Kirk still longed for an old-fashioned shower now and then), Kirk strode onto the bridge, nodding to Sulu and Chekov. "No lingering aftereffects from our little adventure, gentlemen?" The helmsman and navigator shook their heads, their slight smiles saying that, like children at an amusement park, they couldn't wait to do it again.

"Captain," said Uhura, again at her usual post, "I have a message from the palace. It's Securitrix Llora, sir."

Kirk thought for a moment. He had intended to make a report to her in a few minutes in an attempt to quell any more ill will—if that was possible at this late date. But she had apparently learned of their raid on her own.

Ah, well. Kirk would console her by making full disclosure of any information obtained from the body in sickbay, if any. "On screen, Lieutenant."

"*Captain.*" Her beauty, the fine lines of her face, was even more stunning when subject to the magnification of the viewscreen; not all faces could stand such merciless scrutiny. But it was clear, as always, that this was the last thing on the securitrix's mind.

"Chief Securitrix," said Kirk, formally. "Please, allow me to apologize for not—"

"*You have nothing to apologize for, Captain, it is I who— Excuse me.*" She turned to look offscreen; Kirk heard a muffled, rapid voice, and saw her features darken in controlled anger, an expression, he reflected wryly, he knew well.

"*You have not been told,*" said Llora, after a few seconds. "*This is my responsibility and my error.*"

"'Told' what?" said Kirk. He rose from the conn slowly, feeling the sudden need to pace, a need that came over him whenever he sensed bad news in the offing.

"*It is your nephew,*" she said, four of the words Kirk most dreaded hearing. "*He appears to have been kidnapped.*"

Chapter Sixteen

"WHERE IS MY NEPHEW?" asked Kirk, minutes later.

"I do not know," confessed Llora.

They stood in the security wing of the Royal Palace, where Kirk—with Spock and McCoy—had beamed immediately upon hearing of Peter's absence.

"He was in your custody," said Kirk. "You guaranteed his well-being, his safety."

"Captain—" said Spock.

Without looking at the Vulcan, Kirk held up a hand for silence. He knew recriminations would do no good, would not further the finding and safe return of Peter—assuming the boy was still . . .

No. Don't even think that.

He put aside his rage and mounting worry and tried to view Llora as a colleague. "What happened?"

"Your nephew was released while I was on training maneuvers," said Llora. "A set of orders for his transferral was received and acknowledged by my staff."

Behind her, a young man began to protest. Llora silenced him with a gesture that, Kirk much later realized, was a mirror image of the gesture he had used to silence Spock. "Forged orders," she continued. "Excellent orders, with no transmission gaps whatsoever, but forged nonetheless."

"Signed by whom?" asked Kirk. There might have been the start of a trail, of a clue that—

"Signed by myself," said Llora, after a few seconds. Silent in the admission of such audacity, Kirk saw her face color slightly, as she tried to fight down her embarrassment.

"May I examine them?" asked Spock, stepping forward.

"You will find nothing—" she said, then caught herself, seeming to remember the situation. "Of course," she said with a nod. "Bekai, bring up the transmission for Mr. Spock." The young man she had silenced earlier nodded eagerly, and Spock proceeded to his side, leaning over the Security Center's console.

"Captain," she said, "I am entirely responsible for this matter."

Yes, you are, Kirk wanted to say. But recriminations were the easy way out, and Kirk had never taken the easy way.

"May I examine his cell?" asked McCoy, courteously. "There may be something to be learned from it." Llora nodded tightly, and another security officer ushered McCoy back to the holding area.

Kirk raised a brow as Spock returned, clicking his tricorder closed. "As the chief securitrix herself said, an excellent job. The coding transmission is flawless, and—though this is not in itself a technical virtue—the timing of the orders' transmission was precisely correct, coming seventeen minutes ago, when Securitrix Llora was not present, and so could not countermand the forged orders."

"But Peter couldn't have just vanished into thin air," said Kirk, on the verge of exasperation.

"On the contrary, Captain, that is exactly what he did do," said Spock. "According to the orders, following his release, Peter was to wait to be beamed aboard the *Enterprise.*"

"Did he beam out from your pad?" asked Kirk, of Llora. "If so—"

"He did not," said Llora, shaking her head. "He was taken by a transporter beam from an outside source. Untraceable by any means."

"Of course," said Kirk, bitterly. "Bones, anything?" he asked, looking up and off.

"Afraid not, Jim," said McCoy. "The cell was clean as a whistle. Hardly any sign he was even there."

"All right," said Kirk, glumly. "Kirk to *Enterprise,*" he said, to his communicator. "Three to beam up."

"Captain," said Llora, "if I or my people can do anything . . ."

Haven't you done enough? he wanted to shout. But that path would yield nothing but childish gratification. "I'll be in touch," he said.

Llora began to put her hand out as if to touch Kirk's, but by the time she finished the gesture, the three Starfleet officers were gone in a swirl of atoms.

"Are you okay, Jim?" asked McCoy, as they exited the turbolift. Spock would never have put the question that way, but the concern in even his face was evident.

"There are two ways to treat pressure," said Kirk, as they entered the conference room. "Succumb to it . . . or use it as a propellant."

"Logical," said Spock, his version of a pat on the back.

"Which means what?" asked McCoy, skeptically.

"Which means my plan is succeeding. Bones, look at the timing of it. Our raid on the Nadorian separatists happened over forty-five minutes ago. Peter was released from prison, when, Spock?"

"Twenty-five minutes, seventeen seconds ago."

"You see? Peter's release and kidnapping has to be a response to the raid. We drew blood. We're too close for comfort—for their comfort, anyway." Kirk rose and began to pace, worried for Peter, but at the same time oddly exhilarated.

"Which means what?" asked McCoy, again. "We sit and wait for the kidnappers to announce their demands?"

"Not at all," Kirk reminded him. "Have you forgotten about the subcutaneous transponder?" It was apparent, from the look on the physician's face, that he had, at least temporarily.

Spock was at once at the conference room console, tying it in to his bridge station. "Lieutenant Uhura," he said, "monitor for the frequency I am sending to your station, widest possible scan."

"Yes, Mr. Spock," came the response. Through the intercom, they could hear the clicking of relays being nimbly tripped. *"I'm sorry, Mr. Spock,"* she said, a few moments later. *"There is no response on that frequency."*

"Uhura, are you sure?" asked Kirk, swinging the console toward him. "There's got to be a signal."

A few seconds later came the answer. *"I'm sorry, Captain. Perhaps the transponder is under heavy shielding, or—"*

"Or maybe they're on to our game," said McCoy, darkly. "So far, they've shown themselves to be pretty sharp, whoever they—"

"Thank you, Uhura, Kirk out," Kirk said numbly.

"Don't blame yourself, Jim," said McCoy. "You can't foresee every change of fortune."

But I thought I could, thought Kirk, *and now it's Peter who will pay the price for my— No, don't think of that. There's got to be another way.*

"Is it possible," asked Kirk, slowly, "to scan for a lone human amid a group of Nadorians?" He raised his eyes to Spock and McCoy.

"Such a scan might be feasible at close range," said Spock, choosing his words carefully, "but from orbit, given the physiological similarities between humans and Nadorians, it is quite impractical."

"Besides," said McCoy, "there are hundreds of Federation citizens, many of them humans, on the planet, Jim. How could you tell which is Peter?"

Kirk nodded sharply, and for several seconds the room was silent. Then the hailing whistle sounded. *"Captain Kirk, a message from the planet's surface."*

Kirk didn't move. After a few seconds, Spock approached the console. "From whom, Lieutenant?"

"Another coded transmission, Mr. Spock, like the one we received before. A burst of less than a second, far too brief to trace point of transmission." At this, Kirk's head snapped around. The earlier transmission had been from Peter, telling them all was well. Perhaps history would repeat itself. . . .

"Go ahead, Lieutenant," said Kirk.

"It's very short, sir, only six words: 'We have him. Take no action.'" Her voice trailed off; it was obvious that she had figured out the intent of the message, but didn't know what to say, if anything, until: *"I'm sorry, sir."*

"Thank you, Lieutenant," said Kirk, after what seemed a very long time. "Kirk out."

Kirk slumped in his chair, like a suddenly deflated balloon. *I'm out of options. And it's Peter who's going to pay.* To a warrior, even a reluctant warrior like himself, such a defeat was doubly galling. To be beaten in battle, to be outthought, outmaneuvered was one thing, to be bested in such a contest was no shame.

But to have your hands tied behind you because your unseen enemy was using your actions to guarantee the fate of a noncombatant . . . this was intolerable. It was as if an army of chess pieces had suddenly broken the boundaries of the board and taken hostages from those watching the game. It wasn't right.

But what was right, and what was done in the name of blind ambition and avarice, seldom overlapped. However, the troops aboard the *Potemkin* would not view Peter's life with the same importance, and Kirk couldn't expect them to. No matter which decision he made, blood would be spilled. . . .

"Blood," he said, as if never having pronounced the word before.

Spock and McCoy exchanged a glance. "Sir?" asked Spock, after a few seconds.

"Report to sickbay, Mr. Spock," said Kirk, rising from his chair to his full height. Something in his voice, in his posture, told his friends that it wasn't over yet.

"Sir?" asked Spock, again, in the exact same tone. "My collapse on the bridge was, I assure you, a one-time occurrence which has not manifested itself again—"

"Doctor, draw a blood sample from Mr. Spock—"

"But, Jim, what—?"

"Don't interrupt. Draw a blood sample from Spock, and filter *out* the remnants of the neural parasite Spock was infected by on the planet Deneva—"

"Indeed," said Spock.

"The same parasite Peter was infected by!" said McCoy. He and Spock exchanged another glance, but with an entirely different meaning.

"If there's more than one person on that planet who's been subjected to the Denevan neural parasite, I'll give up my command," said Kirk.

"Your captaincy is in little danger," said Spock. "The odds of such an occurrence are greater than—"

"Shut up, Spock," said McCoy. "Let's get you down to sickbay—captain's orders."

"Do you not have the pertinent medical data on file, Doctor?"

"Oh, I do," said McCoy, dryly, "but a fresh batch of data never hurt." He squeezed the Vulcan's forearm between thumb and forefinger. "At least, it never hurt *me*."

"May I assume your operating instruments will be properly sterilized this time?" asked Spock, archly, as they headed for the door.

"I may even sharpen them," replied McCoy, brightly.

Their voices faded away as Kirk turned to the console to order a landing party, keenly aware of the conflicting forces at play here. The same monster that had taken Sam's life might now be responsible for saving the life of his son.

"Fortunately," said Spock, in an ironic tone, "the virulence of the Denevan neural parasite renders it particularly susceptible to scans."

"Less talk and more scanning," said McCoy, impatiently.

"I am capable of both, Doctor," replied Spock. He stood at his post on the bridge, Kirk and McCoy flanking him on either side. The relevant data had been prepared by sickbay's medical scanners and fed into the bridge computer, which now, tied into the ship's scanners, was poring over the entire planet of Nador, inch by inch.

"Scan of eastern continent completed," said Spock. "Presence of Denevan neural parasite not detected."

"Sulu," said Kirk, "bring us over the planet's main continent and decrease orbit to three thousand kilometers. It stands to reason that Peter will be held at the insurrectionists' main base, and that that base won't be too far from the capital."

"Aye, sir."

"Scanning the main continent," said Spock. For too many seconds he remained silent. Then: "I have detected the Denevan neural parasite, Captain."

Kirk thumbed a button on Spock's console. "Kirk to Chief Giotto. Meet me in the transporter room."

"We'll be right there, Captain," filtered back Giotto's voice.

"Spock, Bones, Sulu, you're with me. Uhura, you have the conn." Sulu rose from his post immediately, winking with a self-satisfied grin at Chekov, who rolled his eyes heavenward.

"Uhura," said Kirk, "as soon as we've beamed down, you will take the *Enterprise* out of orbit—"

"Out of orbit, sir? But what about—"

"—at one-half impulse power. The instant you have left the Nadorian solar system, you will immediately reverse course and return with all deliberate speed, placing the Nadorian moon between the ship and the planet and avoiding all contact with any vessels. You will then remain there until you receive further orders. Is that clear?"

"Yes, sir," said Uhura with a nod, comprehension dawning in her features. "You want to make it look to Peter's captors as though we're running away."

"With our nacelles between our legs," said Kirk, with a grim nod. "It's time we took off the kid gloves when dealing with these people. How far out is the *Potemkin?*"

"Still twenty-five hours, at least, sir," said Uhura.

"We may be able to save those troops from getting their boots dirty yet," said Kirk intently as he headed for the turbolift. "Let's go, gentlemen. The insurrectionists have something of ours, and I intend to get it back."

But as they entered the transporter room, Kirk's pace slowed. Waiting for them were Chief Giotto and Lieutenant Sinclair.

"Lieutenant," said Kirk, briskly, "why don't you sit this one out?"

"Sir?" Giotto and Sinclair said in the same instant, and the same baffled tone.

"Not to second-guess you, Chief," said Kirk, "but don't you think someone else deserves to see some action?"

As Sinclair drifted away from the group, Giotto turned to Kirk. In his voice could be heard his respect for both the office and the man vying for supremacy over his anger. "Sir, what's Sinclair done?"

"To my knowledge, nothing," replied Kirk.

"She's going to think she's done something wrong, that she's being disciplined," said Giotto.

"Nothing of the sort," said Kirk. "But I have my reasons."

"Which are?" asked McCoy, pointedly.

"Which are, at the present moment, solely the captain's business," said Kirk, in the same tone. "Mr. Scott," he said raising his voice, "would you care to accompany us?"

"About time I got asked t'dance," said Scotty, strapping on a weapons belt. "I thought I'd be a wallflower fer sure."

"I wouldn't hear of it," said Kirk, dryly. "Mr. Kyle, if you'll do the honors?"

"Your touchdown point seems to be some sort of large storage facility on the edge of the city, sir," said Kyle, examining the transporter console.

"Give us some cover, if you can," said Kirk.

"I'm reading an area that appears to be obscured from view and a safe distance from any life-forms. I think I can set you down there."

"That sounds good. Phasers on stun," he said, to the landing party. "We'll have the advantage of surprise, but that won't last long."

"Maybe we can hit them below the belt," said McCoy, in a voice only Kirk could hear, "just like you did to Sinclair."

"That's enough, Doctor," said Kirk. "Energize."

The last thing McCoy saw before his vision blurred was Sinclair, heading for the door, in the uncertain gait of a woman who has just realized she's walking through a minefield.

Kyle had done an excellent job of putting them down, Kirk realized, as his vision adjusted to the new setting. They seemed to be in a building of some sort, a cool, cavernous place, with small sounds echoing from all directions. Not a great deal different from the cavern they had left hours ago, but this setting had the advantage of a wider field of vision.

Of course, that could work against us, too, Kirk thought, as he saw the stranger out of the corner of his eye. He wheeled and leveled his phaser, but the same instincts that had so often saved the life of himself and of his crew—the same instincts even Spock valued, while admitting he could not understand them—caused his finger to pause on the activator button.

The stranger was looking right at them, that was obvious, even though he was only silhouetted, but he hadn't moved. "Spock," Kirk whispered, motioning his first officer forward.

"Not human, Captain," said Spock, seconds later. "A statue. Of ancient origin, of the same derivation as those we saw in the Royal Palace."

"Look at them all," whispered Sulu. The structure, which seemed to be a warehouse, seemed to stretch off for nearly an acre; it contained hundreds of statues, each of them as beautiful as those whose beauty Kirk had enjoyed in the palace.

"That might be part of the motive behind this whole mess, Captain," said Giotto, softly. "It wouldn't be the first time a smuggling ring has been behind a plot to upset a government."

Kirk nodded and motioned them forward. The *Enterprise* team crept ahead like a single organism with six tentacles, each one feeling, sensing, examining the terrain ahead before continuing.

"Bones," hissed Kirk. "Any reading on Peter?"

McCoy checked his medical tricorder and nodded. "I'm reading the Deneva parasite factor ahead a couple of hundred meters, inside some sort of other structure."

"Fine," nodded Kirk, "let's—"

"Captain," came Spock's urgent whisper, "I read eleven life-forms, three approaching—"

The beam from the controlled force weapon lanced out of the semi-darkness, burning clear through the load-bearing beam Kirk was behind. The split second gave him enough time to roll clear.

He returned fire, allowing himself a moment to glance over his shoulder. The other five members of the landing party were scattering for cover, looking for posts from which to return fire.

Kirk shook his head ruefully. He had been so concerned for Peter that his first action was to check for his nephew's presence, rather than that of hostiles. That was a good way to get them all killed, Peter included. He let his anger with himself take the form of a stinging beam of phaser 2, flung at a furtive movement in the gloom, but heard nothing strike the floor in response.

Giotto had taken Scotty and Sulu with him and fanned out behind and to one side of the rest of the landing party, deploying them with hand signals.

They prowled noiselessly among the stone forest, watching for moving shadows, occasionally letting off a phaser beam, more often dodging controlled force beams—or trying to. Their progress across the warehouse floor was far slower than it should have been. If Kirk didn't reach Peter before they did . . .

"Captain," hissed Scotty, over the communicator, "Giotto's down."

"On my way," said McCoy, who wasn't far away.

"Blast it," said Kirk, fervently, "they know the terrain, we don't. We can use the statues as cover, but so can they, so there's no—" His voice trailed off.

"Captain?" asked Spock.

"Rule Number One in combat, Spock," said Kirk, adjusting his phaser. "Never let the enemy make the rules." He swept his phaser beam in a wide arc around him, screaming energy meeting and disintegrating any statues it happened to touch.

"Captain," said Spock, in a regretful tone, "are you certain—?"

"I like art as much as the next man, Spock," replied Kirk, "but this is war. Fire."

They advanced, firing at selected statues at random, to avoid giving their enemy a clear idea as to their presence. Around them, random fire came from all sides, the act of desperate people with no other recourse. *They're panicking,* Kirk thought. *That will make them careless—but more dangerous.*

In the cleared path before him, Kirk could see something. It was a gray object, a hut, or—no, a small ship! Its hull, rather than sleekly curving and tapering, was oddly faceted, almost a little clumsy-looking, as though her builders had had nothing to work with but straight pieces. Spock's first supposition was correct: It was this that gave the ship a refractive index of nearly zero, making it virtually invisible to sensors. Right now, one of its flat panels had opened. From a small hatch he could see shadowy forms entering at great haste.

"Come on, Spock!" he shouted. No need for stealth now. Cutting their way through a small cadre of what seemed to be hired thugs, none of them with much of a taste for combat, Kirk neared the ship, making out two rather bulky forms in the gloom.

"Counselors Docos and Hanor," commented Spock.

"I guess there are some issues they're able to reach agreement on," said Kirk, grimly. "This is Kirk!" he shouted, advancing on the small craft. "Drop your weapons!"

From Hanor's meaty hand dropped a small weapon—Kirk doubted if she even knew how to fire it. Her ugly features held a sneer of superiority, even in surrender. "Very well," she croaked.

"I disagree," said Docos, his delicate features, which had always seemed unaccustomed to the ways of diplomacy, seemed far more comfortable here. He tucked his right hand deep into his royal blue robes, seizing Hanor from behind with his left hand. His right hand withdrew, now brandishing an object that glinted in the dim light.

"Docos, let her go," said Kirk. Behind him he could hear the rest of the landing party cautiously approach.

Docos did not seem to have heard Kirk. He looked to one side and slightly behind himself, deeper into the ship, his expression first inquisitive. Then he nodded.

Overhead there was suddenly a great rumbling as a portion of the warehouse ceiling began to roll back, revealing a concealed door. At the same moment, the engines of the small craft began to fire up.

"Let her go!" shouted Kirk, over the whine of the engines.

Docos retreated a few steps more deeply into the ship, the blade still at Hanor's throat. Then he seemed to relent; he stepped forward a little, then abruptly swept the object that glinted in the light across Hanor's throat. She collapsed, shoved forward by Docos at the same time, the steps of his hasty retreat covered by the rumbling of the hatch closing.

"Fire!" said Kirk. The landing party aimed phasers at the vessel and let loose. Energy splashed across the ship, turning its gray hull crimson.

The little craft suddenly seemed to leap off the floor of the warehouse, like a fat toad after a fly. Mounted blasters crumbled the roof, its door still not fully open, and hunks of the ceiling rained around the landing party.

The ship wobbled in the night air for a moment, righted itself, and flew off.

Kirk watched the ship—and with it, Peter—flee into the sky even as he waved McCoy forward to Counselor Hanor.

She was still alive, incredibly. "Don't try to talk," said McCoy, uselessly. She seemed to want to, despite the fact that with each word she bled more freely, a filigree of red bubbles foaming out to mingle with the rusty orange of her robe.

"We formed an alliance," she gasped, then managed a ghastly semblance of a chuckle at her own stupidity. "Docos and I wished to restore power to the old tribes after your starship left . . . the smuggled statuary was a way of attaining funding for we three . . ."

"'We *three*,'" said Kirk, jumping on the admission. "Who, Counselor? You, Docos—and who else?"

But she could say nothing else.

"She's dead, Jim." Her face was as ugly in death as it had been in life, but was now just another gargoyle that had joined a crowd of equally lifeless statuary.

Kirk was already speaking urgently into his communicator, most of his being concentrating on the task at hand, a small part praying, unknown to the rest of him, that it wasn't too late. "Kirk to *Enterprise!* Emergency!"

For a long moment, nothing but static. Then, wending its way through the noise of space:

"Captain, this is Uhura."

"Uhura, reverse course, beam us up as soon as possible! Understood?"

"Yes, sir. We've only just left orbit, I think we have you—"

The next thing Kirk knew was materializing in the transporter room aboard the *Enterprise*. "Spock, Sulu, you're with me," he called, leaping off the pad. "Bones, take care of Giotto."

"I'm not hurt, Captain," said Giotto.

"I'll be the judge of that," said McCoy, firmly.

"Scotty," called Kirk, as he headed out the hatch, "get to engineering, I have a feeling it's going to get rough."

"No surprises *there*," grumbled the Scotsman, dashing out of the transporter room.

"Full sensor spread," ordered Kirk minutes later, as he took the conn. "Maximum dispersion. Screen on."

As Sulu returned to his helm position, he saw that Lieutenant Sherwood was filling in for him. He caught her eye and jerked his head to one side with a little grin. She vacated the chair rapidly, winking at him.

Spock was at his station, hands flying over his console while he peered into his viewer.

"Any sign of them, Spock?"

"Negative, Captain. This ship seems as elusive as their earlier vessel, and they will doubtless have learned to compensate for the strategy that proved successful then."

"There's at least one difference between this ship and the old one," said Kirk. "We put a pretty good crease in the hull of this one. That may give us their scent."

"Indeed." Spock was back at his console, as naturally as if it had been an extension of himself, adjusting for this new variable. "Such relative ease in detection was one of the prime factors in Starfleet's abandonment of refractive hulls to attain stealth technique. The index of refraction must be so precisely calculated that damage from battle or even meteors can disable the system. If the refractive dissonance is sufficient, we may be able to . . ." A pause. "I have them, Captain. Putting them on screen now."

A small, glowing speck flashed into existence above Nador, and heading away fast. "Intercept course," said Kirk. "Battle stations. Go to red alert. Spock, have they seen us?"

"I do not believe so, Captain. Though they are beginning to pick up speed, their course is continuous along a straight line, indicating that hurry rather than stealth is their main objective."

"Neither will be enough," murmured Kirk, grimly. "Raise shields."

"Captain, I'm receiving a hail from them."

"On screen," said Kirk, though he had a sinking feeling he knew the upshot of any communiqué they would wish to send.

"Captain Kirk," came the voice of Counselor Docos, a moment before his face appeared on the viewscreen. *"How good of you to supply us with an escort. Not that we'll need one once we leave our solar system. Privacy, you know."*

"Escort?" Kirk laughed, contemptuously. "Back to the planet, certainly. To either a Federation jail or a Nadorian prison—that's a jurisdictional dispute I don't care to get involved in."

"I said 'escort,'" repeated Docos, with a confidence that told Kirk he was not only aware of the ace up his sleeve, but willing to exploit it. *"We have your nephew."*

"So you do," said Kirk, in what he hoped was a sufficiently casual tone. "And I'm giving you a chance to surrender and turn him over. Such an action on your part will be noted on our records, and may work in your favor at your trial—"

"And if you don't let us go, he will die," said Docos, coldly.

At least it's out in the open now, thought Kirk. *No more dancing around it.* Despite the stakes, there was always something to be said for knowing exactly where you stood.

"I wouldn't recommend that," said Kirk, smiling grimly.

To his surprise, Docos laughed. *"I'm sure you wouldn't, Captain, but you'll forgive me if, as captain of this ship, I choose my own strategies."*

"Choose any strategy you like," replied Kirk. He rose from the conn and walked to the viewscreen, hands crossed behind him. "But know that I will not allow anyone—including my own flesh and blood—to be used as a hostage."

"But . . ." Docos seemed taken aback by this, as if talking to an obstinate child who refused to understand. *"But I'll kill him."*

"At which point," said Spock, "you will no longer have any hold over the captain."

Bless you Spock, thought Kirk. "And at which point," said Kirk, emphasizing each word carefully, "I will no longer be inclined to negotiate. That's my counsel . . . Counselor."

Docos turned to look at someone beside him on the small bridge, and shouted something. Before his syllables could fade, his image vanished.

"They're fleeing, sir," said Sulu. "Doubling their speed."

"Right after them," said Kirk, returning to the conn.

"I hope Counselor Docos is a logical man," said Spock.

"That makes two of us," said Kirk, taking a deep breath.

In sickbay, Prince Abon moved the pawn into position. "Check and mate," he said. "Another game?"

"No," said Prince Delor. He rose and stretched, a moment passing before he realized he had very nearly gotten used to the ability to rise and stretch on his own. "I'm bored," he said, with the conviction of one who had always been surrounded by persons whose job it was to relieve that ennui.

"So am I," said Abon, "but it won't do any good to dwell on it."

"And the back of my neck itches worse than ever," said Delor. "It even burns a little—" He stopped in midsentence, realizing the import of his words, and looked at his twin, whose expression, commingling shock and horror, mirrored his exactly.

They reached for the button to summon Dr. McCoy at the same time, but Delor got there first.

"Closing, sir," said Sulu.

"Their status?"

"Raising shields, but not arming weapons," said Spock, after a moment.

"Prepare tractor beam," said Kirk. *By God, it worked, it—*

At that moment, the *Enterprise* was shaken by a blow whose percussive force rang throughout the entire ship.

"What was that?" asked Kirk, quickly. "Have they fired?"

"No, sir," said Spock. "I have the source of the assault on screen."

The image on the screen shifted and Kirk saw, to his horror, another of the roiling psionic storms hovering before them, its mass underneath its surface shot through with power, as it loosed another bolt at them.

Chapter Seventeen

"McCOY!" SHOUTED KIRK, stabbing a button on his console. "What the devil's going on down there?"

"I warned you!" crackled back McCoy's voice. *"The twins can't control it, Jim, and—"*

"What about that neural link of yours?" A new tremor shook the ship, stronger than before. Kirk could see damage-report lights winking to life on Uhura's board.

"Will you let me finish? The neural link burned out as soon as the storm appeared again, and just replacing it won't do any damn good."

"Then try drugs, or—"

"I'm already running some tests on some simulations. McCoy out."

"All power to shields," said Kirk. "Try to keep the Nadorian ship in range."

"That won't be difficult, sir," said Sulu, as the ship shivered again. *That wasn't a blast from the storm,* thought Kirk.

"Photon torpedoes, Captain," supplied Spock, as Kirk turned to him. "From Counselor Docos's ship."

"Bastard," said Kirk, his tone half-admiring. Most

petty thugs would have taken advantage of such an interruption by just running, and hoping the *Enterprise* couldn't catch them. Beneath Counselor Docos's robes, however, seemed to beat a gambler's heart.

A fact, Kirk thought grimly, *I hope to be able to confirm personally.*

"Ready a fusillade of photon torpedoes," said Kirk.

"Photon torpedoes ready, Captain," said Chekov, a moment later. "Shall I—?"

"Fire on my orders only," said Kirk, sharply. "Fire them one at a time, and while doing so, maneuver the *Enterprise* so *their* ship is between us and the storm. We'll see if we can get one of our enemies to do our work for us. Clear?"

"Yes, sir," said Sulu, admiringly. Kirk saw him exchanging an expectant glance with Chekov.

"Use maneuvering thrusters if you have to," said Kirk, feeling the ship rumble again through the arms of his chair. "Nice and slow—but not too slow. Begin maneuvering," beneath him he felt the *Enterprise* move again, this time a steady, controlled motion, "and fire."

Photon torpedoes lanced at the enemy ship several times over the next couple of minutes, doing little damage, but apparently keeping Docos from realizing that the *Enterprise* was slowly but surely changing its position, forcing the Nadorian ship to do so also.

"Another attack from the storm, Captain," reported Spock, unnecessarily, as the ship shuddered.

"Maneuvering complete, Captain," announced Sulu. On the screen, Kirk nodded tightly; he could see Docos's ship some distance away, and beyond it the storm cloud, boiling like the surface of a new sun.

"I am reading increased energy emissions from the storm," said Spock.

"Hold on to something," said Kirk, "and hope."

The storm erupted suddenly, discharging another burst of psionic energy. Faster than it would take to describe it, Kirk saw the tendrils leap out toward Docos's ship.

Then they gracefully curved *around* Docos's ship, to collide head-on with the *Enterprise.*

Over the collision, Scotty's voice came from the intercom. *"We can't take much more of this, sir."*

"Understood, Scotty, I'll try to get you some relief." Clicking off, Kirk turned to Spock. "Get to sickbay. Do *something.* If the princes are generating those storms, stop them any way you can, short of killing them."

"Moving one to a sufficiently distant venue might prove effective," said Spock, as the deck shook beneath him anew. "The distance within which their psionic powers function cannot be infinite."

"Too much distance, not enough time," said Kirk, shaking his head. "We need another option."

"Understood," said Spock, as the turbolift door closed behind him.

"Why?" Kirk muttered to himself, as he paced the bridge. "Why did Docos turn to fight?"

"Even a Cossack would turn to fight if something he loved was endangered," said Chekov.

"Mr. Chekov," said Kirk, after a few seconds, "remind me to put you in for a raise." He hammered one of the console buttons on his chair. "Kirk to cargo hold."

"Lieutenant Sinclair here, sir," came a clear, cool voice from the intercom.

"Lieutenant," said Kirk, slowly and clearly, "listen carefully, I'm only going to have time to say this once. . . ."

* * *

"What the devil do you think you're doing?"

Their Serene Highnesses Princes Abon and Delor looked up, guiltily. "Nothing," said Delor, unconvincingly.

"This is 'nothing'?" asked McCoy. He charged between the twins, seizing the hypospray that lay on the counter before them, and examining its contents. "I thought so. This is tetralubisol." He turned to face the twins angrily. "I don't know how this got here, but if you had used the hypospray, it would have— Oh." He shook his head, even more angry, and barely trusting himself to speak. "No. There's got to be another way. I don't believe in martyrs."

"It's your fault," said Abon, to Delor. "If we had only been able to decide—"

"How can you 'decide' something like that?" asked McCoy, disposing of the toxic lubricant. "What did you do, draw straws?"

"We flipped a coin," said Abon, pointing to a golden circlet on the counter before them. "But we forgot something."

Another tremor shook the ship as McCoy picked up the coin. Despite the tension, he smiled.

On one side of the coin was the face of Prince Abon—or was it Prince Delor? On its obverse was the face of Prince Delor—or was it Prince Abon?

The door hissed open and McCoy looked up. "Doctor," said Spock, "I have come to assist you."

"With these two," said McCoy, "even you may not be enough."

"Are you ready, Mr. Sulu?" asked Kirk, over the protestations of the ship as it was struck anew. *She can't take much more of this,* thought Kirk. *None of us can.*

"Aye, sir," said Sulu, in a baffled tone. "Phasers are ready."

"Fire," said Kirk. A phaser beam snaked onto the screen, barely perceptible, narrowed as it was to a beam of pinpoint accuracy.

"Keep us steady," said Kirk. "Keep hammering the same position on their shields."

"We're through, sir," said Sulu, a few seconds later.

"Kirk to cargo hold—activate cargo transporters *now.* Sulu—*drop all shields!*"

Sulu touched the deflector shields' override button on his console, his finger trembling only a little in the process.

Deprived of shields, the *Enterprise* shook even worse under the dual hammerings from the storm and the enemy's weapons. On the screen, Kirk could see both foes before him, as if deliberate allies, united in a single cause.

Then, suddenly, it happened. Another bunch of energy tendrils shot out from the storm, almost lazily, past the Nadorian ship, toward the *Enterprise*—

—then stopped, and doubled back, striking Docos's ship dead center.

"Captain," said Chekov, with a gasp. "What—?"

"We've got the advantage for once," said Kirk, "let's not lose it. Keep pounding them. Sulu, raise shields."

"Ayc, sir." They were still reeling a little from the weapons of Docos's ship, but having that storm off their backs was a big help. Now the *Enterprise* used the psionic storm as an ally, hammering the Nadorian ship between bursts from the roiling mass behind it.

"Their shields are down, sir," said Sulu, seconds later.

"About time," said Kirk, punching a button on his console. "Transporter room, scan the enemy ship and lock on my nephew."

"Can't, sir," crackled back Kyle's voice. "Too much radiation from the other ship."

"Understood, Kirk out." He thought for a moment, then turned to the console again. "Bones, we're paying a visit to the other ship—uninvited. Join the party."

"But . . . the storm is still active, Jim."

"I know," Kirk replied grimly. "And tell Spock to pull some miracle out of his ears, quickly. We're going to be right on the bull's-eye.

"Ship to ship," Kirk said, tersely. "Counselor Docos, this is Kirk. Surrender or prepare to be boarded."

The image on the screen rolled and popped in and out before finally focusing on Docos. Had it not been for the voice, Kirk wouldn't have recognized him; his features were taut and grim, his face streaked with blood and smoke.

But the old defiance was there. "Go to hell, Kirk. Earth or Nadorian—I don't care which." Then the screen went dead.

"Sir," said Sulu, "he's activated a self-destruct device. I read a five-minute fuse on it."

"Then we'd better do this quickly," Kirk said, matter-of-factly. "Uhura, you have the conn. Sulu, you're with me."

This time it was Chekov who gave Sulu a sympathetic glance.

"Damage report, Sinclair?" asked Lieutenant Kevin Riley.

"Only my pride," replied Sinclair, glumly.

"I heard," Riley said sympathetically, leaning against

the console in the cargo hold. "Kirk benched you just as you were about to suit up, huh?"

"If that means what I think it does, yes," said Sinclair. "It wasn't so much that he did it, it was that he didn't have any reason for doing it. And in front of the others . . ." She shook her head and shrugged helplessly. "If I just knew what it is I'd done. A fine career with Starfleet I've got." She sighed. "Just once, I would have liked to sit at the helm."

"Now listen here, my fine colleen," said Riley, ratcheting his Irish accent up a notch or two. "The same thing happened to me last year. I found myself ordered to report to the depths of the ship, and I spent half my time wondering if it was my fault."

Sinclair looked up at his narrow face inquisitively. "But didn't Kirk do that because—?"

"Because he wanted me out of the way," said Riley, "that's right. And I'll bet it'll turn out he's got a good reason for the way he treated you, too. Believe me, Kirk wouldn't discipline one of his crew without letting them know why."

"Maybe so," she said, with a slow nod. Then she looked up and smiled. A rather wan smile, but better than nothing. "Thanks for coming down, Riley."

The accent was back when he asked, "Could I do anything less for my favorite blonde?"

Sinclair eyed him critically. "I thought Sherwood was your favorite blonde."

"Ah, she's my favorite *strawberry* blonde," said Riley, with a twinkle in his eye, "but you're my favorite blonde."

Sinclair chuckled and went back to her damage report, her efficiency somewhat impaired by trying to determine why the captain had ordered those specific contents of the cargo hold beamed over to the enemy ship.

* * *

"Has Spock found a way to stop that storm yet?" asked Kirk, as McCoy entered the transporter room.

"Not yet," said McCoy, strapping on a weapons belt and taking his place on the pad. "Maybe with us over there, it'll give him a little incentive."

"Four minutes, thirty seconds, sir," said Sulu.

"It's almost like Spock never left," said McCoy, dryly.

"Scotty, keep a lock on us at all times. Be ready for immediate retrieval."

"I'll try, Captain," said Scotty, who was waiting in the transporter room when Kirk arrived, "but with all that radiation flyin' around, I canna make any promises."

"I wish you'd lie about our chances, just once," said Kirk, with a sigh. "Energize."

The interior of Counselor Docos's ship was consistent with Nadorian architecture, Kirk noted. Not that it was of much help.

But the halls had an unfinished look; some of the walls were bare of paneling, leaving conduits and wiring exposed, indicating that this model had been brought online perhaps before it was quite ready.

"What do they power this ship with, coal?" asked McCoy dryly. The hand he drew through the air left a trail behind it. "I don't think there's supposed to be this much smoke in the air."

"They're going down and fast," said Sulu. "This ship might not even make it through the self-destruct countdown."

"Then the need for haste stands," replied Kirk. "Bones, anything on the tricorder?"

"At this close a range . . . yes, I'm getting something," said McCoy, peering at the instrument. "Down the corridor, deeper into the ship."

"Watch out for the crew," said Kirk, cautiously edging his way down a hall. "They won't be in any mood to receive visitors."

But as they rounded a corridor, the first thing they saw were four crew members, both of the hard-bitten sort that made such effective thugs. "Hands up," said Kirk.

They whipped around to the unfamiliar voice and saw the Starfleet personnel, hands beginning to bring weapons to bear. Kirk was prepared for a fight, until he saw their faces, which reflected an amalgam of uncertainty and spacesickness. It occurred to Kirk that they might never have been off-planet before.

Their hands continued rising, over their heads. "We surrender," said one, in a liquid tone that indicated that he had either recently been sick to his stomach or soon would be.

"Weapons on the deck," said Kirk, "then we'll talk."

"You've got to take us with you," said the other. "This ship can't last much longer."

They probably don't know about the self-destruct mechanism, thought Kirk. *So much for only the captain going down with his ship.*

"We'll do what we can," said Kirk. "No promises."

The first made a sound of outrage that was somewhere between a roar and a gurgling noise, diving for his weapon as he did so. The boarding party brought their own weapons up, just as the ship was shaken from side to side by a fresh tantrum from the storm. Kirk was thrown to the deck, Sulu, McCoy, and the crew with him.

"Mr. Spock!" gasped Nurse Chapel. "Can you stop the—?"

"I am aware of my responsibilities, Nurse," replied Spock, entering the surgical room behind McCoy's office. There sat the Princes Abon and Delor, uneasily riding out the storm and, from their expressions, not much liking it.

They've probably never been in such danger, Chapel realized. *An assassin after you is one thing. That's a definable menace. But a storm like this one, a sample of the universe's fury* . . . Yet they were trying not to show what must have been their quite real terror.

"Your Serene Highnesses," said Spock, half-bowing to the monarchs in a way that seemed abbreviated, yet fully respectful.

"Mr. Spock," said Delor, giving a smile that more closely resembled a rictus, "I fear we have not yet had a chance to have our chat concerning Nadorian logic."

"I may still have the pleasure of such a discussion," said Spock, "once these circumstances have reached their conclusion."

"Provided Delor and I are around to see that conclusion," said Abon, in a small voice.

"Your Highness, I am under orders to see that just that event occurs," replied Spock. He moved a chair to a position not far from Prince Delor's. "Will you please be seated?"

Abon slowly began to lower himself into the chair, never taking his eyes off Spock. He nearly stumbled as the fury of the psionic storm lashed out at the *Enterprise* anew, but regained his bearings quickly.

"Sickbay's stores are at your disposal, Mr. Spock," said Chapel, from the doorway. "Dr. McCoy thought you might want to fashion a new kind of neural depressant, or—"

"Unfortunately, Nurse, there is no time for such

experimentation," replied Spock. "However, you may be of service by assuring Their Serene Highnesses and I are undisturbed—"

"Of course, Mr. Spock."

"—even by yourself."

"Of course, sir." Chapel pulled a seat to her and sat down. After all, he hadn't said anything about leaving. From her vantage point, Spock's back was to her, Prince Abon to his left, Prince Delor to his right. He had a plan—he always had a plan—but what it was, Nurse Chapel had no idea. Spock seemed to be gathering himself, to be meditating, his hands raised before him, as if . . .

Suddenly, Spock's left hand, fingers splayed, neared the face of Prince Abon with a speed that nearly defied description, but a self-assuredness that did not startle the monarch.

"Prince Abon—my mind to your mind, your thoughts to my thoughts," he began.

Chapel began to gasp, but caught it. She wanted to remain, now more so than ever, as she realized the strategy he was undertaking—and its risk.

"Prince Delor," said Spock, his voice ringing stoically in the walls of sickbay, "my mind to your mind . . . your thoughts . . . to my thoughts . . ."

Chapel always worried when Spock performed the Vulcan mind-meld, knowing there was a chance, however small, that the mind he entered might become inextricably mingled with his own, rendering both subjects permanently demented—or worse.

But to meld with two subjects at once? Chapel had never heard of it being done and had certainly never seen such a thing done. Yet as Spock's fingers touched the faces of the young princes, seemingly joined to their flesh, as their minds were being joined, she realized their only chance lay in Spock's ability to . . . to "reconjoin" the princes mentally, as they had been once conjoined physically, using himself as the conduit.

Rather than scrabble around for his phaser, which was what they expected him to do, Kirk simply launched himself at the crewmen, sprawling into the four of them at once. Sulu and McCoy took the hint, joining the ungainly fray as the ship's deck danced under them from the storm's fury.

Kirk had his hands around one thug's wrists, holding him back, though not for long. The thug's struggles slowly relaxed, as if exhausted. Kirk released his grip slightly, then threw himself to one side. As expected, the crewman, thinking he had caught Kirk off-guard, lunged toward him, trying to hammer Kirk's forehead with his. Instead, the thug's forehead collided with that of another crewman who was sneaking up behind Kirk, causing a sharp crack that was audible even over the groaning of the ship.

The two sank to the floor as Kirk rose, to see Sulu and McCoy dusting themselves off, their foes unconscious at their feet. "I'm getting too old for this," said McCoy with a grumble.

Sulu glanced at his tricorder. "Not unless we're gone in one and a half minutes, you won't."

They tore down the hall, McCoy and his medical tricorder in the lead.

"Here," said McCoy. "Peter's in here, Jim."

The door to the cabin was swinging back and forth as the ship convulsed, a sign Kirk didn't like. He edged toward it from the side, pushing it open. "Peter?" he asked.

His instincts saved him again; he dodged to the right, narrowly avoiding a beam of controlled force. Kirk thrust his phaser forward and said, "Drop it, Docos."

Then he saw that the muzzle of the weapon was now securely placed against Peter's left temple. Kirk remembered that scene for a long time; Peter's left arm bore a long, jagged wound where the subcutaneous transponder had been removed with less than a surgeon's skill. Counselor Docos stood behind Peter, his stubby legs set wide apart to maintain his balance, his body reeling slightly back and forth with its own interior motion as the ship rocked. *He must have been a sailing man,* thought Kirk. "Let him go, Docos," said Kirk.

"This time I'm calling your bluff, Captain," growled Docos. His face was smudged with smoke, but the hatred in his gaze came through just fine. "Drop your weapons, or he will die."

"Don't do it, Uncle Jim," said Peter. He tried for defiance, but all he could manage was a whisper.

"Try me," said Docos. "I don't even have to aim, anyone I hit is an enemy."

"It doesn't have to end this way, Docos," said Kirk.

"It won't," replied Docos, his eyes briefly fixed on something far away. Then they focused again on Kirk. "Weapons down."

"Uhura!" said Chekov. "Look!"

"I can see it, Chekov." Uhura leaned forward in the conn. The storm had begun to shrink, to diminish like a puddle of rainwater in the summer sun. It continued to withdraw in upon itself, until it winked out of existence entirely.

"Drop shields," said Uhura, immediately. "All power to transporters." She tapped a stud on the arm of the captain's chair. "Mr. Scott, any sign of the Captain?"

"Not yet," came Scotty's fervent voice, *"and they've only got thirty seconds left."*

Kirk nodded to McCoy and Sulu. He kneeled slowly, hands spread wide, placing his phaser on the floor, as his men followed his example.

Then, suddenly, the surging of the beleaguered ship ceased.

Counselor Docos, used to the deck's constant dance, was taken off-balance by Peter, who shifted to one side and knocked Docos's weapon out of his hand. Before it hit the ground, Kirk was on him.

"Now, Docos," said Kirk, "I want a name. *Who's behind this?"*

Kirk felt a sudden, odd burning in his arm, and jerked away, in time to see the stiletto-like blade Docos had whipped from beneath his robes narrowly miss his right eye. "Stay away!" he shrieked.

"Captain, ten seconds!" shouted Sulu.

Kirk stepped toward Docos, expecting an attack, but not the one that transpired. Docos brought the blade, shining with blood, up, reversed it, and neatly skewered his own throat.

"Scotty," Kirk shouted, to his communicator, "four to beam, *now!* And the cargo, too!" He felt the deck begin to buckle under him and thought that, for once, he had cut it too fine, that the odds had finally caught up with him, that the gods of chance had, at long last, turned their backs on him. . . .

The next thing he knew he was in the transporter room on the *Enterprise,* looking at Scotty, who was taking air in in long gasps, as if he'd just run a marathon.

Kirk wheeled around, saw McCoy, Sulu . . . and

Peter. Uncertain whether he wanted to club him or hug him, Kirk settled for the latter. Plenty of time for the former later.

"How about that move?" Peter was saying, as Kirk moved across the transporter room. "Pretty good, huh? You taught me that!"

Kirk grinned back as he accessed the small viewscreen set in the transporter room wall. On it, the Nadorian ship was being swallowed up in a fireball that grew from within itself, like a sort of ravaging disease that consumed its host from within.

"Kirk to Spock," said Kirk, into the intercom.

"Spock here, Captain."

"However you shut off the storm, good work."

"Thank you, sir. However, I cannot guarantee how long the results will remain effective."

"Then we'd better get this over with. Meet me here as soon as you can."

"Understoo—"

"Not so fast," said McCoy. "You're not going anywhere until I take a look at that arm."

Kirk looked behind him and saw a trail of red droplets from the transporter pad to the console. "Peter, are you hurt?"

"It's not me, Uncle Jim," said Peter.

Kirk looked at his tunic and saw a red stain growing across his left arm, much like the explosion that swallowed the Nadorian ship. He leaned against the console; suddenly he did feel a little tired.

"Make it five minutes, Spock."

Chapter Eighteen

"I'M SORRY, CAPTAIN," said Uhura, some minutes later. "There's no response."

"You're sure?" asked Kirk, unconsciously scratching the new skin over his wound. "You tried the exact same frequency the smugglers used before . . . ?"

"The frequency is precisely the same, Captain," said Spock, looking up from the monitor at his bridge position, "as is the strength and duration of the signal. It would be logical to assume that the person you seek to involve is aware of the death of Counselor Docos as well as the explosion of the smuggling ship, and has therefore become aware of your intent."

Kirk nodded, bitterly. He had hoped that by broadcasting on the frequency the smugglers had used before, that one specific party would respond, said involvement leading to capture and evidence for a conviction.

"Sometimes," he said, making light of his disappointment, "they just don't play by the rules."

"But there must be something we can do," said McCoy. "There's all the evidence—"

"None of which is conclusive, Doctor," said Spock, inexorably. "Another stratagem will have to be devised. Logic indicates—"

"Not logic, Mr. Spock," said Kirk, suddenly snapping his fingers. "Emotion is the key here." He turned and began to stride to the turbolift, then stopped halfway and looked behind him. "Coming, gentlemen?"

"The last time I saw that look in your eye, you came up with corbomite," said McCoy with a grin, as he joined Kirk. "I wouldn't miss this for the world."

Spock sighed. "I must confess to being curious."

When they materialized in the throne room of the Royal Palace, Kirk saw that everyone whose presence he had requested was there: Regent Lonal, trying to look as though he belonged on the throne; Commissioner and Janine Roget, the commissioner looking somewhat harried, as the end of the smuggling ring had produced a flurry of calls from diverse officials on and off planet; Chief Securitrix Llora, who stood just to one side and behind Regent Lonal, whether to keep him safe or to keep him honest Kirk wasn't quite sure; and the Lady Pataal, who finally seemed to have stopped crying, but whose countenance still looked entirely too mournful for such an attractive young woman.

"Captain," said Lonal, stiffly.

"Prince Lonal," said Kirk, half-bowing to the regent, giving the first word a faint, sardonic emphasis. Then Kirk turned to greet the others, all of whom save Llora were seated.

"There still remains some unfinished business to this affair," began Kirk.

"'Some'?" scoffed Llora. "Our monarchs have been

assassinated, one of the highest members of government has been revealed to be responsible, and another is also one of his victims. I think your way with an understatement is wonderful, Captain."

Kirk did not rise to the bait, but nodded, gallantly. "Nonetheless, the sooner we start, the sooner we'll be done." He took out his communicator. "Kirk to *Enterprise.*"

"Scott here, Captain."

"Beam down that cargo we discussed, Mr. Scott."

"Aye, sir."

Kirk broke contact, put his communicator away, and waited. For a long moment, nothing happened. Then the trilling of the transporter signal hit the range audible to humans and two columns of light began to coalesce a few feet to one side of Kirk.

Lonal, of course, already knew the secret. On three of the other four faces were reflected nothing but pure astonishment. But across the fifth, almost too briefly to be perceived, played first a mask of pure dread and horror, then, oddly, one of relief, before the lid clamped down, before a savage instinct said: *It's not over yet.*

But that moment of animal terror had not gone unperceived by Kirk. Deep within his being, he smiled. *This might work.*

"I give you," said Kirk, "Their Serene Highnesses, Prince Abon and Prince Delor."

The princes stood there for a moment, hands behind their backs, as they surveyed the room.

Then Delor said: "We will be needing another throne, Lonal."

Lonal shot out of the chair as if it had been electrified. No one else moved.

Then the Lady Pataal rose, her motion causing the

dumbstruck Rogets to realize their gaffe; they imitated her movement.

The young woman walked to within a few feet of the princes, curtsying deeply. Her head was down, giving no clue as to her mental state.

Then she rose, approached Prince Abon, and, in violation of all protocol, gave the young monarch a kiss on the cheek, the joy radiating from her face belying the tears that flowed down it.

"Your Highnesses," stammered Lonal, "we are of course delighted to see you alive and well."

"Thank you, *Regent*," said Abon, giving every impression of actually buying it. "It is good to be back." His eyes swept across the room, including the young woman before him, and he smiled and breathed deeply.

"But how can this be?" asked Commissioner Roget. "Or, more to the point, why?"

"An excellent question, Commissioner," nodded Kirk. "It was part of a ruse, naturally, to draw fire away from the princes. Once the conspirator thought them dead, they were no longer targeted for assassination."

Around the room, heads nodded. "It obviously worked," said Mrs. Roget.

"And very well," said Kirk. "For a time, the conspirator, thinking the princes dead, returned to the original goal."

"But," said Prince Delor, "I thought our deaths were the conspirator's goal."

"That's where we all went wrong," said Kirk, striding back and forth across the throne room. "In thinking social upset was the main goal." He grinned at the monarchs, shrugging apologetically. "I'm sorry to have to tell you, Your Highnesses, that your deaths were a secondary part of the plan—but I'm delighted to be able to tell you."

"Then what was this so-called original goal?" asked Lonal, a little color returning to his face.

"Nothing more than old-fashioned financial gain," said Kirk. "The deaths of Princes Abon and Delor, the toppling of the throne, the involvement of the Federation, all these placed distant second on the conspirator's agenda."

"You keep speaking of 'the conspirator,'" said Roget, irritably. "It was Counselor Docos . . . wasn't it?"

"It was not, Commissioner," said Spock. "Docos possessed neither the wit nor the will to conceive and execute such a plan. He did, however, make an able henchman, before a reversal of fortune, as well as fear of exposure and imprisonment, led him to a quite unnecessary suicide."

"The conspirator's plan was, as noted, nothing more than financial gain," said Kirk. "It was assumed the smuggling of Nadorian statuary off the planet was a way of financing the overthrow of the throne. In fact, it was quite the other way around: the attempted overthrow of the throne distracted attention from the smuggling ring."

"But this smuggling ring seems to have been quite inefficient," said Llora. "Their first ship was destroyed by you, when you first approached the planet, and no fragments of statuary were found. . . ."

"I theorize that the ship was either returning from delivering smuggled statuary to its distributors," supplied Spock, "or the smugglers were able to transport the statuary, as well."

"And when Docos tried to escape," continued Llora,

"your report said he did not attempt to take any statuary with him."

"That was what led me to the truth," nodded Kirk. "When Docos tried to escape, why *didn't* he take any of the statues with him? His initial intent wasn't to attack us; his ship didn't turn to face the *Enterprise* until he was almost away. He clearly intended to leave Nador forever, so nothing in his past life would have been of any use to him. Surely the statues would have been a great financial help to him in starting a new life, elsewhere in the galaxy. But he didn't take them with him."

"Well, Captain?" asked Commissioner Roget.

"He didn't," said Kirk, "because he knew the statuary was dangerous."

"Dangerous?" asked Lonal, intrigued despite himself. His eyes kept going back and forth to the princes, as though he expected them to take a swing at him. "Their possession was dangerous because it was stolen material, yes, but—"

"For more than legal reasons," Kirk interrupted. "Their very possession was physically dangerous to him. Why? Look what happened when another of the psychic storms manifested itself. The storm attacked the *Enterprise,* but left the smugglers' ship untouched, even though it was as close to the storm as we were, sometimes closer.

"It occurred to me," said Kirk, "that perhaps the sites the storms chose to strike were *not* random, as we at first thought. There may be an excellent reason why the storms struck the sites they did. When we were under assault up there, I ran through the list of locales where the storms attacked—Spock?"

"The *U.S.S. Enterprise,*" began the science officer,

without consulting a list, "the Royal Palace of Nador, the Nadonan Heritage Museum, the Nadorian Art Students' League—"

"Thank you, Mr. Spock, that will be sufficient. 'Why,' I asked myself, during combat, 'did the storm assault *these* locations particularly?' The answer: Because all of them contained ancient Nadorian statuary."

"But—" began Securitrix Llora.

Kirk held up a hand, silencing her. "But why should those areas be struck by the storm? Well, we knew that the storm itself was created by the unleashed psionic potential of the formerly conjoined princes. In fact, that's why the princes were conjoined, to contain that psionic potential. Is it possible that the statues, which were created by the psionic abilities of former generations of Nadorian sculptors, still held some affinity for other psionic manifestations? That the storms were drawn by the statuary?"

Kirk shrugged and gave that disarmingly boyish smile which he had learned to use so well over the years. "I didn't *know,* of course. I couldn't be certain. But the odds were against us at that point." He gave a glance at Spock. "I didn't even have the time to check my theory with my science officer; I was willing to take a chance on almost anything to save my ship.

"So I transported some crates over to Docos's craft from the *Enterprise,* and that seemed to have done the trick. The storms ignored us, and began attacking him. Docos took none of the Nadorian statuary with him, because he was conversant with your peoples' history of psionic abilities and figured out the connection long before I did. Any doubts he may have had were dispelled when the energy bolts from the storm circled around his ship to attack *us*. And that's when my suspicions were confirmed, too."

"But, Captain," said Prince Delor, "if this supposition of yours was true . . ."

" . . . your ship would had to have been carrying Nadorian statuary!" said Prince Abon, cutting in.

"I was going to say that!" said Delor.

"That's exactly right, Your Highnesses," said Kirk with a nod. "The *Enterprise* was carrying Nadorian statuary. I should have realized this when I recalled that the first storm attacked the cargo hold. I assumed the storm was a kind of weapon, that it was being directed against the princes . . . but what if it was instead drawn to Nadorian statuary *in* the hold?"

"But that is forbidden," said Regent Lonal indignantly, now on firmer ground. "Ancient Nadorian statuary cannot be removed from the planet without a valid export permit. Captain, is your Federation in the habit of trafficking in stolen goods?"

"Certainly not," said Kirk, "all cargo transported aboard the *Enterprise* is automatically scanned to prevent just that—except in one case," said Kirk, surveying the crowd. "In the case," he said, "of cargo being shipped under the seal of diplomatic immunity."

And all heads turned, like iron filings drawn by a magnet, to look at Federation Commissioner Sylvan Roget.

"Captain, I assure you, none of our personal goods contained smuggled Nadorian statuary. . . ."

"Kirk to *Enterprise*," said Kirk, into his communicator. "Energize, Mr. Scott."

Again the air tingled and solidified, this time into a large crate bearing a number of Federation stamps and secured with a single impressive-looking gold seal.

"Examine it, Commissioner," said Kirk. "Is the seal on that crate secured with your authorization?"

"It is," said Roget, "but I still maintain—"

"Then open it," said Kirk, in the same inexorable tone.

Roget looked around the room, shrugged, and approached the crate. He punched an authorization code into the small pad on the crate's side, and said, "Roget, Sylvan, Federation Commissioner. Authorization A-four."

The seal parted and the crate's sides fell open, revealing what most observers at first took to be a pair of human beings, so realistically were the contours of the forms fashioned. But then light struck the forms fully, revealing them to be a pair of statues of a handsome, godlike man and a young girl, the god handing the girl a small, four-winged bird, two figures Kirk took to be from Nadorian mythology.

"*The Bestowment of Conscience,*" gasped the Lady Pataal. "That was thought lost for years."

"And we know where it was, don't we, Commissioner?" asked Kirk.

"Kirk, I know nothing of this—" said Roget. For the first time since Kirk had met him, he seemed at a loss for words, even undignified.

"The evidence says otherwise, Commissioner," said Spock. "Such a violation of trust, not to mention of your Federation oath, will surely mean a trial, perhaps even a sentence to a penal colony."

"But I didn't—"

"Then who?" demanded Kirk. "The fact that whoever was behind Peter's kidnapping knew to look for a subcutaneous transponder pointed to someone with Federation training, someone who knew we might try such a strategy. If not you, who, Commissioner?"

"I don't know, but it wasn't—"

"He's telling the truth," cut in another, sharper voice. Mrs. Roget stepped forward, her voice louder than Kirk had ever heard it. "It's not his fault, it's mine. It was my idea, my plan."

"Janine?" said her husband, looking at her as if seeing her for the first time. "But our duty . . ."

"Your duty, Sylvan, not mine," she said emphatically, shaking her head. "An ambassador's pension is nothing, these days . . . not after the way we've been living, all these years. I just wanted to create a nest egg for our retirement. With your contacts in the palace, it wasn't difficult. It wasn't until after the first ship was intercepted that I got the idea of sending out the statues under your diplomatic seal." She smiled, nostalgically, as if at a time decades gone. "You always left all those details to me."

"Your 'nest egg' nearly hatched a civil war," said McCoy, indignantly.

"I never intended any of that," said Mrs. Roget, shaking her head. "After I brought that fool Docos into it, he recruited Counsclor Hanor, and they began acting on their own, advancing their own 'cause.' I knew what they were doing, but by then I couldn't stop them. I tried to, but they said they'd bring Sylvan down with them. . . ." Streaks of what looked like silver began running down her cheeks. Then she stopped, wiped her face, smoothed back a few strands of errant hair, and drew herself to her full height. "But it wasn't Sylvan's fault. Let his record remain clear. It was mine." Her left hand tentatively began creeping up her husband's arm, like a small animal that is afraid of rejection.

But Sylvan Roget seized her hand strongly, yet tenderly. "We'll face this together, dearest," he said. "Captain, as the ranking Federation representative present, we turn ourselves over to you."

"Accepted," said Kirk, his voice like steel. To have shown them any sympathy, any pity, he knew, would have been more than they could bear. He turned his back on them as he took out his communicator. "Kirk to *Enterprise*. Five to beam up. . . ."

Chapter Nineteen

Captain's Log, Stardate 3375.6

Few missions, I confess, have left me with emotions as mixed as those of this assignment on Nador. I am glad to have prevented the assassination of a planet's monarchs, but saddened by the cost to the Federation of a loyal and valued member of its diplomatic corps, through no fault of his own. The handover ceremony went as planned—for a welcome change—and the Nadorian people have been officially admitted to the Federation. Captain Konstantin of the *Potemkin* has been notified that the troops he is transporting will not be needed.

"THERE IS ONE MORE MATTER left to be resolved, Your Highnesses," said Spock.

Both Princes Abon and Delor nodded, seated in the old throne from which they delivered so many pronouncements for so many years. Kirk didn't quite think that their desire to sit in that throne, which placed them back-to-back, stemmed from nostalgia, but rather from the need to perform a mutual duty one last time, at once as a kind of memento, and a last farewell.

"We are well aware of this, Mr. Spock," said Prince Abon.

"But are you sure that your mind-meld would be unable to prevent the psionic storms from coming back?" asked Prince Delor.

"I am a scientist, and science does not deal in absolute certainties," said Spock. "But I cannot guarantee the efficacy of a Vulcan mind-meld to prevent future occurrences, no. Such a storm could return at any moment, and the only method Dr. McCoy and I believe certain to forestall this—aside from the death of one of the participants—is the separation of Your Highnesses by a considerable distance."

"By 'considerable,'" asked Delor, "you mean—?"

"Several million miles at the very least," said McCoy.

"I would call that distance quite considerable," said Abon.

"In our first meeting, I mentioned the characters from Earth mythology, the twins Castor and Pollux," said Spock, "called the Dioscuri. It seems to me a solution might be found there."

"How so, Mr. Spock?" asked Abon.

"The twin Castor was a mortal, while his brother, Pollux, was immortal. When Castor was slain in a conflict, Pollux asked his father, Zeus, for the gift of sharing his immortality with his brother. They spent alternate days in Hades and on Olympus."

"You suggest one of us go off-planet, Mr. Spock?"

"That would seem the only way to attain the distance between your twin necessary, Prince Delor."

"'Off-planet,'" said Abon, almost reminiscently. "To

wander the stars, exploring, experimenting . . . It seems like a good life, eh, Captain?"

"I've never regretted it," said Kirk.

"I shall miss you, brother," said Delor, rising and facing his twin. "But we both know the proper decision."

"I wish someone would tell me," said McCoy. "I know that you, Prince Abon, were inquiring about space travel—"

"But it is clearly Abon who would make the better ruler of Nador," said Delor, "the best monarch to guide our people through the process of becoming members of the Federation." He sighed and looked around. "I must confess, as often as I wished to be free of this place forever, I shall miss it."

"As we shall miss you," said Prince Abon. "But know that as Nadorian's Ambassador to the Galaxy, you will carry the full force of the throne behind you."

Delor nodded graciously, the turned to look into the shadows. "My lady," he said, "may I ask a boon?"

"How may I serve you, Your Highness?" asked the Lady Pataal, emerging from the shadows that gathered at the edge of the room. Her friend, Yeoman Tonia Barrows, followed her nearly into the light, but stopped a few feet short.

"I ask you to accompany me," said Delor, extending a hand. "Space would seem not so vast had I someone to share it with."

"Your Highness . . ." began Pataal, walking forward and kneeling at his feet. "I am honored . . . but I cannot."

"Cannot?" asked Delor. He said the word as if for the first time.

The Lady Pataal shook her head. "Will not, then. Forgive me, Highness, but I have realized it is not you that I love." She stood and looked at Prince Abon, a slight quaver coming to her voice. "It is Prince Abon."

Delor's eyes closed and he was still for a moment. Then he nodded. "A monarch may command anything but loyalty and love." He turned and extended a hand to his brother. "Good fortune to you both."

Pataal and Yeoman Barrows hugged as the princes shook hands.

"But I have one favor to ask," said Delor. "On our birthday, brother, let us arrange to view the constellation of Gemini."

"Agreed," nodded Abon, a slight catch in his voice. "It may be that that ritual will ease the loneliness I will feel for you."

This time the brothers embraced, and it seemed quite natural to Kirk to see them so conjoined.

"Captain," a voice called to Kirk as he left the throne room, "may I have a word?"

Both Spock and McCoy, recognizing that cool voice, glanced over at Kirk, who nodded. "Of course, Chief Securitrix," said Kirk, turning to face Llora.

"Our relations have not always been the most peaceable these past few days," said the chief securitrix, "but I do thank you for the help you have given my planet and my people."

"Thank you," said Kirk. "Perhaps we shall have a chance to repair our relations, someday."

"I hope so," she replied, simply. Then she extended her right hand. "Good luck."

Kirk took her hand, which was warm and soft, and, not at all to his surprise, strong. He met its pressure for a few seconds while his eyes met her gaze. After a few seconds she released the grip and walked away. "Thank you for showing me the stars," she said.

* * *

"Gentlemen," said Kirk, in his quarters on the *Enterprise* a few minutes later, "to success."

"To success," echoed three voices, clinking champagne glasses, then imbibing their contents.

"An excellent vintage," said Spock.

"It's no mint julep," said McCoy with a grin, "but it's not bad."

"It's very good," agreed Peter Kirk.

Three sets of eyes turned as one to him.

"Know a lot about drinking, do you, Peter?" asked McCoy.

"A little," said Peter, with a disarming, familiar smile. "About as much as I know about women."

"Watch out for this one," said McCoy, turning to Kirk.

"I've already found that out," replied Kirk.

"Well," said Peter, after a long pause, "maybe I'll just turn in now."

"Good idea," said Kirk, with a wink. "Good night."

"Good night, Uncle Jim," said Peter, at the cabin door. "And thanks—for everything."

"I made your father a promise," said Kirk.

"Sirs, if you'll excuse me," said Spock, "I have duty on the bridge."

"I'll join you," said Kirk, setting down his glass.

"You go ahead, Spock," said McCoy. "I'd like to speak to Jim for a minute."

"Well, Bones," asked Kirk, after the Vulcan had left, "what's the mystery?"

"No mystery at all," said McCoy, "not anymore. Not when I knew where to look."

"You're orbiting a little too far over my head, Doctor," said Kirk, dryly. "What's this all about?"

McCoy shrugged. "I should have seen it immediately. Not your concern for Peter—he's family, after all. But the way you cut Sinclair out of the action when his whereabouts were unknown, the way you insisted only on experienced hands, this nonsense about wanting to be closer to the younger crew . . ."

"Is this going somewhere, McCoy?" asked Kirk, rising. "If not—"

"Jim, that day you approached the new crewmen in the mess hall . . . I know it was his birthday."

On his way to the cabin door, Kirk stopped as if he'd taken full stun. The door opened, waited a few seconds, then closed again.

"It's not your fault," said McCoy. "That you weren't there. And trying to become pals with the younger crew won't make up for it."

Kirk turned, and it had been a long time since McCoy had seen such hurt in a man's eyes. "He's my son, Bones. I should be there."

"I know how you feel, Jim," said McCoy, and it wasn't until much later that Kirk realized his friend wasn't just making sympathetic noise; he had a daughter he hadn't seen in years. "But you and Carol agreed . . ."

"Damn our agreement. I should be there. Teaching him to throw a ball, to ride a horse . . ." He picked up one of the champagne glasses, made a fist around its stem, then set it down, slowly, his fingers uncoiling. "I should be there. Carol has David . . . who do I have?"

"You have the *Enterprise*," said McCoy. "And Spock and me. And Peter."

"I suppose that's better than nothing," said Kirk, "but that doesn't make it any easier."

"Apologizing might make it a little easier," said McCoy.

"To who?" asked Kirk, baffled.

"To a certain lieutenant who thinks she's being disciplined for no reason," said McCoy. "You owe her an explanation."

Kirk spread his hands. "Bones, what'll I tell her?"

McCoy shrugged, but smiled encouragingly as he headed for the door. "I'm sure you'll think of something. Right now, the gesture is more important than the truth."

On his way out, McCoy caught just the edge of Kirk's voice: "Uhura, put me through to Lieutenant Sinclair. . . ."

"Captain, Prince Delor's craft is leaving orbit and sending us best wishes."

"Visual, Lieutenant," said Kirk. A moment later, the face of the prince occupied the viewscreen, and it occurred to Kirk that he would have known it was Delor, not Abon, even without having been told. Perhaps the separation—in more ways than one— would be good for them.

"Captain," said the prince, *"thank you once again for your assistance in launching this craft. Your Mr. Scott said it would take at least four days, but the work was completed in one."*

"Our pleasure, Your Highness," replied Kirk. "You're in for the adventure of your life. Just try to have a little fun once in a while."

"Yes, sir." The prince smiled. *"Nador's Pride out."*

"You wanted to see me, sir?" came a voice from behind Kirk, quavering slightly.

"Yes, Lieutenant," said Kirk, swiveling the conn to face the turbolift, and Sinclair. The muscles of her throat and jaw were working, but she stood as rigid as a tree.

Across the bridge, no one moved. Then they realized they weren't moving, and tried to give the impression of movement, while straining to hear the conversation.

It wasn't necessary for them to strain. "Mr. Chekov is running a diagnostic check on the phaser banks," said Kirk, indicating the vacant post next to Sulu. "Take the navigation console, Lieutenant."

She glanced at the helm briefly; then she turned back to Kirk. "Yes, sir," she said, and took the seat next to Sulu.

Kirk tossed a quick wink to McCoy, over at Spock's station, who returned a grin and a nod.

"Prepare to leave orbit, Mr. Sulu," said Kirk.

"Aye, sir, course laid in."

"Captain," said Spock, approaching him, "let me congratulate you on your fine work in deducing who was behind the smuggling ring. The method in which you built a case against Commissioner Roget, in order to elicit a confession from Mrs. Roget, was particularly effective."

"Thank you, Mr. Spock. I knew Roget wasn't behind the smuggling ring, of course; he had too many chances to impede our efforts and took none of them. But with no solid proof against his wife, making her come to her husband's defense seemed the most direct way of getting a confession."

"Flawlessly logical, sir," said Spock. "I must confess surprise that I did not think of it myself."

"I relied on you quite heavily during this mission, Spock. I figured it was about time I started pulling my own weight."

Spock nodded and turned to leave.

"Besides," Kirk added slyly, "nobody's perfect."

"Just a minute, Spock," said McCoy, nearing the

conn. "You're saying that Jim figured all that out by logic? He was playing a good, old-fashioned hunch, pure and simple. The way he played on Mrs. Roget's love for her husband—"

"I must disagree, Doctor," said Spock, with just the merest hint of perfectly controlled annoyance and forbearance. "The captain's reasoning—"

"Just a moment, you two," said Kirk. "Isn't it possible it was a little of *both?* That it was . . . a logical hunch?"

For a moment, Spock and McCoy stared at Kirk. Then, with perfect timing, they turned toward each other.

"Now he is being insulting," said Spock.

"I agree," said McCoy, "and we don't have to take it."

The two turned their backs on Kirk and walked away.

Kirk turned to the viewscreen, shaking his head. "Take us out of orbit, Mr. Sulu. Then go to warp factor one."

"Aye, sir."

Kirk looked around him, feeling the throb of the ship's power pulse through the arms of the conn. Perhaps it wasn't a home and family, but it was better than nothing. A good deal better, in fact.

The *U.S.S. Enterprise* left orbit and leaped hungrily for the stars.

About the Author

A *Star Trek* fan since 8:30:01 P.M. on September 8, 1966, Mike W. Barr is perhaps the first writer to have written every one of the first four incarnations of *Star Trek—Star Trek, Star Trek: The Next Generation, Star Trek: Deep Space Nine,* and *Star Trek: Voyager*—in comic book form or any other. Mike's first professional sale was to *Ellery Queen's Mystery Magazine,* and mystery author Ellery Queen remains one of his major influences. A comic book writer for many years, Mike's credits include the first comic book version of *Star Trek* that was commercially viable and critically acclaimed; *Camelot 3000,* the first comic book maxi-series, with artist Brian Bolland; *Batman: Son of the Demon,* the graphic novel whose proceeds restored DC Comics to first place in sales after fifteen years, with artist Jerry Bingham; *Batman and the Outsiders* with artist Jim Aparo; *Detective Comics* with artist Alan Davis; *The Maze Agency* with artists Adam Hughes and Rick Magyar; and *Mantra* for the Malibu Ultraverse. His *Batman* scripts have been adapted for the movie *Batman: Mask of the Phantasm* and for several episodes of the *Batman* cartoon show. He has also written Internet animation scripts for Stan Lee Media and Icebox. His current comics projects include his new creation, *Psi-Mage and the Verdict,* and his Internet comic strip, *Sorcerer of Fortune,* available at www.adventurestrips.com. He is working on more novel projects, both originals and *Star Trek.* Mike is not offended by the term "Trekkie."

Look for STAR TREK fiction from Pocket Books

Star Trek®

Star Trek®: The Original Series

Star Trek: The Next Generation®

Star Trek: Voyager®

Enterprise®

Star Trek®: New Frontier

Star Trek®: Stargazer

Star Trek®: Starfleet Corps of Engineers (eBooks)

#12 • *Some Assembly Required* • Scott Ciencin & Dan Jolley
No Surrender (paperback) • various
#13 • *No Surrender* • Jeff Mariotte
#14 • *Caveat Emptor* • Ian Edginton
#15 • *Past Life* • Robert Greenberger
#16 • *Oaths* • Glenn Hauman
#17 • *Foundations, Book One* • Dayton Ward & Kevin Dilmore
#18 • *Foundations, Book Two* • Dayton Ward & Kevin Dilmore
#19 • *Foundations, Book Three* • Dayton Ward & Kevin Dilmore
#20 • *Enigma Ship* • J. Steven York & Christina F. York
#21 • *War Stories, Book One* • Keith R.A. DeCandido
#22 • *War Stories, Book Two* • Keith R.A. DeCandido
#23 • *Wildfire, Book One* • David Mack
#24 • *Wildfire, Book Two* • David Mack
#25 • *Home Fires* • Dayton Ward & Kevin Dilmore

Star Trek®: Invasion!

#1 • *First Strike* • Diane Carey
#2 • *The Soldiers of Fear* • Dean Wesley Smith & Kristine Kathryn Rusch
#3 • *Time's Enemy* • L.A. Graf
#4 • *The Final Fury* • Dafydd ab Hugh
Invasion! Omnibus • various

Star Trek®: Day of Honor

#1 • *Ancient Blood* • Diane Carey
#2 • *Armageddon Sky* • L.A. Graf
#3 • *Her Klingon Soul* • Michael Jan Friedman
#4 • *Treaty's Law* • Dean Wesley Smith & Kristine Kathryn Rusch
The Television Episode • Michael Jan Friedman
Day of Honor Omnibus • various

Star Trek®: The Captain's Table

#1 • *War Dragons* • L.A. Graf
#2 • *Dujonian's Hoard* • Michael Jan Friedman
#3 • *The Mist* • Dean Wesley Smith & Kristine Kathryn Rusch
#4 • *Fire Ship* • Diane Carey
#5 • *Once Burned* • Peter David
#6 • *Where Sea Meets Sky* • Jerry Oltion
The Captain's Table Omnibus • various

Star Trek®: The Dominion War

Star Trek®: Section 31™

Star Trek®: Gateways

Star Trek®: The Badlands

Star Trek®: Dark Passions

Star Trek®: The Brave and the Bold

Star Trek® Omnibus Editions

Other Star Trek® Fiction